Books by Frederick Buechner

Novels

Non-Fiction

LION COUNTRY

FREDERICK BUECHNER
LION COUNTRY

Atheneum *New York* *1971*

For Harry Ford

LION COUNTRY

CHAPTER ONE

HALFWAY down the subway stairs, he turned. There was a smell of stale urine. It was raining on Lexington Avenue. He said, " 'All things are lawful for me, but all things edify not.' One Corinthians ten."

He had his hand on the stair rail and was looking at me over his shoulder. As he spoke, his right eyelid fluttered part way down, then up again, and I thought he was winking. He was not. It was involuntary, just a lazy eyelid that slid partly shut sometimes. If it happened in conjunction with a smile, it looked as though that one eye knew something a lot funnier than what the rest of him was smiling at and was fighting the impulse to doze off and dream about it.

He said, "We'll be seeing you," and then continued on down the stairs, a fleshy, scrubbed man in a tight black raincoat with a narrow-brimmed hat, dimly Tyrolean, on the top of his head. Happy Hooligan. *We'll be seeing you.* I remember the way he said *we* when there was obviously only one of him there. I remember the urine smell on the subway stairs and the rain and the way he turned and said—not as an afterthought but as though it was the main thing he had wanted to say all along and he had only just now found the right way to say it—"Everything I do is lawful."

Leo Bebb. He was all by himself, and because I had only that day for the first time met him face to face, I had no way of knowing who his *we* included. But I came to know in some detail later, and when I close my eyes now and try to conjure up again that moment at the subway entrance, I don't exactly see the others on the stairs with him but I sense them waiting for him in the shadows a dozen steps or so farther down. In reality they were all at that time safe, to use the word rather loosely, in Armadillo, Florida, but I nonetheless picture them waiting for Bebb there in the flatulent bowels of the IRT—Sharon, that willowy carnivore, that sleepy-limbed huntress, that hierodule; and Lucille, the mother, with her black glasses and wet, liverish lips; and Brownie with his china teeth smiling his unrelentingly seraphic smile. Bebb descends to them like Orpheus with his lyre, and in the dark they reach out their hands to him like the souls of the dead, whether in menace or entreaty I cannot say, while up there at the entrance to the underworld I also reach out my hands. The truth of it is that I probably had my hands in my pockets

4

feeling for taxi money, but I remember waiting to watch him disappear, and that, I suppose, was a kind of reaching out. Bebb twanged once or twice on the lyre strings: *All things are lawful for me*—climbing down into the breathy, warm dark—*but all things edify not*. He was going to hell. Lawfully, of course, and on an errand that, for all I know, he may even then have understood.

He had granted me my interview that afternoon in a lunchroom between Third and Lexington in the Forties someplace, all tiled walls and floor like a men's room with fluorescent lights that turned our lips blue. I had ordered tea, Bebb chocolate milk which he sweetened with sugar. The man at the counter who took our order had silvery hair and a silvery, ageless face. "You know what he is, don't you?" Bebb asked when we had taken seats on either side of a formica slide so narrow that we could not both drink at the same time without the risk of touching foreheads. "That one there," he said, nodding back over his shoulder. "He's from outer space." I had raised the teacup to my lips, and Bebb put one bitten thumb on the near rim of the saucer, pushing down to make the far rim rise. "He got here in one of these. *Maybe.*" One finger in the air. "It's when the hair and face are all one color you can usually tell."

"Silver," I said.

"He's one of the silver ones," Bebb said. "There are gold ones too and other types. In Scripture they are called angels. There are quite a few of them around and always have been, but they don't mean us any harm. Often quite the opposite. Ask me any questions you want to. That's what we're here for."

His mouth snapped shut like something on hinges, a

nutcracker man's mouth or the mouth of one of those
wooden bottle-stoppers carved into faces that they pour
whiskey out of sometimes in bars. A workable, Tweedle-
dum mouth with the lines at the corners, the hinge
marks, making an almost perfect H with the tight lips.
A face plump but firm, pale but not sick pale. He was
high-polish bald and had hardly a trace of facial hair,
beard or eyebrows even. The eyes were jazzy and wide
open and expectant, as if he'd just pulled a rabbit out of
a hat or was waiting for me to. It could have been the
face, I thought, of a fat and very clean nun who had
nearly decided to break her vows.

"You ordain people," I said.

Bebb said, "I ordained you."

As indeed he had. I had seen his ad—*"Put yourself on
God's payroll—go to work for Jesus* NOW*"*—and had
answered it, enclosing the suggested love offering plus a
stamped, self-addressed envelope. Ten days later from
the Church of Holy Love, Inc., in Armadillo, Florida, I
received an ordination certificate with my name written
on it by Brownie in purple ink and a mimeographed letter informing me that as a minister I was now entitled to
conduct weddings and funerals and christenings and give
last rites and administer the sacraments. There were
also two mimeographed order blanks, one on blue paper,
the other on pink. The blue one was for a pamphlet entitled *Worthy of His Hire*, which was billed as explaining in detail various types of tax exemptions and ecclesiastical discounts and draft deferments available to
ministers. The pink one was for a catalogue of mail-
order courses offered by Gospel Faith College and a
description of the degrees that the College was in a

6

position to award, together with the fees and requirements for each.

"I suppose you must come under a lot of fire," I said. "Ordaining anybody who answers your ad."

"Anybody," Bebb said. "Anybody *male.*" That cautionary finger again. "Scripture doesn't say anything about ordaining females. But anybody else, it doesn't matter. When people say I've probably ordained all kinds of crooks and misfits—pimps, sodomites, blackmailers and pickpockets for all I know, you name it—I say judge not that ye be not judged. That's God's business. I am here to save souls. I am here to save your soul, Antonio Parr. What kind of a name do you call that anyway?"

Antonio Parr. An Italian mother, an American father, both long since dead. A World War I romance. That kind of a name, I explained to him. And a face to go with it. An El Greco face, Ellie called it, Ellie the fair, the lily maid of my long bachelorhood. An elongated, olive-skinned (she would not have said sallow) face with eyes that she said she always thought of as rolled heavenward and brimming with whatever the eyes of El Greco faces brim with. Rolled heavenward anyway, heaven knows, those caramel-colored eyes I inherited from my mother, and my shoulders shrugged, my hands outstretched palms up: So *now* what? What next? What not next? I think of the old joke about the communist agitator walking in Central Park. A bird flies over and drops a load on his head, and he shakes his ragged fist and cries out, "For the rich you sing!" What not next?

At the time of my first meeting with Bebb I was

7

starting out on my scrap-iron period. Old ratchets, wheels, tongs, strappings, hasps, hinges and nails, whatever I could lay my hands on I would paint with Rustoleum black and then assemble in various interesting and I hoped entertaining ways. I resorted as little as possible to welding but used balance wherever I could or the natural capacity of one odd shape to fit somehow into or on top of or through another—entirely autobiographical, in other words—the idea being to leave the lover of my art (of me?) free to rearrange it with love in any artful way he chose. Permanence, I believed, was the enemy, and no one, least of all poor, unwelded Ellie, could say I failed to live my faith.

I had not long since passed through my teaching period (English instructor and dormitory head at a small coeducational boarding school where with a kind of determined camaraderie teachers and students called each other by their first names), and I had recently moved into the city partly to be near my sister, who was then dying, and partly to set out on my writing period. It was when I was just giving up on my fourth novel— the three earlier ones had never gotten past page 34, an apparently fatal number for me and also my age at the time—that I began edging into scrap-iron. Bebb's ad caught me thus astraddle, and I answered it because I hoped that it would provide me with copy. I would set novels aside, I thought, and try my hand at journalistic exposé. I was ready, in other words, to try out yet another of my periods.

Put yourself on God's payroll: this burning bush tucked in among the hemorrhoid cures and dashboard Virgins and neckties that glowed in the dark. At every level I could have been held accountable on, it struck me as inspired rascality ripe for my exposing—except that I can believe now that in some subterranean way I may have been interested not only in exposing it but also perhaps in, shall we say, sampling it. At least I remember that when I received my ordination certificate and with it license to bury and marry, I found myself almost right away wondering crazily who and where and when. The Reverend Antonio Parr, I thought. The Peculiarly Reverend, the Preposterously Reverend Parr.

I suppose I had been prudent long enough, prudent and earnest and in some miscellaneous sense faithful although welded to nothing: balanced precariously on top—in only the most remote and metaphorical sense, I assure you—of my poor Ellie and our seven-year understanding which promised to lead neither of us quickly anywhere. Ellie and her causes. We marched on Washington in '63 and on the Pentagon in '67 and in between times supported liberal candidates of as many races, colors and creeds as possible and even gave blood together. Ellie's came out in a steady, blue stream whereas mine took hours, and once when they handed me my orange juice afterwards, I fainted. Both orphaned early ourselves, we talked often of starting a school for orphans, an all-year-round school where we would be teachers and parents both, and many an evening during those many years we met in her Manhattan House apartment to lay, if nothing else, our plans.

Sometimes when we tired of planning, I would recline on the floor and she would play the piano—she played very well but was shy about it, played almost exclusively for me—and when I picture her, I am apt to picture her there. A tall, long-necked girl with her hair to her shoulders rather like Tenniel's Alice just after she has bitten into the cake marked *Eat Me*, my poor Ellie sits there at the piano with her fingers on the keys and one foot on the pedal. It is this foot that I see most clearly, a rather generous-sized foot in a heelless brocade slipper working up and down on the soft pedal while I lie there on the floor watching it at eye-level. In answering Bebb's ad, I am sure that I was, among other things, hungry for fortissimo.

Certainly no such thought was in my mind, however, as Bebb and I were sitting there blue-lipped in that dismal eatery and he looked up at me across the formica and said, "I am here to save your soul, Antonio Parr." It was only with effort that I kept my eyes from rolling heavenward at the sudden rush of adrenalin and guilt. After my ordination I had written back that the next time his crusade took him to New York—the Church of Holy Love, Inc., his ad indicated, had many mansions —I would welcome the opportunity to discuss with him various possible directions that I imagined my ministry might take. And here he was talking about saving my soul, and there I was with every secret intention of holding his up to public ridicule and condemnation.

He said, "There are some folks don't care how they abuse a man. They're going to call you a crook, some of them, and say you're using the gospel ministry for sucker bait. Sticks and stones will hurt my bones!" That tidy, fat, nun's face—or was it Fatty Arbuckle's or Juliet's nurse?—those tight little hinges his mouth worked on, snip-snap, those quick and overexcited magician's eyes as he rolled up his sleeve and prepared to grab down into his truck topper. He said, "Bad names aren't ever going to bother me." He lowered his voice. "Sure some of the brethern got itchy fingers, no question about it. Matthew ten sixteen. 'Behold, I send you forth as sheep in the midst of *wolves*,' Antonio. 'Be ye therefore wise as serpents and harmless as doves.' You just bet there are wolves in it strictly for the kill. But I'm in it to bring folks to Jesus. I guess the Almighty can handle the wolves all right." There, did I see? Holding it up by its long pink ears, his face a triumph, a challenge. Could anyone go him one better than that? He lowered a teaspoon delicately into his glass so that a little of the chocolate milk skimmed over into the bowl of the spoon where the sugar was.

"You've got to eat," I said. "How do you make a living out of all this? Is it the love offerings?"

"Love . . . Listen," he said, laying a finger on my sleeve. "Ninety percent of the answers I get to the ad don't have any love offering. And I ordain them anyway. Now you ask me how do I make a living, and that means how do *you* make one too. There's no reason on earth why you shouldn't ask it. Remember the ox, Antonio. 'Thou shalt not muzzle the ox when it treadeth out the corn.' Deuteronomy twenty-five four. *Maybe*," he said, the finger again, "or twenty-four five. Be wise as a serpent, Antonio Parr. *How* you make a living, that's for later when I know you better and know where your talents lie. Give me time. But what you *do* with your living once you make it, that's for now. You plow it right back into the church, that's what you do with it, and then the I.R.S. can't touch it with a ten-foot pole. Church money is for the church to spend any way it sees fit, and when it comes to your own church, you're the one calls the tune. Set up a discretionary fund, and as long as you're discreet you can dish it out wherever the Spirit guideth. There's plenty of poor families could use a piece of it. Tell me about yourself now, Antonio," he said, his lazy eyelid for the first time in my presence misbehaving. "Do you have a poor family?"

My family was dying, Miriam by name, my twin, and to that extent, I suppose, it could hardly have been poorer—all the family I had or can even well remember having except for her children, two young, pale boys who since the divorce had lived with their father in Westchester because their mother was in no shape to have them live with her. Myeloma was what she was dying of, a complaint that in her case came in like a lamb and went out like a lion. The Merck Manual, a handbook of horrors that no hypochondriac can afford to live either with or without, says of it that "pain may be its only symptom," a phrase that seems to me as curiously noble as anything in Greek tragedy. It is a fatal disorder which has to do with bones, although just what it was going to have to do with and to her bones, ultimately, I am happy to say that neither I nor, I assume, she knew until some time later. As soon as I left Bebb at the subway, watching him until he'd disappeared into the shadows like Orpheus, I took a taxi up to the hospital to see her.

It was November and getting on toward dusk by this

time. The picture window in her room was of glass tinted to tinge the most cloudless sky with the illusion of approaching storms. On a table in front of it was a vase of copper-colored chrysanthemums. It couldn't have been later than five or so, but already from the corridors came the rumble and click of tray carts laden with supper, a comforting sound. I felt like Cyrano coming to the Convent to bring Roxane the news of the court, his white plume concealing the fatal wound as the autumn leaves fall and he recites, *"Comme elles tombent bien,"* except that in this case the fatal wound was not Cyrano's.

Miriam my sister, my twin, that Mater Dolorosa with her cigarette between her fingers and her black hair spidered out on the pillow. She gave me her left hand to kiss, her name typed out on the plastic bracelet at her wrist. She said, "They can't be expecting it to go on a hell of a lot longer, Tono. They've given up on the cobalt now. I suppose the idea's not to throw good money after bad," and that laid the ghost for that visit, the ghost which always troubled the air in between us, especially the air in between our faces, until one of us named its name. There was a time when she would simply show me where on her back and chest they had marked out with something that looked like iodine the areas for radiation. It was like showing me the map of a journey she was planning to take alone.

"The queerest thing is this feeling I have I'm *going* someplace," she said, "instead of just out, like a match. I should have been a better Catholic. Maybe I'd understand more. All last night I kept dreaming about doors opening."

"Vaginas," I said. "I thought everybody knew that."

She said, "Listen, I'm through with that stuff for good."

Then the nurse came in with her tray, and she became our nurse, mine as well as Miriam's. We were children, and it was suppertime. It seemed to be nearly always suppertime when we were children, suppertime in winter especially, with the lights in the apartment going on at twilight and, fifteen stories down, the muffled baritone of horns as the Park Avenue traffic moved home, an entirely different sound from the morning horns. There was something pastoral about it at the end of day—the lowing herd winding slowly o'er the lea, leaving the world to darkness, and to Miriam and me. And always a nurse coming in, any one of a long dynasty of nurses, and we would have our supper to the accompaniment of the Lone Ranger or Uncle Don or Mr. Keen, Tracer of Lost Persons. If you opened a window, the air smelled gritty-cold and bitter like an iron gate. In the apartment it smelled of lamb chops and fur.

The nurse said, "You eat up now. We want to keep our strength up."

"It's like having a baby," Miriam said. "Only the baby I'm going to have is me."

At school they were always asking us what it was like to be twins. Could we read each other's minds, and if one of us was hurt, did the other one feel the pain? There was some movie about this. If one of us was shot, would the other one die? If one of us had myeloma, would the other one's bones break? The answer, I was to learn, was yes and no.

"You're my baby," the nurse said, taking the cigarette

from between my sister's fingers. It had gone out.

The nurse turned on the lamp by the bed and then had Miriam sit up to receive the tray which she rolled up over her lap. A shadow deep in one cheek and down the bridge of her nose, her black hair unbrushed and oddly clumped in back where she had been lying on it, she looked like a young Jewess. I thought of Rachel in Ramah weeping for her children, and I thought of the two small, pale boys living with their pale father in Westchester. Miriam rarely if ever mentioned them, let alone wept for them as far as I know. It was as if she had written off everything except this room and what happened in it, what was going to happen in it. She had herself become her only children.

While she picked at her supper, I told her about the time with Bebb that I had just come from and the secret plans I had for dismembering him. For some reason, I had not mentioned before about answering his ad and receiving the certificate of ordination through the mail, and when I was on the point of explaining it to her here, I found myself thinking better of it. Instead I put it simply that when I read he was in town, I had written for an appointment. Was it out of some fear that if I told her I had been ordained, even by a charlatan, she would look to me for something more than I felt I had in me to give—some deathbed expertise, the "sweet reprieve and ransom" that Father Hopkins describes having tendered to Felix Randall the farrier in a poem my sometime English students invariably loathed? Or was it a deeper fear still that she would laugh more definitively at the slapstick of it than somehow I quite could myself at that point, which was of course the real slapstick of it? I don't know. I know only that I moved on quickly to the interview itself with that plump and implausible man in that appallingly plausible joint. The silver-faced visitor from outer space slinging hash at the counter. The sizzle and smell of French fries frying, and just the idea, let alone the act, of putting sugar in chocolate milk, while through the window I could see the rain coming down hard on Lexington Avenue.

Bebb followed his chocolate milk with a wheel of Danish, and it was when he finished that, I told Miriam, that he got down to what I rapidly concluded must have been his chief purpose in being there with me at all.

He said, "Antonio, I'm commencing to get the feel of you a little. You've had me doing most of the talking, but I've been watching your face and your eyes and they've told me many things—*more* things," he had a way of interrupting himself as if taking you down through deeper and deeper levels always nearer to some remarkable truth, "*maybe,*" he interrupted again, taking me yet another step nearer, "more things than maybe you'd ever dream of telling me yourself." Whereupon I had the eerie sensation for a moment that I who was there to expose him was on the point of being exposed myself as being there under pretenses so false as to border on the supernatural.

"You are a sensitive man. You have a tender heart. You've got it upstairs. You are a good listener. What does that add up to? Teaching, Antonio. I see your ministry as first and foremost a teaching ministry."

He had to catch a plane back to West Palm in a couple of hours, he said, and therefore would come quickly to the point. His proposition was for me to start

16

a branch of Gospel Faith College on my own. I would do the canvassing of students myself and would offer the standard Gospel Faith curriculum, for which I would receive the standard Gospel Faith tuition fees. If my students passed muster, I would forward their names to Bebb in Armadillo, and he would send them their diplomas. When my branch started paying off, I could pass on whatever I thought was fair. He knew, he said, that when I started cashing in, I would not forget the Mother Church. This was the first time I had seen him give any sign of emotion, or at least that is what I took it to be. "The Mother Church," he had said, and this was the phrase that seemed to hit him. He glanced down at his empty plate and with all ten fingers, working out from the center, divided the crumbs from his Danish into two small piles.

Without looking up, he said, "Foxes have holes, Antonio, and the birds of the air have nests, but for a while when you first start out, you may not have any place to lay your head. Only faith. You better believe that I know whereof I speak." With his face bowed, I was able for the first time to look at the rest of him—the jacket of his black tropic-weight suit straining under the arms, the handkerchief in his breast pocket folded into four neat points so that the monogram B showed.

Partly for information, partly to recall him to a role that I felt better equipped to cope with, I questioned him about the legality of the operation. Was he accredited to offer degrees? It brought him to life again.

"Inc.," he said. "Inc., Antonio. The Church of Holy Love, *Inc.* Once you've got yourself incorporated, you can offer any degree you've got a mind to—almost," he said, breaking in upon himself, "any degree. Almost any degree to almost anybody—anybody who can meet the fee, that is. They're not all going to be Harvard graduates, Antonio, but Jesus Christ wasn't a Harvard graduate either."

Feeling at this point that even if I angered him, he had given me already rope enough to hang him with, I risked a more direct approach. I said, "It sounds a little like a diploma mill, doesn't it, Mr. Bebb?"

It was less the substance of his answer that surprised me than the tone and manner of it. His voice went soft and conciliatory, the hinges of his mouth working looser, and for the first time I could imagine him actually working at his trade, asking the blessing in somebody's kitchen or pronouncing the benediction in a funeral parlor. He said, "It's a mill, all right, but the product isn't diplomas. The product is people who are ready to go all the way with Jesus, hundred-percenters like yourself, Antonio. What comes into the mill is raw cotton. What goes out is something helps keep folks warm and dry when the winter comes."

Rising abruptly and putting his hat on the back of his head as he tried to work his arm into the inside-out sleeve of his raincoat, he said that I was not to rush into such an important decision half-cocked but should take it to the Lord in prayer. In the meanwhile, he would have me sent all the information I might need about the courses themselves and how to administer them. Better still, if there were any chance that I could get down to Armadillo, he would personally show me the whole process in actual operation from A to Z. He did not press this, just threw it out while I was paying the check—it seemed to me that as Judas it was the least I could do—and he did not refer to it again. I walked him to the subway.

"It smells like half New York dropped by here last night to take a leak," he said when we got there. We shook hands in the rain, and then I watched him go downstairs to where he turned and said that all things were lawful for him but all things edified not—that foolish hat on top of his head and the tight-fitting black raincoat that couldn't give him much protection, I thought, against that chill November. That one lazy and somehow hilarious eyelid with the nether world looming at his back.

"*Lasciate ogni speranza, voi ch'entrate,*" I said to Miriam, bringing an edited rambling version of this account to an end, and only then did I see what had become of her while I was too busy talking to notice.

The shadow in her cheek and the shadow of her nose had met so that one whole side of her face was virtually missing. The remaining eye had gone from oval to parallelogram. It was not looking out any more. It was looking in. Her expression, as nearly as I can describe it, was one of utter disbelief. She was obviously listening not to me but to her own contractions. She was preparing for the time when she would be delivered of herself. It was not the final labor yet, but it was a full dress rehearsal.

CHAPTER TWO

THREE YEARS BEFORE, for Christmas, Ellie had given me a cat which she delivered to my door with a card around its neck on which, so help me God, she had written, that chaste and comprehensively innocent girl, that she hoped I could use a little pussy. *O tempora, O mores,* shaking my ragged fist in an agony of wild and savage mirth, my El Greco eyes rolled heavenward. For the rich you sing! The cat was a rather handsomely endowed tom which I could never bring myself to have altered. One of us out of action at a time, I felt, was enough. I named him Tom.

When I got home from my visit to Miriam at the

hospital, I discovered that Tom had gotten a fish-hook in his eyelid. There were lots of fish-hooks lying around ready to dip into Rustoleum black for use with my scrap-iron creations, and by some series of gross miscalculations Tom had tangled with one of them. It was a whole day of eyes as I look back on it—first Bebb's, then Miriam's, and now Tom's, although, strictly speaking, in Tom's case as in Bebb's, it was not the eye but the eyelid. It was only when I moved the hook around, trying to extricate it, that the eye itself seemed in danger, and that was why after several unsuccessful attempts with Tom squirming under one arm, I called up the vet. His office was closed by this hour, but he said he thought he could handle it at home if I wanted to bring Tom down. I even brought him down in a taxi, I was that grateful to him in a way for rescuing me with a malaise so circumscribed and manageable from that disheveling afternoon.

When the first shot of anesthetic made no impression on him, the vet gave him a second which in a relatively short time knocked him cold. The vet then pushed the hook through to where he was able to cut off the barb and pulled it back out easily. He rubbed the eye with some ointment, I paid him, and in no time at all I was out on the street again with Tom unconscious in my arms.

It might be some time, the vet had said, before the double shot wore off. In the meantime Tom should be kept warm and in a place where he could do himself no mischief in case he was groggy and irrational when he began to come to. I took him to Ellie's. God knows I had no wish at that moment for political discussion or piano music or orphanage planning, but Manhattan House was a good deal nearer where we were than home was, and, trying to put myself in Tom's shoes, I decided that Ellie's would be a more reassuring place to come to in with its wall-to-wall carpets and maid service than our own flat, which was all sharp corners and hard surfaces and a great many other fish-hooks which could only stir up painful memories. Ellie seemed delighted to see us. It had been her afternoon at the U.N., she said—she did volunteer work at the information desk—and she had just been wishing that she had somebody around to unwind with.

Ellie unwinding. The imagination runs free. Unwinding like a clock which has been wound so tight that it won't run till you give it a shake? Unwinding like a ball of string which for years has dreamed of just lying around, festooned over sofas and carpets and beds? Somebody to unwind with, she said as I came in with poor, limp Tom in my arms, and I thought of two alarm clocks going off together until the last languid rattle announces that all passion is spent. I thought of two unraveled balls of twine all messed up together in a wicked tangle on that fuzzy gold rug. And who knows but what on that particular evening with the small November rain raining down outside, with Miriam heavy on my heart and the U.N. heavy on Ellie's, some switch might have been tripped, some tender and little-used muscle set to twitching somewhere. That Victorian face —those ringlets almost to her shoulders, those Christmas-bright eyes and orderly little seed-pearl teeth. She called up and ordered Beef Stroganoff for two. I poured out two scotch-and-sodas in those narrow highball glasses of hers with a single tear-drop in the base. We laid Tom near the radiator on a Turkish towel.

Nothing the vet said had prepared me for the performance that took place when life began to stir in him again. He was drunk. He was Dionysiac. He staggered around cross-eyed with never more than two legs working at a time. He knocked himself silly against the legs of tables and chairs. He fell over on his side like a rag to lie there heaving with his eyes rolled up until the god in him got him started off again. He was entirely indifferent to our attempts, once he had fallen down, to cozen him into staying down. And he made no noise. If he had yammered and whined, it would have been better, at least better for us. But he was silent in his mad staggering—silent and relentless and drunk. The life-agony was upon him.

Though usually a model of continence, he had not yet regained control of his functions, and there were damp spots here and there on the golden rug. Tom himself, with what may have been as much sweat and tears as anything else, looked half soaked. Except for a few random wisps that stuck out like pinfeathers, his fur clung flat to his sides, and I realized for the first time how much of his bristling and impressive bulk was —as with the rest of us, I suppose—the sheerest fluff. He went weaving around from pillar to post looking half starved in addition to everything else, and I must say that Ellie was magnificent throughout. Another woman might have looked first to the damp spots, but her concern was all for Tom. She warmed a saucer of milk for him, and when he fell into it whiskers first, his front legs buckling, she tried to hold him steady so he could drink. He lapped at it a couple of times and then choked. She put him in her lap, wet and raving as he was, and tried to stroke peace back into him with those lovely Tennysonian hands. She helped him back to his feet when all his own strugglings toward that end failed. And finally she laid him on her apricot-colored bed, where with pillows from the chaise-longue on one side and a bolster held in place by an armchair on the other, she at last consented to leave him—asleep, as nearly as we could tell—convinced that here at least he could come to no grief. By the time we got back to our flat scotch-and-sodas, whatever might have been possible between us before, however remotely, was possible no longer.

It was over the Beef Stroganoff that I told her about seeing Bebb that afternoon. She had been in on the whole business ever since my original answer to his ad and had encouraged my plan to expose him in print. My scrap-iron and my novels had both left her cold—lacking, as she quite accurately saw it, anything much in the way of social relevance—but at the idea of my bringing a crook to justice she was enthusiastic. As it turned out, she had even done some investigating of her own.

After a morning of digging through newspaper files at the Public Library, she had come across a short piece in the old *Journal-American* which she had had photostated and presented to me that evening. The incongruity of it as I look back—Ellie sitting there bright-eyed on her beige couch, so Brearley and Vassar, so *cotillion*, and in her hand, holding it out to me like a dance card, that tawdry relic datelined Miami some eleven years back and, like the subway entrance where I said goodbye to

Bebb, smelling of stale piss.

Remembering it, I see the honey-dipped mommas and hash-browned poppas sitting in their rockers like J. P. Morgan on the throne of Minos as they watch the traffic simmer along. I see the window-shopping typists with their hair up in rollers under souvenir bandanas or those mobcaps aflutter with gauzy fish scales. I see fried clams and papaya-juice stands and stuffed baby alligators and vast neo-Babylonian lobbies, see Assyrians hung like bulls in their Jantzens and oiled from their huaraches up to their thundering wings and blue-black beards. And I see Bebb.

Bebb is standing in a side street near the back entrance to a restaurant. There are pails of sweet-and-sour garbage, lobster shells, drifts of wastepaper, all smelling of rancid butter. There is a windowless stucco wall, blinding in the sun. Some children are playing with a tennis ball. Bebb has on a white linen cap with a green-lined visor and little perforated panels at either side to let the air in. He has on a Harry Truman sport shirt with a camera slung around his neck and the kind of sunglasses that look like mirrors from the outside. At this moment they are mirroring the children. He is smiling his climactic magician's smile, his most effulgent and tight-hinged allez-oop of an H, as he reaches down with one hand to pull the rabbit out of the hat. Only it is not a rabbit that he pulls out and not a hat that he pulls it out of. It is a bunch of white grapes. It is a handful of suet. Squab and pale, it nestles like plovers in his treasuring grip, like plovers' eggs.

The first child to notice yells to the others, or maybe just the opposite—stops yelling. They all stop and turn, the tennis ball abandoned among the lobster shells and wastepaper. With the blinding wall at his back and his looking-glass goggles, he stands there wigwagging at them, his hand no quicker than their eyes. They run away helter-skelter, skinny and barebacked, like newspaper blowing in the wind. Do they? Or maybe they stand there enthralled with their ribs sucked in. Tattletale-tits. And did they even tell their tattle right, get it straight what that prestidigitator was up to, what that plump and preposterous showman was in his madness trying to show? God only knows. Sebastian full of arrows, Ursula baring her breast, Bebb with his fist full of fire . . .

Ellie. She read the thing out loud to me and then dropped it into my lap where I sat beside her on the couch. "Little *children*," she said, drawing her shoulders up as though she suddenly felt a cold draft. "Honestly, Tono, whatever you do with this, he's got it coming. Why, the man's a monster," and the air between us turned so dark and heavy with her indignation that for a moment it was as if I was myself Bebb.

At the time, I am almost certain, no such surrealist fancy took me, but now, recollecting it in tranquility, I can't help wondering what extraordinary events would have followed and how both our lives and, for all I know, life itself might have been unimaginably changed if I had at that exact point actually played Bebb there, stolen Bebb's act. By a kind of sympathetic magic his crime had momentarily, in Ellie's eyes, become my crime, and what if in full view of those same eyes I had, like Bebb, committed it, pulled my own rabbit out of my own hat? Hey presto! Now you see it, now you don't, in reverse. The gaudy *what-if*'s of history. What if Eisenhower had taken a black child in each hand and personally led them up the steps of the Little Rock Central High School? What if Barabbas had not been the one to have his execution stayed? But the point, I suppose, is that, given the people we are and the nature of our times, we can't do or be anything other than what we are, at least not anything much. It's as if something in the very nature of chronos almost physically prevents our occasional little stabs at anachronism, and if I had had any impulse at that moment to pull a Bebb on my goggling Ellie, the chances are the very air itself would have somehow stayed my hand. And yet one plays the tantalizing game anyway . . . What if I had suddenly set my rabbit free, alive and quivering on the couch between us . . . something whose time had not yet come, was perhaps never to come at all, coming? These turning points at which the whole world might have turned. *Comme elles tombent bien,* at least in the memory's convent garden, like golden leaves from a tree that is past leafing.

In any case no such thoughts, I am reasonably certain, crossed my mind at the time. Ellie's moral indignation became my own—indeed, even faded by comparison with mine, because in a moment her face softened into that little frown of hers—half question, half answer—and she said, "The man's sick, of course. He needs help." I felt no such tender concern myself. On the contrary. That Bebb was a charlatan I of course had no doubt, but it must have been that as a charlatan *priest* I expected his charlatanry at least to go decently cassocked. This scabrous new revelation shocked me so deeply that I believe that at some level I must have taken him for a version, at least, of the genuine article, and thus it was now I who suddenly became the molested child. No exposure could have been more indecent than that of my own trusting innocence. By some act of misguided faith, some residual image of even the charlatan priest as hopelessly if obscurely priestly, I must have actually believed him when he turned on those malodorous stairs and assured me that everything he did was lawful—not capital L lawful, maybe, but lawful enough. When I discovered from the *Journal-American* that the case was indeed quite otherwise, I felt that I, the would-be betrayer, had been betrayed.

And then it was the ludicrousness of the thing that struck me. Bebb the ordainer of thousands, Bebb the bestower of advanced theological degrees, above all Bebb as in his physical presence he had appeared to me that very day all trussed up in his tight black raincoat with his handkerchief in four tidy points, so scrubbed and hairless and in spite of everything somehow so *Protestant*—this same Bebb caught with his pants, in a manner of speaking, down. This picture in my mind supplanted everything else for me, and I burst into laughter which Ellie's earnest incomprehension, I'm afraid, only served to intensify. I can even believe that at this moment I might have given up the whole idea of writing an exposé. It is hard to launch a crusade with your funnybone. And there were the unfinished novels, after all, and all that scrap-iron to do something with, maybe try for a one-man show at one of the uptown galleries. I might even have decided to go back to teaching again. Who knows? But then, as twice before that day, Tom fatefully intervened.

Ellie said she thought she heard queer noises coming from the bedroom, and I followed her in to investigate. The noise turned out to be Tom's breathing, as unnerving a sound as I have ever heard. You expect to hear a dog pant as you expect to hear and see and smell almost anything a dog does because dogs wear their hearts on their sleeves, but here was a cat panting—a cat who had never before even let it be known that he breathed, a cat who, like all cats, had always played his cards tight to his chest, who had never to my knowledge—except for this post-operative lapse—made a single undignified gesture.

And here he was apparently fighting for life like any peasant, his mouth ajar, his teeth bared and dry. He was lying on his side on Ellie's apricot spread with his front paws stretched as far as they would stretch forward and his back paws as far as they would stretch backward, as though he were running at a great speed or hung up in a taxidermist's icebox awaiting treatment. He looked very long and very flat, and his ribs were fluttering in and out and his breath coming in hoarse, rapid grunts. He was smiling eerily. There seemed nothing for us to do except stand there and watch—this rare and forbidden sight of a cat struggling with death.

O Miriam, Miriam, my sister, my love . . . I am not and was not then a sentimental man. I do not often, after the fashion of the sentimental, throb more than God does over things. I do not weep at weddings. At the funerals of people I love, I rarely give death more than its due, which is to say I am usually able to stop just this side of where tears for the dead become tears for yourself, for everything and for nothing, those nineteenth-century tears which it is really rather a treat to shed. I take no credit for this. I suspect it comes simply from overexposure at an early age—both my parents were dead by the time I was twelve. Nevertheless, as I stood there in Ellie's bedroom with the clipping about Bebb still in my hand and that same hand around Ellie's shoulder as if we were old war comrades, I suddenly saw the thing that was happening to poor Tom on the bed as Miriam's thing.

From my teaching days I remember De Quincey's essay on the knocking at the gate in *Macbeth*, how he says it is only when the real world floods back in the form of the knocking and the drunken porter's bad jokes about the effects of alcohol on tumescence that you realize the full horror of Duncan's murder. It was only here with Tom that I really *saw* my sister as she had lain there in the hospital with half her face missing, only here that I knew fully and felt in my bones what was happening to her there. It was like walking downstairs in the dark when you think you have one more step to go and take that step only to find that it's not there because you're at the bottom already. The jolt of it is so total that you feel it in your teeth. What I felt in my teeth there in that vestal bedroom of Ellie's was my sister's death. The struggle on the bed was no longer Tom's.

I tightened my grip on Ellie's shoulders, slipped my hand up into her shampoo-sweet hair and pressed her head in against mine, temple to temple our two skulls touching hard. I wanted to tell her about Miriam, about her living and her dying and how it was when we were children together in the wintertime with the horns honking homeward and how her hair raying out on the hospital pillow was Medusa's now in my more than memory because it was turning me to stone; but I couldn't. I could never speak easily about one of those women to the other. I could never speak to one about the other without twinges of guilt. And the reason, I suppose, is that with both of them I was more than a little in love.

In love with my twin? Does that mean that I was in love somehow with myself? I do not think so, although I have heard of queerer things in my time. At most, I believe, I was only in love with the female part of myself, the part I wouldn't let weep at weddings. Or in love with the childhood we had shared, with the children we had been, those lost persons that it would take Mr. Keen himself to trace. Did I want to go to bed with her? —that oddly touching phrase we use, the one Adam used, surely, of his sister Eve before the unpleasantness over the apple. If so, then only, I think, to that hospital bed perhaps where in no John Donne sense but quite straightforwardly we might die in each other's arms, the gemini, babes in the wood pushing thirty-five, with the dry leaves falling to cover us. *Comme elles tombent bien.*

I didn't speak to Ellie about any of this, didn't so much as mention Miriam's name, as we stood there in bony, cranial embrace watching what I could only believe were poor Tom's last few moments as himself. What I did say was "That sonofabitch Bebb. I'll skin him alive if it's the last thing I do." Skin him alive. As Miriam was fond of saying, there's a lot of Wop in me, and although my customary manner is mostly recitative, I do on occasion burst, at least internally, into aria. I was suddenly Rigoletto vowing vengeance on Gilda's betrayer—*Maledizione!* with the full orchestra pulsing around me and my fist as well as my eyes raised heaven-ward. *Maledizione!*—the fool's curse. The jester's revenge. And in my bloodshot and grief-crazed eyes the betrayer, the villain, the one who was somehow responsible for what was happening there on those two sad beds which in my mind had become one, was Bebb. I vowed his destruction. I would skin him alive. "That horny old bastard," I said, not sparing Ellie's blushes, not even aware of them. Wop opera, Miriam would have said. And been right.

Why Bebb? In Hindu iconography, I have read somewhere, the mind of man is portrayed as a monkey swinging from tree to tree, witless, purposeless, grabbing out at whatever new branch happens to come to hand, which I take to mean that it is not we who control our thoughts but circumstances that control them. Let me smell bacon frying, and in spite of myself I am hungry; wave a red flag at me, and I am mad as hell. Or subtler stimuli—a drop in barometric pressure, the look in somebody's eye, the state of my digestion—and willy-nilly I am whatever they make me. Since hearing Ellie read the *Journal-American* piece, my attitude toward Bebb had passed from shocked indignation to horrified amusement and now to Verdian bloodlust. Why? Maybe just because these were the branches that presented themselves. In other words, the flat scotch-and-sodas, the smell of Ellie's hair, the damp spots on the rug—all these may have had as much to do with my feelings about Bebb as Bebb did himself. And yet, although I doubt I could have explained it at the time, I think there was a kind of crazy logic to it too. We are none of us entirely simian.

32

If Bebb had been a real priest instead of a phony, he might have been able to help. I suppose that would be the briefest statement of it. Help who? Help Miriam and Tom in their dying, or at least help me in my helpless watching. Help how? I don't know how, but if Bebb had been real instead of phony, he would have known. If there had been any priests anywhere who were real, they might have been able to help. I think my unreasonable reasoning may have gone even as far as that, making Bebb personally responsible for the failure of the priesthood in general, blaming Bebb personally for the bankruptcy of God. I would probably not have put it that way at the time, but I suspect this was part of what lay behind my shaking fist and bloodshot glance.

It was a crazy business, of course—looking for holy help to this plucked and perverted fraud with his lazy eye—but it had to do, I think, with my being Catholic. Like Miriam, I was not a good Catholic. I still attended an occasional mass and dropped into St. Patrick's once in a while to light a kind of rabbit's-foot candle to Saint Anthony, who, as both my patron saint and the saint who watches over lost things, seemed worthy of my special attention. But I hadn't made a confession or received the sacrament for years. Yet still from my early training—especially, I suppose, from my poor mother, who like an old photograph has so faded in my memory that I can hardly tell the light of her from the dark of her any more—I had this notion that once a priest always a priest, that however far Bebb had fallen, he still bore the mark upon him like an old tattoo or an appendix scar. He *should* have been able to help. He *should* have been real. And if he had been real—the more I think about it, the more I believe this may have been the real nub of it—then I would also have been real.

That mimeographed letter I received along with my certificate of ordination informing me that now I was entitled to marry and bury and baptize—and, by extension, certainly to give absolution, to heal even, all these things that my sister and Tom rolled into one so desperately needed—if Bebb had been a real priest, then I whom he had however absurdly ordained would however absurdly have been able to do these things. I would have been a real priest myself. All of which is a roundabout way of saying that I think I blamed Bebb for my own inadequacy. I vowed to skin him alive because a hard death was taking place under my nose and there was not a blessed thing I could do about it.

Tom didn't die, as things turned out. It was apparently only the effect of the anesthetic wearing off, after all. Soon his breathing started to return to normal. He closed his mouth, thereby dismantling the unearthly smile and replacing it with what I have always thought of as his Egyptian expression—archaic, enigmatic, and slightly near-sighted. Then he fell asleep.

But I continued to vow revenge anyway, and back in the living room again, where the Beef Stroganoff had gone cold and waxy on our plates, I kept Ellie up way past her bedtime laying my plans. I would not stop at any one-shot assault on Bebb, I told her—the kind of satirical account of my own dealings with him that I had originally planned. I would do a series of articles—a book even, if I had to. I would take him up on his suggestion that I make the trip to Armadillo. I would observe the whole operation from A to Z, as he had put it, and then back to A again as many times as might be necessary to find out all there was to find out. I would dig up the full story of the Miami incident. The *Journal-American* reported only that Bebb had pleaded not guilty and was awaiting trial, and Ellie said that she could find no follow-up in later issues. I would do the follow-up myself.

I would pump his enemies. I would bribe his associates. I would destroy him utterly—and with him every priest everywhere and God and, in some sense, I suppose, myself—for helplessly abandoning my twin sister to her ungodly labor.

My aria turned into a duet then—Ellie answering my vindictive vibrato with little trills of encouragement interspersed with occasional chest tones calling for restraint. I mustn't over-react, she said, and the man was obviously sick besides. It was Tom who transformed us into a trio. He wandered back into the living room in his most urbane manner, looking, except for a slight dampness around the hindquarters, as though nothing untoward had happened. He miaowed several times to indicate not that he needed food—he needed nothing—but that if we were to offer it, he would find it not uncongenial.

It was on the way to the kitchen that Ellie found on the dining-room floor a mess that he must have left there earlier when the madness was upon him. He ate Portuguese sardines in the kitchen while Ellie and I cleaned it up—a foul-smelling thing which not even several different types of household cleaner were able to remove entirely. When we finally kissed goodnight at the elevator, it was in a cloud of cat and Mr. Klean.

CHAPTER THREE

I DECIDED not to let Bebb know in advance that I was coming. Having only just returned from his trip to New York, he would be unlikely yet to have gone off anywhere else, and I would be almost sure to catch him at home. More to the point, I thought, I would be almost sure to catch him by surprise, catch him in the act, whatever exactly I imagined the act might be.

The morning after my supper with Ellie, therefore, I arranged to board Tom at the vet's and got myself a roomette on a train leaving for Florida that very afternoon. There seemed no point in delaying. Anybody else would have taken a plane, but I am a coward about flying. Statistically speaking, I am told, you are safer in the air than in your own bathtub, but for me all such statistics come down in the end to either you crash or you don't, fifty-fifty, and I prefer to take my chances in the bathtub. And I have always liked trains anyway. Nobody can get at you in a train. You are in the world but not of it as you flash by as free and impermanent as the silver meteor for which my train that day was named.

Before I left, I stopped in at the hospital again to tell Miriam what I was up to. I always dreaded our good-byes, even as trivial a one as this, fearing that it would be not *a rivederci* but *addio,* and obviously this was often on her mind too—the unimaginable possibility that we were looking at each other for the last time. The doctors admitted to me that they had run through their whole bag of tricks to the point where the only one left was to keep her as comfortable as possible until the end, which might come in a matter of a week or two, they said, or might go on for months. And yet when I saw her that morning of my departure for Armadillo, she couldn't have looked better.

I knew, as I'm sure my sister did too, that these remissions, as in their antiseptic but I suppose ultimately humane jargon the doctors called them, were only temporary, but they were on the face of it such hopeful times that I always thought maybe, once you got that much hope in a face, it might seep down in to where the cancer was and work a miracle. They were like watching *Romeo and Juliet* allowing yourself for a moment to hope that somehow this time Juliet will wake up from Friar Laurence's potion before Romeo swallows his death.

Miriam was sitting up in bed reading the papers when I came in. She had put on lipstick and a bed-jacket, and her hair was brushed and tied back with a piece of florist's ribbon from one of the plants somebody had sent her. We did not even find it necessary to lay the usual ghost by naming it, and she surprised me by asking if I had brought the martinis. When she was first hospitalized, I had brought them quite often, put the gin and vermouth together at home and then gotten glasses and ice from the nurses. The doctors were all for it. But for weeks now the very thought of gin had made her feel like throwing up—it was the cobalt, she said—and I had long since given the custom up. There was a bar across the street, however, where I had no trouble getting what we needed, and our meeting was in some ways the easiest we had had for a long time.

Without mentioning either Ellie or the *Journal* piece, I told her I was going to Florida for a couple of days to do the article on Bebb, but she didn't seem to remember about him from the day before, and her remission clearly did not involve her being interested enough in the world beyond that room to want me to tell her again. She started talking instead about her children, and that in itself I thought was a hopeful sign.

She said, "Tono, I worry like hell about those kids. The woman he's got taking care of them for him is such a menace with that big bust of hers bouncing around and that voice you could lance a boil with. And Charlie's such a shrinking violet by comparison, besides which he's asleep most of the time anyway. The castrating mother—I mean *her*—and the castrated father. I'm scared to death they're going to turn those boys into fairies. The situation's got all the makings, God knows."

Although I was on perfectly friendly terms with my ex-brother-in-law and knew Miriam would have liked me to see the boys more often, I hadn't been out there for months. Still, it did seem to me that in the original sense of the term at least there was something fairy-like about them—something transparent and insubstantial, a spidery quietness that seemed more than just shyness. They watched you with their mother's dark eyes and didn't smile much. Chris twelve, and Tony, my namesake, ten —they were like old men in their little gray suits, like little businessmen without any business.

I told my sister that I didn't think she had anything to worry about. After all, they had a father who loved them and was around most of the time—he did scripts for some educational TV people out there, working mostly at home—and although the Bouncing Bust wasn't going to win any popularity contests, she was good-hearted and conscientious.

"It's Charlie," Miriam said. "Tono, the man's a bleeding ghost. I'm not being a bitch—I cut loose, and that's that. But to bring up two boys . . . Do you know what I *mean* when I say he sleeps most of the time? I mean he often doesn't get up till noon, and when he naps, he doesn't just nap when it's raining or something but right in the middle of a sunny afternoon, for God's sake, with the kids and me roaming around in bathing suits right under his window. Sleep's his escape from life, Tono. Someday they'll have to come wake him up and tell him he's dead." And tell him she was dead, I suppose she also meant, though of course she didn't say so.

39

She went on to tell me more about Charlie Blaine than I think she had ever told me before—Charlie asleep in his underwear; Charlie with his allergies, taking his kapok pillow with him when he went off on overnight trips; Charlie as a lover, both importunate and oddly passionless, as though, like sleep, he found her body desirable not in itself but as a way of escape. Although she never said so, not even indirectly, I felt sure that I knew why she was going on at such length. She wanted me to see for myself that her children couldn't be left in their father's hands permanently after she was dead, these children who had my blood in their veins as well as his and hers. She wanted me to say, if possible without her having to ask me to, that I would somehow arrange to take them on myself. I felt sure this was in her mind, and for a few moments I came very close to saying I would do it, or at least making it easy for her to ask me if I would.

She had to stop talking when the nurse came in to put a thermometer in her mouth, and during that silence it was on the tip of my tongue to say that maybe Charlie and I could at least work out an arrangement for sharing the children between us. But I didn't. It meant permanence, for one thing—the pieces no longer balanced one on top of the other in various interchangeable ways. And it suggested marriage—if I were to make a home for them, the least I could do would be to provide them with a mother.

I could marry Ellie, if she would have me, and settle, as the saying goes, down, settle in, after all my various scrap-iron and teaching and novelizing periods settle for, at last, one final period to do me the rest of my life.

But not even for Miriam was I willing or even able to make such a promise, and I suspect that may be why she didn't ask me to in so many words, not wanting to give it the terrible sanctity of what would have amounted to a deathbed request. So, heartlessly, I changed the subject back to my trip again, and we finished our martinis over that.

When it came time to go home and pack, she said, "For two cents I'd get the hell out of here and go with you," and for a wild moment I think we both considered this almost seriously. Why shouldn't she simply get the hell out of that bed and come with me? For all we knew, maybe she was no more fatally sick than I was—diagnoses had gone haywire before—or even if she was that sick, why shouldn't she die on the way to Florida instead of here, if that's what she wanted? The doctors had no right to stop her—she was paying them, after all; they weren't paying her. But then the moment passed, and she reached her arms out toward me.

I leaned down, and she put her hands on my shoulders and kissed me once on each cheek. She said, "*Ciao*, Antonio."

The last glimpse I had of her was reaching over to the bedside table to stub out her cigarette and waving at me with her other hand. It was a rather absent-minded, informal wave, as I think back on it, because she was looking not at me but at the ashtray. And I remember the florist's bright ribbon in her hair.

All this was what lay behind me, and Bebb was of course what lay ahead of me when I got on the train a few hours later, but I thought of neither very much once we pulled out of the old Penn Station and were safely on our way. It is what I like about trains. You are neither here nor there, and you are neither this nor that. You are in between. I mean in between not just in a geographical sense, of course, but like an actor waiting in the wings for his cue to re-enter, or a disembodied spirit drifting between incarnations like an unconfirmed rumor. Who you were last and who you are going to have to be next hardly matter. The drifting is all. And if you are in a roomette such as mine was, once you have shown the conductor your ticket and told the porter when you want to be woken up in the morning, you can maintain this state of things almost indefinitely. Except for the train people, who don't care, there is no one in the world who knows where you are. You can slide the door shut or zip up the curtain, and there is no one in the world who is likely to bother you.

So I sat there in a kind of trance with my legs stretched out and my feet up on the closed lid of the john, looking through the window at that sad and to me oddly moving wilderness that you pass through when you first come out of the tunnel into Jersey. I felt like Dante being ferried across into limbo with the spirits of the doomed fluttering about him *come d'autunno si levan le foglie,* as he says—those autumn leaves again. And that tundra, those scrubby, colorless flatlands stretching away under the November sky. Those drab and dreamlike cities off in the distance—Jersey City, Hoboken, Secaucus? I know them only by name and have seen them only through the windows of year after year of trains. I do not know one from the other or even that they stand where I think they do. Maybe they are on the other side of some other river. The gray sky with here and there some industrial Stonehenge black as soot against it. Once in a while a tower shooting up jets of fire. One of the few memories I have of my father is of his telling me once that during the Depression the poor people came and lived out there somewhere in shelters made of tin cans and old piano crates, and I thought of them there trying to keep warm on a raw and lonesome afternoon like this. I wondered idly if my father had actually seen them himself through just such a hastening window as mine. And then as nearly as is ever possible this side of dreamless sleep, I stopped thinking about anything, and the Hindu monkey gave up his pointless swinging and just hung there limp by the tail. Schenectady, Schenectady, Schenectady, went the wheels on the tracks just as Reginald Gardiner used to say they did, and I watched the dusk gather over Newark, was it? or Elizabeth, Rahway, Metuchen, those places that for all I knew existed only in my mind and barely there, so vacant and remote my mind had become, like the landscape we were passing.

When, just as darkness was falling, the buzzer went off over my head, I not only could not guess what it was, I could not for the moment even guess what I was—a man, a disembodied spirit, a pane of dusty glass. I am just under six feet two in my stocking feet with long, cross-country legs, and it took me a moment or two to unfold myself from where I had one knee wedged up underneath the window sill and the other foot braced against the collapsible sink. When I slid open the door, what I found standing there in the otherwise empty

43

corridor was a girl. As nearly as I could tell at first glance, she was naked.

She was not entirely naked, as it turned out. She was wearing a bathing suit of sorts and a pair of those Japanese sandals with a peg that comes up between your toes. She can't have been more than nineteen or twenty but very poised in a sort of semi-professional way. I could imagine her as a Rockette or doing summer stock in some Berkshire resort. Except for a little too much eye make-up for my taste, she was very pretty, with a good tan and what I took to be genuine sun-streaks in her hair. She handed me a leaflet and explained that the train was some sort of tourist special with TV in the club car, a movie for the kiddies, bingo, and fashion models. She was also giving out reservations for supper. There was a choice of two sittings, she told me, and I chose the later one.

Noticing that she had only a few reservation checks left in her hand, I concluded that she must be nearing the end of her run and asked her if this was so. I must have hit what was uppermost in her own mind because she gave me the prettiest and most unprofessional smile in the world—she was a Rockette no longer but coming barefoot off a tennis court in cut-down blue jeans with her shirttail out—and "Thank God, *yes*," she said. "What I need now is a drink."

The what-if's of history. Though it is a game that is usually played in retrospect, there are occasions when you find yourself playing it on the spot, as, indeed, I did there in that empty corridor. There I was, no longer in the first blush, certainly, but in pretty good shape, all considered—I made it a habit to get laps in around the reservoir at least once a week, and I've always been careful about my diet. And there on that grim November afternoon *she* was, that summer's day of a girl, that Persephone, too old to be my daughter and too young to be my wife, clad only in those two little garlands of lilac and rose and the Japanese sandals with the peg between the toes, saying what she needed most now was a drink. What if I asked her to have one in my roomette with me? Not knowing what I might find in Armadillo, I had packed a fifth of Dewar's in my bag. I could ring for glasses and ice, or we could use paper cups like a picnic in the park. Manet's *Le Déjeuner sur l'Herbe* flashed into my mind—those two *Deuxième Empire* dandies in their frock coats and that marvelous woman looking over her bare shoulder with nothing on but a dim smile.

What if she accepted my invitation? What if it was what she had been waiting for since the beginning? I remember that I got as far as the words "What if" themselves, but how I was planning to finish the sentence I am no longer sure. "What if I asked you to have one with me?" maybe, but maybe just "What if they ask to see your birth certificate?"—something foolish and avuncular like that. Probably I was not sure even at the time what I was going to say, and now I will never know, because a porter appeared in the corridor then with an armful of bed linen and pillows, and thinking, I suppose, that the girl was in a hurry to get through with her duties, he flattened himself out against the wall to give her room to pass. I see him there like a bank teller in a movie stick-up with his hands and cheek pressed tight to the wall. It was a gallantry too strenuous to ignore, and giving me the more professional of her two smiles, the girl squeezed by him, chastely keeping her back to his as she did so, and disappeared through one of those hissing pneumatic doors. What if? What if? Who knows.

I had not thought before this of having a drink at all, but back in the roomette again, I decided I needed one. I had it in one of the paper cups, neat, and it not only tasted of the paper but in some ways, I think, was the loneliest drink of my life. It was dark outside by now, and I watched the lights go by, wondering whether we were in New Jersey still or had crossed into Pennsylvania. I couldn't remember stopping at Trenton, but maybe the tourist specials didn't stop there or I had been too caught up in my reveries to notice. I had not one drink but three before I was done, and what made them loneliest was the thought that except for my ineptitude—or was it fate?—the girl might have been there with me. If the girl had never buzzed at my door, I would have been sitting there with nobody—zero. As it was, I was sitting there with minus one.

I have never been a more than ordinarily sensual man. As a boy away at school I was brought up in the cold-shower and laps-before-breakfast tradition, and growing up with a twin sister took some of the heat off too. I knew what girls *looked* like anyway, and Miriam was never bashful about telling me what it felt like to be one. Later on, as a bachelor and virtual celibate, the secret of my success was the obvious one. I kept busy. Girls didn't need sex so much when they had the period, Miriam told me when we were young, and I discovered that this biological mercy held true also for me. The teaching period, the novel period, the scrap-iron period —as long as they were upon me, I was comparatively safe. And, like anything else, of course, continence tends to become a habit.

On the other hand, in the same place probably as where I came across the Hindu idea of the mind of man as a monkey in the trees, I came across a discussion of chastity among holy men. For year after year, I learned, and from incarnation to incarnation, they resist so successfully all the temptations of the flesh to come their way that eventually they reach the point where even the subtlest and most irresistible has almost no power to attract them. In fact, by this time there is almost no element of self left in them to attract. But even among holy men, apparently, *almost* is a key word. As long as they are on their guard, they are safe. As long as they see the shimmering young ranee or fragrant-limbed houri coming from far enough away to give them time to prepare for the encounter, they have nothing to fear. But take them by surprise, let the temptress leap out unexpectedly from behind a piece of temple statuary, and in case after case the game is lost. All the vast quantities of psychic energy that they have accumulated at such enormous cost through life after life of total abstinence are released in an instant to be squandered in one great orgy that may go on for centuries. It is a tale with both its comic and its tragic dimensions.

In my case, too, it was the unexpectedness of the thing that was largely responsible for what happened—being jolted out of my twilight musings by that deafening buzzer and then opening the sliding door to find the girl there in that reverberation of a bathing suit. Add to that the three papery scotches and the loneliness of them. Add to that also the fact, I am told, that one reason truck drivers are reputedly so lascivious is that the constant vibration of the engine works darkly on their prostates as, for all I know, my seat over a wheel of the tourist special was working darkly on mine. Add to that the character of the roomette itself. What had been a hermit's cell, a corner away from time and a window on the world, became suddenly an adolescent's dream. The intense privacy of it—the door could be locked, and no one had any reason to break in on me anyway. The anonymity of it, the almost physical sense of all the others who had sat there with similar stirrings before me. Even the architectural features of it: the mirror on the inside of the door, which turned my legs and thighs into those of a complaisant stranger or, with no more stretch of the imagination than I was then capable of, into Persephone's tanned legs. The collapsible sink, the neat little stack of Pullman towels . . .

I did nothing, of course. I just sat there quietly enough with the scotch in my hand and looked out the window, I suppose, although it was too dark to see much. But in my head I peopled that little room with lurid what-if's from as far back as my childhood. And Persephone! How we dallied with each other there as the train sped southward—the ingenuity, the indefatigability, that little handful of rose and lilac hanging like a bride's bouquet from the electric fan above the door. The ignominy of it, I thought—those adolescent fantasies at my stage of the game. And the sadness of it too, the unutterable sadness of all that aching life caught on a train between periods with no place to go.

48

I went to bed early after a sandwich in the club car for supper, but sleep gave me little respite. I kept waking up with station lights in my face or the clank and jostle of cars being changed, the shock of coming to a standstill after the cradling jounce of the rails. And in between times I dreamed.

The girl in the bathing suit was in the hospital and I wanted to see her desperately but had a hard time persuading the doctors to let me in. When they finally consented, I found her lying in bed with nothing but a blank where her face should have been. She reached out one hand toward me, but when I took it in mine, it turned out to be not a hand but a fish-hook.

In another dream I was riding in the train with my father, who, it seemed, had never actually died at all. It had been just some complicated misunderstanding that I wasn't able to understand fully. He kept pointing through the window and whispering to me to keep watching because we were about to pass the house where I had been born. But I could see no houses—just the barren Jersey flats with the Pulaski Skyway arching across it in the distance.

But the dream that I remember most vividly and that for obvious reasons disturbed me most took place on a stretch of tropical beach which I recognized somehow as Armadillo. Chris and Tony, my two young nephews, were there. They had very grave expressions on their faces and were sitting in straight-backed chairs with their backs to the sea. They were dressed in dark suits, and I realized they must have come down for their mother's funeral. Charlie, their father, lay asleep at their feet with his face buried in his arms. I was standing in front of them dressed also for a funeral, and their gaze was fixed steadily upon me. Little by little I was undressing. First I took off my tie and jacket, then my shirt, my socks and shoes and trousers, so that finally I had nothing on but my undershorts. There was a cool breeze blowing in off the water, but the sand beneath my bare feet felt warm.

After a while the boys stood up woodenly as though to sing a hymn or at the entrance of the priest, and at that point I dropped my undershorts and stood there completely naked with their solemn dark eyes watching me. Then I lay belly down in the warm sand and started trying to work myself slowly into it like a worm with the early bird hot on its tail. Harder and faster I pushed until suddenly I felt something unspeakable happening to me and cried out to them, "See me! See me!" as though my life depended on it, or perhaps what I cried out was "Semen! Semen!" I do not know which it was, and that's quite all right by me. It was the first dream of its kind that I had had for years, and it woke me up with the sound of that forlorn cry still echoing in my ears.

As I turned on the ghostly blue night-light to look at my watch and so on, I felt sure that I would fit right into things at Armadillo.

CHAPTER FOUR

WHEN I WOKE UP the next morning, it was summer. Just
by the way the sunshine flashed off the hoods and roofs
of cars you would have known it. The temperature in
the train was about the same as when we left New York,
but you could feel the difference anyway—something
soft in the air, some sense of promise that had not been
there before. I could hear Southern voices in the corridor, a man and a woman talking together. They must
have gotten on during the night when I was asleep. The
unhurried phrases trailing off at the end, the even-toned,
bedspread-smoothing, grocery-listing rumble and rise of
their courtly morning voices outside my closed door—

there is no more reassuring sound in the world as far as I know, and if ever somebody has to tell me that I have only a few more weeks to live or the world is about to come to an end, I hope it is a Southerner who does it. It was just the right sound to wake up to after my *Walpurgisnacht*. And breakfast in the dining car was also just right.

The sun almost blinded me, flashing off the white tablecloth and swinging back and forth like a little wafer of fire in the water pitcher, and the parts of me that I could feel it warm on were the parts that I could see reflected in the window as we raced through Georgia—my mouth and chin, the knuckles of one hand and part of my sleeve. Throwing weight-watching to the winds, I ordered both grits and cornbread with my ham and eggs, and the waiter who brought it was the king of an African tribe with a voice like Paul Robeson's in *Othello*. I felt decadent and Mediterranean in his presence and thought how if life were based more on the natural order of things, I would be keeping him cool with a fan made of chicken feathers. I also thought how Ellie would have approved of that feeling.

When we stopped at Jacksonville, I got out on the platform to stretch my legs, and although I had already seen that it was summer through the window, the shock of actually feeling it for myself quite overwhelmed me. I was a child getting out of his last class on the last day of school. I was old Dr. Manette released after all those years from the Bastille. I was the jolly green giant. There was a man selling oranges in net bags, dozens of them heaped up on a luggage cart, and they were so orange, they were so Southern and summery and round, that I couldn't resist buying some although of course I had no possible use for them where I was going. There must have been a good dozen and a half of them in the net bag. I could give them to Bebb as a kind of hostess present, I thought, but, considering the purpose of my visit, that seemed deceitful and Judas-like. Beware of Wops bearing gifts, my sister Miriam might have said.

It is curious how many changes of heart I was able to have about Bebb when you think that I had seen the man only once and had no reason to believe that he had changed in any way himself during the short time since. But when I got back to my roomette again with the bag of oranges, I found myself feeling almost sorry for him. Here I was, a smart-aleck from the North with a college education and a small private income, and not much to show for either of them. And there he was—a crook certainly, a degenerate apparently, but God only knew with what provocation. The way he had put sugar in his chocolate milk as though to make up for a grim and candyless childhood. That black raincoat that couldn't possibly have been enough to keep him warm. I pictured him growing up in one of the drab towns that now and then the railroad tracks cut through—a filling station, a movie theater, the rows of houses facing the tracks with their jigsaw porches and sagging steps. The wonder of it seemed suddenly not that he had sunk so low but that he had come so far—flying to New York and heaven only knew where-all else to keep tabs on his far-flung if devious interests, the ads that carried his name all over the nation. And when you came right down to it, was there any real harm in what he was doing, or was the disapproval of people like Ellie and me mainly just aesthetic? If he played on the weakness of men, it was at least only on their weakness for . . . what? For the prestige that went with diplomas and ecclesiastical titles; for the easy success and quick approval that are among men's more innocent dreams; in the long run maybe only on their weakness, however slapstick and obscure, for God. Why not? It was hard, suddenly, to blame him for what he was.

And yet with Miriam on my mind and my own helplessness to be of any real use to her, it was still not hard for me to blame him for what he was not and for what I was therefore not either. For the first time I found myself wondering why I had answered his crazy ad to begin with. Was it, as I had thought, just to find fuel for my new journalistic period? Or had I answered it more in the way that I lit an occasional candle to Saint Anthony, hoping against all reason that in a world where there was obviously no magic any more, the flickering little wick in its ruby glass cup might still manage to cast a holy spell if only on myself?

In any case, the problem of what to do with the oranges solved itself when we finally pulled into West Palm Beach that afternoon. There, standing prettily on one of the little metal stairs they let down from the cars and leaning out from it with one hand grasping the pull-rail and the other shading her eyes like an old print of a sailor in the rigging, was the bathing-suit girl. She was fully dressed at this point in a powder-blue railroad uniform. My first reaction, I admit, was to run and hide as though I had seduced her in reality instead of just in my florid imaginings, but then I thought better of it. I went up and handed her my bag of oranges, which she took before she realized, I think, what it was or that I was giving it to her to keep. "These are for you," I said. "They're full of vitamin D, the sunshine vitamin," and then I stepped away quickly before she had a chance to give them back or protest.

I do not think that she recognized me or that such impulsive gestures from male passengers were anything new to her, but I treasure the look that passed between us as the train started to pull out. It was the kind of look that is possible maybe only for people who feel sure they will never set eyes on each other again, the kind of look that is sometimes exchanged between the windows of two trains as they speed in the same direction along parallel tracks and come for a moment abreast of each other. For that moment, anyway, there were no secrets between us, no curtain discreetly zipped or camouflaging chatter. We seemed to stand more helplessly naked to each other's gaze than in my most lurid fantasies the evening before, and maybe that was what it was all about, I thought. The aching loins, the tigers in the blood, maybe in the end it is not so much the possession of another's full nakedness that we hunger for but just the presence of another's full humanity, and the chance to be known ourselves as fully human. I like to think that there may have been even a touch of *what if* in her glance as well as in mine. She didn't smile or say thank you as the train started slowly carrying her off with my oranges in her arms, but that may well be just because she didn't need to. Persephone.

They gave me a choice of cars at the Hertz garage, and the one I chose was a two-door convertible the color of frozen custard with white-wall tires and upholstery as red as the inside of a mouth. It seemed to fit my mood, which was a combination of sheer lightheartedness at the weather and the sense of vacation together with a rather desperate hilarity as I realized that I no longer had any clear idea what I was on my way to Armadillo to accomplish or how I would go about accomplishing it once I got there. But at least I enjoyed driving along the Sunshine State Parkway with the top down and my hair stinging my forehead in the warm wind. Once I left the parkway, there was a long stretch of back roads with some complicated turns, but I had no trouble finding my way and arrived at Armadillo in something less than an hour after setting off from West Palm.

O Armadillo, Armadillo . . . thou that killest the prophets and stonest them that are sent unto thee. If I forget thee, let my right hand forget her cunning. If I do not remember thee, let my tongue cleave to the roof of my mouth . . . What I see in my mind most clearly as I try to remember is a certain stretch of sidewalk. The main shopping street comes to an end where some railroad tracks cut across it, but beyond the tracks the sidewalk continues a quarter of a mile or more along one side of a pot-holed macadam road that leads south toward Fort Lauderdale. It is a wide sidewalk made of marble slabs with crab-grass growing up between them and spider-webbing all over the place. There are concrete benches every once in a while, the concrete stained with bird-droppings and the weathered green slats flaked and splintery and in some cases missing altogether. At regular intervals there are streetlamps, ornamental streetlamps with fluted shafts once painted the same green as the benches but with just an occasional flake or two still sticking on them to suggest the original color. Curlicued wrought-iron brackets jut out from the tops of the shafts to hold the light globes, but the globes are not there any more or were perhaps never installed to begin with, just in each case a few stiff black wires hanging down.

The sidewalk eventually peters out somewhere in the scrubby grass. It doesn't go anywhere. It doesn't serve any purpose and never did because the town it was originally laid down to serve never got out that far. During the land boom in the twenties, apparently, there were dreams for Armadillo that never materialized, and the building lots that were to have been for millionaire villas and luxury hotels are nothing much now but palmettos and creepers and the kind of junk people throw out of car windows. When I think of Armadillo, it is of this sidewalk I think first—a native American ruin and not entirely without a kind of appeal as it rambles off into the scrub, going nowhere.

Not knowing where to find Bebb, of course, and not even sure that I wanted to find him just yet, I cruised around for a while in my fancy car, trying to get the feel of the place. If it had been late June nearer the coast, it was mid-July or August here—not so much that the sun was hotter but that as far as I could see there was no place to escape from it. The main street, where the shops were, was all one- and two-story buildings with false fronts sticking up like garage attendants' pompadours and only an occasional tin awning's worth of skimpy shade. Everything seemed made out of stucco or cinderblock and bleached to about the same shade of oystery white, which caught the sun and reflected it back so dazzlingly from all directions that the only way to escape it was to wait for night or die. I drove around town with my eyes squinted half shut to keep out the hellish glare until finally the perspiration started to make them water and smart so that when I parked in front of a drugstore and went in to buy a pair of dark glasses, the clerk looked at me queerly, as though he thought I was weeping.

The Mother Church I happened on quite by accident. A few miles out of town along the same road that the sidewalk bordered, there was a little complex of buildings dominated by a souvenir shop, a long, shed-like affair that displayed coconut husks carved and painted to look like cannibals' faces, rugs with peacocks and sunsets and Red Indians on them, grass skirts, baskets of all kinds, and many novelty items like shrunken heads hung up by their long hair and Florida scenes composed entirely of real seashells. There was also a barber shop with a tankful of miniature turtles in the window—one of them was trying to clamber up the glass with his hind feet braced on a companion's shell, but he fell over backward as I watched him. There was also a 1930's modern building with curved walls painted swimming-pool blue and lots of glass brick instead of windows. Projecting far enough out from the side of the building to be visible from in front there was an almost life-sized cross made of frosted glass that looked as though it could be lit up from inside. On the vertical member, printed vertically, was the word HOLY and on the cross-piece, printed horizontally and sharing the same O, was the word LOVE with a small red heart preceding the L to make the design symmetrical. It looked not unlike the trademark stamped on Bayer aspirin tablets.

Napoleon gazing on the Sphinx could not have had a keener sense of history than I did sitting there in red-leatherette luxury with the steering wheel hot in my hand and peering up at Bebb's cross through my new dark glasses. What had brought me to this place anyway? There was my discovering Bebb's ad at a peculiarly receptive moment in my life, of course, and then step by step our meeting in the Lexington Avenue lunchroom, Ellie's digging up the *Journal-American* piece, even Tom's getting the fish-hook in his eyelid and the fact that the vet's apartment was not far from Manhattan House—a perfectly plausible train of subtly interlocking circumstances whose consequence had been to land me here between the souvenir store and the fire-insurance building with the Florida sun in my eyes. A simple or not so simple matter of cause and effect—inevitable, impersonal, and automatic. Karma, as those bedeviled holy men would call it. And yet, as Napoleon must surely have felt it there in the sands of Egypt, in addition to the sense of history there was a sense of destiny—a feeling that, no matter what the circumstances, no matter if Tom had not tangled with the fish-hook, or even if I had not seen Bebb's ad, I was bound to end up here anyway. Mysterious powers. The silvery-faced soda-jerk whom Bebb had identified as a visitor from outer space. It was another of my operatic moments. I approached the door to the church like Don Alvaro in *La Forza del Destino*. And it was unlocked.

Inside, the Mother Church seemed to consist of a single low-ceilinged room, empty and smelling dimly of floor wax. About forty folding chairs set up in tidy rows filled it just about to capacity. The sunshine came bright through the glass brick, and thus there was plenty of light in the place even though there was no way to see either in or out. The pink color of the walls reminded me of denture gums. At the far side, opposite the entrance, there was an altar table and a lectern. A box marked LOVE OFFERINGS stood near the door, and above it hung a rug like the ones for sale outside except that instead of a Red Indian or a sunset it bore a picture of Jesus Christ. It was a three-quarters view, head and shoulders, that showed him with a very high forehead and long hair that shone with much brushing and had a wave it it. He looked a little like Charlton Heston and was wearing a simple homespun garment with what I believe is called a *bateau* neckline. There was a faint glow around his head, and his gaze was directed off to the right and a little above the horizontal toward a spot which there in Bebb's church happened to be occupied by a hot-air register.

I sat down in one of the folding chairs in the front row, and because my eyes still smarted from all the open-car wind and sun, I closed them. It was extremely quiet in there, the kind of quiet you are apt to find in empty theaters or restaurants or even empty classrooms, as I remember them from my teaching days, places empty which you usually think of as full, places where the very absence of people becomes a kind of lulling presence. Quite without premeditation—the fact that it was a church, after all, and that my eyes were closed must have tripped some forgotten thermostat—I found myself saying a Hail Mary. "Pray for us now and at the

60

hour of our death," I whispered. And pray for Miriam, I added, at the hour of hers, and I thought of her waving that off-hand wave at me while she was stubbing out her cigarette, and wondered if it was possible that I might never see her again. I had a feeling that it was supposed to be a heresy to pray for the dead, but I decided that this might just be a Protestant idea and prayed for my father and mother anyway. I remembered my father on the train in my dream and how it turned out that he hadn't died at all but that it had just been a complicated misunderstanding. Maybe death itself, I thought . . . just a complicated misunderstanding. I even said a prayer for Tom, which I was almost sure was heretical—Tom penned up in one of those little cages at the vet's. I wondered if his eyelid was sore.

Then I felt a hand on my shoulder and heard a voice say, "Blessed are those who mourn, for they shall be comforted." I thought for an instant that it must be Bebb himself, but as soon as I opened my eyes I saw that it was not. It was a man about Bebb's age, in his fifties somewhere, wearing shorts and a sport shirt. He had the most dazzling set of false teeth I had ever seen and was wearing a pair of glasses that were rimless except across the tops, where the rims were heavy and straight and gave him a very intense and earnest look. He said, "I am Laverne Brown, the assistant pastor. The many friends that the Lord has blessed me with all call me Brownie."

Standing up, I told him my name, and we shook hands.

"Your eyes are red," he said.

"It's this Florida sunshine of yours," I explained,

"and I got sweat in them from my eyebrows when I was squinting."

"We were given eyebrows to keep the sweat out, not to put it in," he said. "Never be ashamed of honest tears, dear." And then he smiled.

Two things—first his smile, and then his calling me dear.

Brownie's smile—that low-hung rack of glittering teeth, that fiercely sincere set of horn-rimmed eyebrows, those pale eyes staring out at you. The smile of a man at a joke he has not quite heard the punch-line of? The smile of a man caught cheating in a pay toilet? The smile of a little man who has just been kicked in the crotch by a big man? It was all of these and none of them. The smile was Brownie and as impossible to do justice to in a few words as Brownie himself was. Yet the smile was also the glasses and the teeth, and if Brownie was in the habit of laying them aside when he went to bed at night and if he then had occasion to smile afterwards, I can almost see the teeth trying to clamber out of the water glass like the miniature turtle in the barber shop and I can almost hear the spectacles pulling themselves across the table by their ear-pieces—the way they say French wines corked up in bottles sparkle each year when spring returns to the vineyard of their origin.

And he called me dear—not just then, during the first few seconds of our acquaintance, but a great many times afterward as well. "Never be ashamed of honest tears, dear," he said, and I thought that first time that I had simply heard him wrong or that "dear" was part of "tears" somehow, possibly a repetition of it for effect. The next few times I thought various other things—

62

that he was talking to somebody else perhaps or that it was not a word at all but just a sound, a verbal *tic douleureux* like one that a professor of mine at college had who would throw in the sound "ayeeee," drawn out at considerable length, about every fourth sentence until it got so we hardly noticed it any more. In any event, whatever explanations I arrived at the first dozen times or so, the point of it is that one way or another I got so used to hearing it that by the time I was forced to conclude that it was clearly "dear" he was saying and clearly me he was saying it to, I was so used to it that it seemed quite natural.

I decided against trying to persuade him any further that I had not been weeping. I had been praying, after all, and I suppose that is a kind of tears. I decided also against asking for Bebb or in any other way tipping my hand at this point. I was interested in different churches and religions from a sociological point of view, I told him, and with some time on my hands here in Armadillo, I thought it would be interesting to find out what was going on around here in that line.

He said, "Well you have certainly come to the right place. There is a whole lot going on around Armadillo in the area of your special interest. Right here at Holy Love, to give you an example. We are a church, as anyone can plainly see, but it might interest you to know that we are also a fully accredited educational institution."

"It interests me very much," I said. "Tell me about it."

"You take Holy Scripture," Brownie said. "The Bible is a frequently misunderstood book. I will give you a simple illustration." His accent was Southern, I decided, but with a lot of the nap worn off. His shorts and the plain, sky-blue sport shirt that he wore hanging outside them had nothing sporty about them. It was clear that he wore them purely for comfort the way a man might go around the house in his underwear. He had a laundered look, scrawny-necked, with arms that were as surprisingly hairy as his bare legs were surprisingly hairless. I caught a whiff of after-shave as he crossed in front of me on his way to the lectern. He opened the Bible that lay upon it.

He said, "I will read from the Apostle Paul to give you a simple illustration. The Epistle to the Romans, chapter twelve, verses nineteen to twenty-one inclusive. 'Dearly beloved, avenge not yourselves, but rather give place unto wrath, because it is written, "Vengeance is mine. I will repay, saith the Lord." ' "

The words came out in a kind of hushabye sing-song that seemed oddly at variance with what I thought was the Apostle's rather forceful tone, and when he reached "saith the Lord," Brownie paused and smiled as though the Lord had just promised a major tax cut. He held up one hand with what looked like several fraternity rings on the fingers and a gold spring-band around his hairy wrist.

"But this is the part I want you to pay special attention to. Verses twenty and twenty-one. 'Therefore if thine enemy hungers, feed him; if he thirsts, give him drink; for in so doing thou shalt heap coals of fire on his head.' 'Thou shalt heap coals of fire on his head,' " he repeated. "Dear, would you be interested in knowing what the Apostle means about heaping coals of fire on your enemy's head?"

I said, "It sounds like one-upmanship to me. Your enemy craps on you, and in return you do all sorts of nice things for him. That makes him feel like a heel." I came within an inch of saying "like a shit" but substituted heel at the last minute. Crap, shit—what was there about Brownie that made me want to use such language? But I do not think he heard it, because all the time I was giving my explanation he was slowly shaking his head back and forth as though he knew in advance that I would explain it wrong and didn't particularly want to listen to me do it.

"That is a very common misinterpretation of this Scripture," he said, "and I'm not surprised to see you fall into it. You say you are interested in religion, so you might be interested in hearing what the Apostle really meant. How can a person know what he really meant? By studying the background and by familiarizing himself with the customs of the times."

Brownie was looking toward me in one direction and the picture of Jesus was looking toward the hot-air register in the other direction, but Brownie turned at this juncture and pointed at the picture. "Treating your enemy nice to make him feel bad. Does that sound like the kind of thing any apostle of *his* would say? I will tell you a little-known fact about the Holy Land back in Saint Paul's time. When winter came and it got cold, not everybody had his own fire. Fuel was sometimes scarce, for one thing, but that wasn't the only problem, because even if you had the fuel, what were you going to light it with? They didn't have matches then, dear. So the custom was this. The baker was the one who had the fire, and he got it started real early in the morning so as to get his ovens hot for baking. Then when folks wanted to start their own fires, all they had to do was go down to the baker's. They would take with them an inexpensive pottery vessel, and for a small consideration the baker would let them have several of his burning coals. They would place these coals in their vessels to take them home, and maybe by now you can guess how they carried them. Yes. They carried them just the way some of our black sisters still carry their washbaskets. On their heads. You can well imagine what a good feeling it was —the warmth from the baker's hot coals traveling down their neck and shoulders on a frosty morning. And when they got home, they used them to start a fire of their own with, as easy as rolling off a log. That clears up a lot of things, doesn't it?" Brownie was smiling—those teeth, those glasses—and looking intently at me.

"The Apostle says, 'If thine enemy hungers, feed him; if thine enemy thirsts, give him drink' because that will give your enemy a nice warm feeling, and he will repent and do likewise unto others. He will take the coals of fire you heaped on his head like the baker and start a fire of his own. If you used this as a sermon text, you could title it like the popular song—'I've got my love to keep me warm.'"

I said, "It's not a meaning that exactly leaps off the page, but it certainly puts the passage in a new light." I had sat down again when Brownie started speaking, but now that he was finished, I felt it put me at a psychological disadvantage. I started to get up, but he motioned me to stay where I was.

He said, "You've got to know the background and the customs."

"You spoke of running an educational institution in

connection with this church," I said. "Am I right in thinking this is part of a course maybe?"

"It is part of two courses," Brownie said. "Exegesis and New Testament Background. It comes up in both."

I said, "Would I be right also in thinking these are correspondence courses, or do you have students actually in residence here in Armadillo?"

"Gospel Faith College," Brownie said in a rather absent-minded way, looking down as he spoke. "Full accreditation from the State Board of Education." He had not answered my question, and at first I thought that it was because he chose not to, but then I saw that he was running his finger down a page of the Bible, evidently looking for something. I don't think he had heard my question.

"Mark, chapter seven reading from verse twenty-four down here to verse thirty. The Syrophenecian woman. This is another case in point, only here the true explanation comes from a knowledge of the original tongue and not from a knowledge of ancient customs. And this time it's not the Apostle Paul. It's Jesus." The way he said Jesus, drawing it out into two distinct syllables, I saw the name G. Zuss in my mind.

Brownie said, "This Syrophenecian woman came to G. Zuss and besought him would he cast forth the devil out of her daughter, she had an unclean spirit in her. . . . This Syrophenecian woman's daughter, she was unclean, dear, and the Syrophenecian woman went and fell at the Master's feet. . . ." He seemed to have been reading ahead of the part he was paraphrasing, but looked back up at me here with his finger marking the place. "Here it is. Listen to what G. Zuss said when the mother finished begging him to heal her girl. He said, 'It is not meet to take the children's bread and cast it to the dogs.' How do you like that?"

"Maybe he had a headache," I said, "or she interrupted him in the middle of something and he felt cross. He was human, after all, whatever else he was."

Brownie said, "He was the Lamb of God, dear. He was the Rose of Sharon," and he spoke the curious old titles in a dreamy way as though they had come drifting into his memory from far away. "He didn't have headaches. And he didn't go around using language like that either. It sounds pretty bad in English, doesn't it?— referring to all the Syrophenecian people as dogs. But that's just the translation. In the original tongue the word isn't 'dog' at all. It's more like a pet name for dogs —like pup or pooch. Poochie," he said, "would be closer to the original meaning of G. Zuss."

"Poochie," I said. "That would take a lot of the sting out."

Brownie said, "There wouldn't be any sting then at all. It was just his little joke—using a pet name like that. And this is supported by the fact he went ahead and cast the unclean spirit out of the girl anyway. In John two four, when G. Zuss and his mother are attending the wedding service in Cana and his mother asks him to do something about the wine running out, G. Zuss says to her, 'Woman, what have I to do with thee!' Now you take the word 'woman' that sounds so spiteful and mean in English . . ."

It was obviously not in my interests to antagonize the man, and details like these of the Gospel Faith curriculum might prove very useful to me later on, but some-

68

thing came to my mind that I couldn't resist throwing at him. It must have been the phrase "original tongue" that did it, because I found myself thinking of the one place in the Gospels, as far as I know, where the words of Jesus are given in the language he's supposed to have actually used. Ellie and I joined the Canterbury Choir group one winter and I remembered them from Schütz's *The Seven Last Words of Christ*, which we did—she in the alto section and I a marginal baritone.

"*'Eli, Eli, lama sabachthani?'*" I said, interrupting him. "You can't get more original than that, and it seems to mean he's calling God a sonofabitch for running out on him. Or was it just an old Jewish custom to ask the Deity theological questions when you were being crucified?"

Brownie said, "*'My God, my God, why hast thou forsaken me?'*" He was not smiling. He had taken off his glasses to wipe them, and without them he looked old and confused in his Youngstown haircut and the oversized sport shirt that hung down over his shoulders. "No, dear," he said, putting back his glasses. "Those terrible words mean just what they say. They mark the moment when he knew that before the resurrection he was going to have to descend into Hell."

"Maybe he was there already," I said.

We were silent for a few moments. Jesus descending into Hell, I thought. Maybe the reason he was so intent on the hot-air register was that it awakened old memories of that trip—the long downward chute, the belching heat. I remembered dimly from catechism class that the reason he had gone down was to save the souls of the good people who had lived too early to be saved by him through the normal earthly channels. Maybe he had found time to save a few of the bad ones too. I hoped that was so and wondered if Brownie might be engaged in similar theological speculations. He had closed the Bible and was standing there with both hands on the cover, staring vacantly at one of the glass-brick windows. Out of nowhere and without looking at me, he said, "You said your name was Antonio Parr, didn't you?"

I said that I had.

"Mr. Bebb's in Texas on the Lord's work. He'll be coming back in a day or two probably. But he left instructions about you before he went."

"Bebb knew I was coming?" I couldn't keep the surprise out of my voice.

Brownie said, "He said if you came while he was gone, to tell you you would be welcome to stay at the Manse."

It is hard to describe the combination of uneasiness and grudging admiration I felt at the thought that Bebb had known I might be coming to Armadillo before I had the faintest idea of coming myself. He had undoubtedly based his assumption on the premise that I was genuinely interested in cashing in on my ordination by starting a diploma mill of my own even if it meant going to Florida to learn how, but though his premise was wrong, the assumption itself had proved right. I was there. Bebb had known something about me that I had not known.

Brownie was smiling at me from the lectern, his eyes pale and watery through his glasses, and I found myself uneasier still at the thought that he too had known something about me that I had not known he knew. From the moment I gave him my name, he knew who I was and what I was ostensibly there for—to learn the

ropes and join Bebb's sordid little team. My story of
being interested in different churches and religions from
a sociological point of view—he must have smiled at me
like an old whore at a sister who, for all her virginal airs,
has obviously been screwed but royally, and by the same
man no less. Bebb, that molester of innocence. But
Brownie gave no sign of holding my duplicity against
me. Specialist as he was in making the rough places of
Scripture smooth, he had probably explained it away
already on the basis of my background and customs or
the tongue I spoke.

And of course there was my true reason for being in
Armadillo—the deeper duplicity that I devoutly believed Brownie could not know nor, heaven help me,
Bebb—which was to skin Bebb alive, as I had put it to
Ellie that fateful Beef Stroganoff evening. And who
could say? Beneath that, perhaps, there was a truer
reason still for my being in Armadillo which even I
did not know any more than Napoleon can have
known what inexorable power had drawn him at last
to the sandy lion-paws of the Sphinx. In any case, it
was such a tricky game I played that I decided against
accepting Bebb's invitation to stay at the Manse, useful as it might have been for my private purposes. I
might talk in my sleep. So I lied again and said I had
made arrangements to stay at the motel I had noticed
on my way into town. I even remembered its name—
the Salamander—in case Brownie should ask me, so
wily had I become.

But he didn't ask me. He put his arm around my
shoulder and walked me to the door, where we made
our farewells under the frosted-glass cross. "Lights
up," he said and pushed a switch just inside the en-

trance. It did. HOLY LOVE with the light shining out from it and the small red heart to make things symmetrical. He turned it off again.

It was late afternoon by now, and the sunlight had gone mellower, more golden, so that I no longer needed my dark glasses. At the souvenir shop a man was gathering in the peacock rugs and shrunken heads for the night. Brownie closed the door of my car for me and then leaned on it with his hairy arms. I was aware of his after-shave again. Those battered eyes under the horn-rimmed eyebrows. Those seraphic teeth.

He said, "Here's what you do. You go on back and get settled at the Salamander Motel. Take your time and wash up, and then when you're ready, you come over to the Manse. Mrs. Bebb will give us supper, and I will show you around myself." We shook hands on it.

Fortunately for my lie to Brownie, there was room for me at the Salamander. I gave them my license number and the address of the apartment Tom and I shared in New York, and then, just as I was about to sign my name on the register, I stopped. Should I or shouldn't I? Was I or wasn't I? I decided then that if I was going to play the game, I might as well play it, and with a ball-point pen that didn't do well over the place where my sweaty hand had hesitated for a moment, I wrote *The Reverend Antonio Parr*. For all I knew, Bebb or Brownie might check it someday. They would have thought it queer if I'd signed myself any other way.

CHAPTER FIVE

IT HAD NEVER occurred to me that Bebb might be
married. Perhaps it was because of some lingering
childhood image of the priesthood that had come
loose in my subconscious and attached itself to him—
the priest as celibate with the Church his only bride
and all men his children. Or perhaps it was because
the one time I had seen him in the city he had seemed
so much on his own, so sure of himself and in charge,
like a parlor magician doing tricks, that it never
crossed my mind he might have a wife who knew all
his tricks by heart, somebody he went away from and
came back to and maybe even depended on, if only

to fold his pocket handkerchief into those four points and keep buttons on his raincoat. I was not prepared even for the idea of a Mrs. Bebb, let alone for its incarnation in Lucille.

Brownie took me in to her. He must have seen me coming, because he was standing on the porch waiting when I pulled up to the curb in my rented convertible. It was one of the older streets in Armadillo, with a few trees big enough to cast some shade, I imagined— the sun was setting as I arrived. Instead of the stucco bungalows and flat-roofed split-levels that I had seen virtually everywhere else, there was a row of good-sized frame houses that must have made it one of the more fashionable parts of town in its day. The Manse itself was a modified Charles Addams with too many windows and a fair amount of scrollwork around the eaves and porch. One corner was rounded off in the suggestion of a turret, and there were dormers and bays in unexpected places. Off to one side but visible from the street was one of those children's gym sets, a rather rusty-looking slide attached to a swing and seesaw. There was also a sandbox with a broken chair in the middle of it, and I found myself wondering whether, having only recently adjusted myself to the fact of Bebb's having a wife, I was going to have to prepare myself now for the possibility of children—roly-poly little replicas of Bebb running around in small black raincoats of their own.

Unfamiliar with the amenities of dining out in Armadillo, I came dressed much as I had been on the train, in a shirt and tie with a seersucker jacket to replace the heavier one I had traveled in. Brownie, on the other hand, had not changed out of his shorts and sport shirt, and the disadvantage was clearly mine. I was the carpetbagger, the fast talker from the North. Brownie was all palm-leaf fans and hot verandas and flies in the honeysuckle. He looked as though he had been working at something—there were two wet stains at his sky-blue armpits, and I thought his glasses were slightly fogged up—but he greeted me cordially, expressing the hope that I had found everything to my liking at the Salamander, and held the screen door for me as we entered the Manse.

As we walked down the dim hall toward what turned out to be Mrs. Bebb's private sitting room at the back of the house, my eye was caught by a doorway standing ajar under the staircase. It was a bathroom, as I had guessed, and glancing in as we passed, I got a glimpse of the toilet. It was the old-fashioned kind with an overhead tank and a pull chain, altogether what I would have expected to find in a house of that vintage, but what I didn't expect to find only because I had forgotten they existed was the toilet seat, which was not form-fitting and white and shaped like the victory wreaths they hang around the necks of racehorses but a little flat ring of varnished brown wood. How it carried me back, that brown toilet seat—carried me back to my childhood and beyond to some Victorian incarnation perhaps—and just as you think of the Capitol by its dome and Saint Patrick's perhaps by its great bronze doors, so it is by that toilet seat that I will always think of the Manse—shiny and brown and out of another world entirely.

Mrs. Bebb's sitting room was at the end of the hall, and Brownie opened the door without knocking. There was the smell of a hot TV set in the air and the un-mistakable intonations of a sports commentator. It was a color set, I discovered when I finally located it, and Mrs. Bebb was sitting in a high-backed wicker armchair at an angle that put her back both to it and to me, so that the first part of her I saw was a thin bare arm slant-ing down straight toward the floor. Just an inch or so above the floor she was holding a tall glass of what looked like Florida orange juice. Speaking louder than usual in order to be heard above the TV—it was a football game, with the color tuned wrong, because the faces of the players looked green and the reds seethed like burning embers—Brownie said, "This is the Reverend Parr. The one I told you about." And then the bare arm rose slowly and retracted, and Lucille Bebb craned around the armchair back to take her first good look at me.

She was wearing dark glasses, and partly because the light in the room was not good—just the remains of a sunset through the window and a single bridge lamp near her chair—her face, like the TV set, looked as if the color had been tuned wrong. The lips I can only describe as liverish, by which I mean not only the maroon color of raw calves' liver but the wet sheen as well. Her complex-ion, consistent with this butcher-shop image, reminded me of a certain kind of bologna Tom and I were both partial to, which is coarse-grained in texture and some-where between pink and gray in hue. She had thin, arched eyebrows that showed above her dark glasses, and she had dropped her lower jaw in what, as with newborn babies, could have been either a smile, I thought, or gas. Because of the glasses I could not be sure which of us she was looking at, but it was to Brownie that her first words were addressed. She said, "Brownie, go get the the man a Tropicana. And on the way out, fix that pukey color. It's making me sick."

I do not remember in any detail what Lucille and I talked about those first few moments of our acquaintance when Brownie left us alone together to do what he was told, but I remember that most of it was done by me. I have always found it disconcerting to speak to someone who is wearing dark glasses, and make it a point if I am wearing them myself either to take them off or at least to lower them when someone comes up to speak to me. Little as we actually make use of it, we ought to have at least the option of looking each other straight in the eye. But Lucille obviously felt no such compunction, and I remember thinking that if I had brought along the sunglasses that I had purchased in Armadillo that afternoon, I would have been tempted to put them on as a counter-measure. Instead, I rattled on about such matters as my trip down and the weather, and such replies as Lucille made were rather brief, as I remember, and always had, no matter how straightforward in content, an air of the arch or cryptic about them by virtue of her habit of dropping that lower jaw.

When Brownie returned with my Tropicana, I discovered to my surprise that although two parts of it were orange juice as I had surmised, the third part of it was gin. Brownie did not bring one for himself and took a seat a little apart from Lucille and me so that he was neither quite in the group nor quite out of it, as though, having brought the two of us together, he was not sure what Bebb would want of him next. He joined in the conversation once in a while, but at nothing like the length he had permitted himself in the church that after-noon, and much of the time, I think, he was watching the football game. Lucille sent him out of the room twice to replenish her Tropicana, but he took several other unexplained trips on his own which made me wonder whether by any chance he was fixing supper.

Lucille seemed rather vague about Bebb when I finally maneuvered the conversation around to him. "Long enough to know better" was her answer when I asked how long they had lived in Armadillo. I asked her if she found that her duties as pastor's wife took up a lot of her time, and she said, "Bebb doesn't need a wife. He's got Brownie." Not wanting to seem suspiciously inquisitive, I told her a little about how Bebb and I had met in New York and how he had generously invited me down to observe his entire operation at first hand.

"He's an operator, that's for sure," she said. "I've lost count how many operations he's pulled off in his time, and once or twice he's got operated on himself, hasn't he, Brownie?"

Brownie smiled somewhat wanly, I thought, looking back at her from the football game. "Spiritual opera-tions," he said. " 'If thy right eye offend thee, pluck it out. For it is profitable for thee that one of thy members should perish and not that thy whole body should be cast into hell.' "

Lucille said, "Brownie, turn that lousy set down. I can't even hear myself think, let alone Scripture."

Going back to the subject of our meeting in the lunch-room, I found myself telling her how interested I had been in Bebb's theory that the soda jerk was a visitor from outer space. It was the first time she showed any real interest in what I was saying.

"A gold or a silver?" she asked.

I said a silver.

"Hear that, Brownie?" she said. "Bebb racked up another silver in New York."

I could not make out whether Brownie's smile was in response to her or to the commercial he was watching, which showed the vapors rising from an acid stomach into the esophagus and causing heartburn.

Lucille said, "He runs into those outer-space people all over the place. They are silvers mostly, but once in a while he finds a gold. The golds are rarer. He says they are here on this planet to keep an eye on things."

"Has he ever talked to one?" I asked. "Does he have any idea whereabouts in outer space they're from?"

Lucille said, "How should I know?" She took a swallow of her Tropicana, looking at me over the rim of her glass.

"Do you believe they're from outer space yourself?" I asked her.

She took her time about answering. She dropped her lower jaw at me and set her Tropicana down on the straw rug. Her last swallow had left her with a little wet mustache. "Do you know what I believe?" she said finally. "It takes one to know one, they say. Sometimes I believe Bebb is from outer space himself."

Brownie, who had gone out of the room on one of his short trips, returned at this point. Lucille said, "How about it, Brownie? What do you believe?"

Brownie looked understandably puzzled. The sweat stains under his arms had spread, and what with the gin and the fact that the windows in the room were all

79

closed, I felt quite warm myself. Brownie said, "What do I believe about what?"

Lucille said, "Did you ever stop to think maybe Bebb was from outer space?"

It was a difficult question. I admired Brownie for simply not answering it. He stood there sweating in the doorway with the TV screen reflected in his glasses and his hairy arms hanging straight at his sides. "Supper is ready" was all he said.

We ate in a high-ceilinged dining room which looked out on the street, where, although it was barely dusk, the lights had come on. Across the street a man in a bathing suit and a golf cap was watering his lawn. I could see my car where I had parked it at the curb, and although it had come into my temporary possession only a few hours before, it seemed a link somehow with the whole world I'd left behind me in New York, and I found the sight of it oddly touching and reassuring. I realized that, such as it was, I missed my world and wondered whether I could put off returning to it until Bebb got back from Texas.

"When did you say your husband was coming home?" I asked Lucille.

She said, "You tell me."

"Probably tomorrow," Brownie said.

"He's got a big Texas rancher on tap down there," Lucille said.

"Oil, dear," Brownie said.

"Anyway," Lucille said, "sure as God made little green apples, he's not going to rush that one."

I decided that I had been right in my guess about Brownie's making supper; at least, there was no sign of anyone else who could have done it, and Lucille hadn't

80

lifted a hand since my arrival except to raise the Tropicanas to her lips. We had corned beef and turnip greens
and corn sticks. If Brownie had done the cooking, he
also did the waiting on table—brought the plates in
and kept our glasses filled with ice water. Lucille sent
him out twice for extra butter for the corn sticks.

We had little conversation during the meal. Still
wearing her dark glasses, Lucille seemed intent on what
she was eating although once or twice I thought I
caught her looking at me, and Brownie was up and down
a good deal. At one point, however, remembering the
gym set in the yard, I asked if the Bebbs had any children. Lucille and Brownie both stopped eating, and
Brownie raised his napkin to his chin, I remember, and
kept it hanging there as though he had forgotten he was
holding it.

Lucille said, "We had a little baby once, but it died."
Her forkful of turnip greens was poised halfway to her
mouth, and her arm looked so thin that I thought I
could probably get my thumb and forefinger around it.
She said, "That's the way it goes, and besides, it was a
long time ago."

Brownie said, "There's Sharon. Don't forget about
Sharon."

"Sharon!" Lucille said, and this time it was unques-
tionably a smile that had disarranged the lower part of
her face. "The man said *children*."

Did she mean that Sharon was not a child, or that she
was not *her* child, or that, though perhaps both a child
and hers, the term *children* seemed somehow misapplied
in Sharon's case? It was hard to tell what Lucille meant
in general, with those impenetrable glasses and the eye-

brows arched above them. For the moment I decided against pursuing the subject further, but Brownie would not let it go.

He said, "Mr. Bebb is like Jesus. He has a very warm spot in his heart for children. He loves having them around. You take a pretty little child, black *or* white, he can get almost anything he wants out of Mr. Bebb anytime."

"Anything," Lucille said. "Day or night."

Brownie said, "I think it is their innocence and their sense of wonder. He loves taking them around and showing them things. The lions, to give you an example. Only last week he took a pack of them out and showed them the lions."

Lucille said, "Soon there won't be anything left in Florida he hasn't shown them."

Just for a moment I had the insane suspicion that they were working the truth nearer and nearer to the open air until at any moment, with shrieks of laughter, they would pull it out in all its throbbing nakedness. Bebb himself would come crawling out from under the table in his Happy Hooligan hat, and the three of them would dance around me committing indecencies. Or was the truth working its own way to the open air through the very vigor of their effort to conceal it, like the harassed lady asking J. P. Morgan if he wanted cream or lemon in his nose? Or was there any truth at all except that, like Jesus, Bebb had a warm spot in his heart for children?

Then Lucille said, "Brownie, get me some more of that ice water. Those Tropicanas always leave me spitting cotton," and Brownie—no wonder the wet spots under his arms, I thought—got up again to do her bidding.

As soon as she had finished her meal, Lucille got up and excused herself. She said she was pleased to meet me, and it occurred to me that maybe she really was pleased, what with just Brownie there to keep her company and the color TV acting up. "Now Brownie will show you around if you want," she said, "but don't expect the Massachusetts Institute of Technology. Maybe Bebb will be back tomorrow. I wonder if he's seen any silvers in Texas." Then we said goodnight, and I could hear her all the way up the stairs, shiny and brown like the toilet seat.

It interested me how neither of them called Bebb by his first name. I wondered if Mr. Bebb was what Brownie called him to his face or just the way he referred to him to outsiders. I wondered if there was anyone anywhere who called him Leo.

The College, as it turned out, was in the garage out back. It was the same vintage as the house but, as Brownie explained, had been converted to this use several years back when the work had grown beyond what could be handled in the Manse. There was an uncompleted sign over the entrance—a white board with all the letters of Gospel Faith blocked out in pencil but only the first two painted in with black, so that from any distance at all the sign seemed to read just GO, whether in evangelical exhortation or dire warning who could say?

Inside, it reminded me of a World War II induction center with its air of impermanence and disheveled urgency. There was a large central room with a couple of desks in it and a number of folding chairs stacked

83

against the wall, and then there were several smaller rooms blocked off with partitions that didn't come even close to reaching the high ceiling. One of these was Brownie's office. There was a desk in it with a sign saying *The Rev. Laverne Brown B.D., S.T.M., Th.D., D.D., Dean,* and a mimeograph machine. On a table there were several piles each of the pink and blue order blanks that I remembered receiving with my ordination certificate, one for the pamphlet on ecclesiastical discounts, tax exemptions and military deferments, and the other for a complete prospectus of Gospel Faith courses. Framed on the wall were a number of Brownie's personal credentials—his Bachelor of Divinity, his Master of Sacred Theology, his Doctor of Divinity, and other certificates, licenses, and testimonials whose exact nature I didn't have time to determine, but all of them, as nearly as I could tell, issued under the seal of Gospel Faith College and signed by Bebb.

Bebb's office, which Brownie took me to next, was slightly smaller, and there were no diplomas of any kind in evidence on the walls. It reminded me of how the Pope, in contrast to the renaissance splendor of his cardinals, sometimes appears in the simplest white skullcap and cassock. Compared with Brownie's, the sign on his desk also had a kind of stark authority about it— just *The Rev. Leo Bebb, International President.* There were some photographs on the walls: Bebb shaking hands with an Indian chief in full regalia; Bebb in a white robe standing in front of what I recognized as the altar table in his church with his hand raised in benediction; Bebb with a visored cap sitting at the center of a semicircle of children on what seemed to be a playing field of some kind. There was one which by the look of the clothes and the sepia cast of the print I recognized as considerably older than the others. Bebb was sitting on the front stoop of a house, squinting into the sun. He was wearing knickerbockers and holding in his lap what I took to be a baby, although with the glare of the sun and the fading of the print it was quite faceless. Beside Bebb, with one hand on his shoulder, was a young woman in a long, filmy-looking dress. She had an unmistakable look of the 1920's about her, with a Mary Pickford mouth and her dark hair shingled, but there was also something soft and timeless in her expression as she gazed down at the white bundle in Bebb's lap. Bebb himself, I noticed, looked remarkably the way he had when I saw him—a few pounds lighter, perhaps, but the same firm, round face and tightly hinged mouth. *This baby . . . this woman . . .* , I could almost hear him say. *All things are lawful for me.*

"Lucille?" I asked Brownie, indicating the young woman in the filmy dress. Brownie nodded. "The years have taken their toll," he said. And thus it must also have been the baby that had died, I assumed. It could almost have been dead when the picture was taken—so small and white and faceless in Bebb's lap. Perhaps it was all the hot sun that day that had killed it.

In a room adjoining Bebb's office there were several tall filing cabinets, and Brownie showed them to me with particular pride. Every ordination that had ever been issued, every degree that had ever been conferred, every course that had ever been taken, it was all on file here, he explained, complete with names and dates and whatever other information seemed useful. Brownie pulled open one of the drawers and removed a manila folder apparently at random. It belonged to somebody named Arthur Krebs, and inside there was a single sheet of paper. It read: "KREBS, Arthur (white). Ordained to Gospel Ministry June 1, 1958. San Quentin. 15 years. Love off. $5.00. N.D."

"San Quentin Prison?" I asked.

Brownie said, "Dear, the Spirit bloweth where it listeth. When a man is behind bars, he has time for reflection. Many things that seemed important to him on the outside do not seem so any more, and vice versa. We do a lot of business with the prisons. Remember the good thief."

"Fifteen years is what he got sent up for, and he coughed up five bucks for the Mother Church, but what about N.D.?" I asked. All the other information was typewritten but N.D. had been added in pencil.

Brownie said, "It is a code that Mr. Bebb uses, and he wrote it in there himself, as you can see. I don't know what all his symbols mean, and I am not at liberty to divulge all I do know, but in this case I don't see any harm can come of it. N.D. stands for No Dice. It means that when Mr. Bebb took the name of Arthur Krebs to the Lord in prayer as he does for everybody he ordains, he received negative vibrations concerning Krebs' future in the Gospel ministry."

"But he ordained him anyway," I said.

Brownie said, "Mr. Bebb ordains everybody who applies as long as they are of the male sex and over eighteen years of age. He may have negative vibrations about a certain individual himself, but he knows that the Lord moves in mysterious ways, dear, and that judgment is his. Mr. Bebb says there is a priest in every man. All you have to do is lay your hands on it, and the Lord will do the rest."

As Brownie replaced Arthur Krebs in the file, it occurred to me that in one of those drawers somewhere there must be a folder on me. Presumably Bebb had taken my name to the Lord in prayer too, and I wondered what that involved. I imagined him taking something like the baby in his arms, something faceless and white, and lifting it up into the hot glare of the sun. Or something like Tom the way he was when I carried him back limp and unconscious from the vet's. And after that, what vibrations had Bebb felt and what symbol had he written next to my name? Would Brownie be able to translate it for me, and would he if he could? It would have been easy enough to ask him, but I didn't, finally— not that I lacked interest so much as that I was too interested. There were some things, I decided, that even a journalistic spy was better off not knowing.

Brownie said, "When Mr. Bebb was away those five years, I kept these files up single-handed, and I can tell you it was no easy task."

I said, "Five years? Where did he go for as long as that? Outer space?"

Brownie had walked ahead of me into the last of the partitioned rooms, which was presumably the College library. Bookshelves lined three walls, and there was a small hand press and a tray of type on a table against the other. Stretching out one arm toward the books as though about to continue his guided tour, Brownie seemed not to have heard my question, so I repeated it. "Those five years he was away," I said. "What was he up to?"

Brownie kept on pointing toward the books, but at

the sound of my voice he turned and looked at me over his sloping shoulder with a smile in some way unlike his usual one, as if it was the smile itself he was smiling at. He said, "The Lord's work, dear," and then went on to ask me if I would like to pick out a book to take back to the Salamander with me. The one that caught my eye caught it because among all the gaudy paperbacks and flashy jackets and compelling titles that seemed to be vying for my attention, it was the only one that looked reserved and scholarly and as if it couldn't have cared less whether I gave it my attention or not. It was an Oxford University Press book entitled *The Apocryphal New Testament* and edited by someone named Montague Rhodes James. "A trustworthy collection of rare writings," the jacket flap announced in moderate tones.

Running my eye down the table of contents, I was struck by at least the rarity of it—Fragments of Early Gospels, Lost Heretical Books, a Coptic Passion Narrative entitled "The Book of the Cock," a miracle story from the Gospel of Thomas entitled "The Children in the Oven," but what made me decide to take it back and read myself to sleep with it at the Salamander Motel that night was less these baroque and provocative titles than a sober biographical note about Montague Rhodes James himself which was also quoted on the jacket from *The Times Literary Supplement*. A competent scholar, an exceptionally learned student, an eminent medievalist, Dr. James was, *The Times* maintained, "pre-eminently fitted to handle this vast and chaotic mass of material." If this was indeed true of him, I thought, then it was Dr. James whom I wanted to go to bed with that night. It was to his sane and orderly scrutiny that I wanted to submit the chaotic mass of impressions that I had gathered from my first day in Armadillo. Brownie said by all means to take him along, and this compact seemed to signal the end of my tour.

When we stepped outside, the night was as warm as bathwater and the moon nearly full. There was a sweet fragrance in the air—magnolia, bougainvillea, oleander? Unlike Ellie, I know nothing about trees and shrubs, but just the names themselves sound fragrant. There were some lights on in the Manse and a few of the other houses along the old street, but otherwise no sign of life. Brownie was silent at my side. It was a singularly tranquil moment, as though the spirit of Montague Rhodes James had already begun its work, and thus I was as unprepared for what happened next as I had been for the sound of the buzzer in my roomette.

I heard the sound of a window being raised and then a girl's voice calling through the dark, a cool, silky voice with a certain laziness in it that seemed to belie the vigor of the words. "Hey, peckerhead," she called. "Shut the door out there this time. You left it open last night, and the place was full of batshit." Then the sound of the window being shut again and a glimpse through the wavy panes of a pair of bare shoulders and a white slip.

Brownie said, "That Sharon. You see if she doesn't get into trouble using language like that for the world to hear." He closed the door to the College behind him and then pulled at the handle until he heard a click.

"Bebb's daughter?" I asked.

"Adopted, dear," Brownie said, and then, after a little pause, "I've never seen a bat in Armadillo."

Poor Brownie. I kept thinking about him as I drove

89

back to the motel. Maybe peckerhead was only a misleading translation and in the original tongue meant something like Honey or Gramps. Maybe he didn't always have to fix supper. It could have been the cook's night out or just that corned beef and turnip greens were his particular specialty. Maybe Bebb and Sharon were usually on hand to help him keep Lucille supplied with Tropicanas. In any case, his smile took on a new dimension for me—the smile not so much of a man who hasn't quite gotten the joke but of a man who after years has finally gotten it.

The main street of Armadillo was empty as I drove slowly through with the top down. I had taken off my seersucker jacket and was perfectly comfortable in my shirt sleeves. It was South, it was midsummer night's dream. But the stucco and cinderblock buildings, the tin awnings and deserted sidewalks, glittered white in the moonlight like new-fallen snow. It was a town of ice I was passing through, and I thought of Dante's ninth circle with Brutus and Cassius and Judas Iscariot stuck fast in their frozen lake.

CHAPTER SIX

MY ROOM at the Salamander Motel reminded me of my roomette on the train. It was considerably larger, of course, but, like the roomette, came fitted out with almost everything a man needs to keep himself going—a bed, a sink, a toilet, an electric fan and, in the case of the Salamander, a TV. It was a room to stand siege in, a fallout shelter, an isolation ward for one. It was a solitary-confinement cell in one of our more progressive prisons, and I thought about Arthur Krebs in his cell at San Quentin and how Brownie had said that being behind bars gave a man time for reflection. I thought of my own overheated reflections on the train coming down and of my dream about the sandy beach. And I thought of Tom in his cramped cage in New York and wondered what imponderables were crossing his mind as he crouched there with his feet and tail tucked under him, outstaring the universe. As for myself, I decided not to attempt any reflecting until after first settling my mind with a shower and a dose of Montague Rhodes James. I took my shower, got into bed, and was on the point of turning to my book when I was distracted by a device on the bedside table that I had not noticed before.

It was a black metal box about the size of a small radio and seemed to be attached to my bed by several stout electric cords. There was a card taped to it which described its nature and purpose. It was called Magic Fingers, and if you dropped a quarter into the slot on top of the box and then lay down on the bed, for the next ten minutes approximately you would receive through the mattress a steady, deep vibration which did wonders for the sore muscles and frayed nerves of travelers like myself. I resolved then and there to put it to the test, but, not being sleepy yet and feeling under some obligation to Dr. James, who, even unread, seemed already to have had a soothing effect on me, I decided to have a look at *The Apocryphal New Testament* first.

There was a good deal of scholarly apparatus plus an introduction to each of the documents, and the gist of it all seemed to be that, though often of ancient origin and wide currency, the entire array of apocryphal gospels, acts, epistles and apocalypses was in essence a pack of pious and fanciful whoppers. The idea of making such a collection in the first place appealed to me, and I felt all the more drawn to Dr. James for having directed his sober, organizational skills to what a lesser man might have considered a frivolous end.

I looked first at the miracle of "The Children in the Oven," which turned out to be rather splendidly unedifying. It told how for unspecified reasons some children ran away from Jesus one day and went and hid themselves in an oven. Jesus chased after them and stumbled on some women who had seen the children go into the house and knew perfectly well where they were hiding but weren't about to give them away. There were nothing but goats in the house, the women said, whereupon Jesus commanded the goats to come out, and when they did, they were goats indeed. Jesus then delivered himself of a rather obscure homily having to do with black sheep and the house of Israel, after which the women asked him if he'd mind changing the goats back into children again. He granted their request, saying, "Come ye children, my playfellows, and let us play together."

I liked the idea of the children running away from Jesus in the first place—"suffer little children" and so on to the contrary notwithstanding, I had always suspected he wasn't Captain Kangaroo—and I liked him for chasing after them and turning them into goats. It threw a scare into them they probably needed. I had a feeling they then played with him only till the first chance they got to give him the slip again, and I had a feeling he was probably just as glad.

I was drawn next to "The Book of the Cock," which, whatever the title had led me to expect, turned out to be a tale which, according to Dr. James, is read in the Abyssinian Church on Maundy Thursdays. At supper one evening Jesus is served a cock that has been cut up in pieces and set before him on a magnificent dish. He is just about to start eating when he notices Judas slipping stealthily out of the room, and as soon as he has gone, Jesus brings the cock back to life with a touch and tells him to tail Judas and find out what's going on. The cock overhears Judas' whole sordid scheme, and then, translating from the Ethiopic, "the cock returned to Bethany and sat down before Jesus and wept bitterly and told all the story."

Lying there in my bed at the Salamander Motel, I could imagine him in the center of the table giving his report to Jesus with his wings outstretched and his comb and wattles askew after the long chase. I could imagine the bitter tears trickling off the end of his beak. The disciples also wept, the text continued, and maybe as much for the cock himself, I thought, as for Jesus. It couldn't have been the easiest tale in the world to tattle. But tears were not the end of it because as soon as the truth about Judas was out, Jesus thanked the cock and placed him in the sky for a thousand years. It was nice to think of the cock, like Romeo, cut out in little stars so all the world, including the world of the henyard, could be in love with night; and it was nice too to think of the Abyssinians remembering him so faithfully for so many centuries, Haile Selassie and all of them. It was a pleasant vision to go to sleep on, and I was on the point of slipping my quarter into the Magic Fingers and turning off the light when my eye was caught by a subtitle listed under "The Gospel of Nicodemus" as "Part II. The Descent into Hell."

I thought immediately of Brownie's reference to this

event in church that afternoon, how it was at the moment Jesus knew he was going to have to descend into Hell that he gave out that terrible cry in his original tongue: *Eli, Eli,* as Ellie and I had so blithely sung it several millennia later with the Canterbury Choir, *lama sabachthani?* And I thought too of the Charlton Heston portrait of Jesus staring grimly at the hot-air register there in the Church of Holy Love while, outside, the miniature turtles and shrunken heads went on with business as usual. Dr. James presented the text in three versions, which he printed one above the other as Latin text A, Latin text B, and Greek. I chose Latin text A because it was printed at the top of the page and looked somewhat fuller than the others.

Sometimes a book you read and the place you read it in become so interwoven in your mind that you can't remember one without remembering the other and in some odd way the book and the place come to reflect each other like facing mirrors, each showing the other in endlessly receding perspective. "The Descent into Hell," on the one hand. That rather stuffy room at the Salamander Motel on the other, with the electric fan going, and the dresser mirror still steamed up from my shower, and my bottle of Dewar's on the windowsill half hidden, God knows why or from whom, behind the curtain. I do not pretend to be able to explain adequately even to myself what each is saying about the other—I certainly don't consider that room any more infernal than many other rooms I have slept in before and since—but to this day I cannot disentangle my first night in Armadillo from the night which Latin A starts out by describing and the events that follow upon it.

Like *Don Giovanni,* it begins in the dark, and, like *Don Giovanni,* it is opera in the grandest manner from beginning to end. In fact, I remember thinking as I read a little further along that in some ways Dr. James might have presented it as a kind of sequel to *Don Giovanni* with the Don, that *galantuomo,* turned Mr. Keen, Tracer of Lost Persons, as he is led down, down, down in the Commendatore's stony grip.

The story begins in the dark with three hysterical rabbis who come rushing in and in breathless *recitativo* try to tell a solemn assembly of priests and Levites about a miracle they have just witnessed. One of the priests rises, a basso in robes reminiscent of *Aïda,* and in a brief passage, with French horns pulsing in the background, asks the rabbis to try to express themselves more clearly. It is here that Rabbi Addas, a baritone, has his first and only aria, since he does not appear again after this opening scene or prologue. With a hand on his heart and his other arm outstretched, he tells how he and his companions were on their way from Galilee into Jordan when they ran into a crowd of men wearing white garments whom they recognized immediately as spirits of the dead. What was their errand here in the land of the living, the rabbis asked them, and the spirits' answer was, "We arose with Christ out of Hell and thereby may ye know that the gates of death and darkness are destroyed."

The assembly of priests and Levites is thrown into an uproar by this news, and in the manner of opera choruses they turn to each other with their beards wagging and their hands gesticulating and murmur fiercely back and forth *rhubarb, rhubarb, rhubarb* perhaps, or whatever syllables sound most like a mob murmuring fiercely in Hebrew. Then the basso priest steps forward again and tells the rabbis to produce the ghosts themselves so that they may verify this extraordinary report and fill in the details. The rabbis are quick to obey and in a moment return with two white-robed figures. Again there is the same kind of horrified stir among the priests and Levites that I associate with such early Gluyas Williams cartoons as "The Day a Cake of Soap Sank at Procter & Gamble's." The basso restores order, however, and the two ghosts are sent off into two different cells, each to write down his own account of what happened in Hell. There is a good deal of pizzicato from the orchestra to suggest the scratching of their quills, followed by a lyric passage from the strings and harp to represent divine inspiration, and finally there bursts forth simultaneously from each of the two cells a triumphantly sustained Amen. The ghosts have finished at precisely the same instant and emerge bearing their scrolls. Taking a scroll in each hand, the basso raises them heavenward with a ghost at each elbow, and the ensuing trio marks the finale of the prologue. Miraculously, the two accounts have turned out to be identical, and "The Truth is One!" the basso priest sings while the ghosts, both tenors, continue their triumphant Amens.

At about this point in my reading, I remember, a fly appeared inside the shade of my bedside lamp. Since a fatal swat is virtually impossible under those circumstances, I flushed him out of the shade and waited for him to land on some more substantial surface. Still crazed by the scorching splendor of the light-bulb, he swooped around the room in braggadocio parabolas until at last he lighted squarely on my bed at about the level of my knees so that I could have swatted him easily without even having to change my position. Maybe it was because the shot was too easy, or maybe it was because the only weapon I had at hand was *The Apocryphal New Testament*, or conceivably, like Uncle Toby Shandy, I simply thought, "This world surely is wide enough to hold both thee and me," but, whatever the reason, I decided to spare him. It may have been that the shock of finding himself still alive was as fatal as the swat would have been or just that I got too absorbed in my reading to notice, but I do not remember being disturbed by him again.

"On a sudden there came a golden heat of the sun and a purple and royal light shining upon us" is the way Latin A describes it. A purple light is hard for me to picture, but red lights and blue lights I have seen on the stage often enough, and I suppose there is no reason why they couldn't be mixed. In any case, the opera proper—a dramatization of the accounts the two ghosts wrote on their scrolls—opens in Hell. Like the gypsies at their campfire in the second act of *Trovatore*, the dead are gathered around in the purple and royal light, and as the curtain rises, you can hear them humming a quiet, somber theme in the key of B minor. They are dead, and the light is dim, and there is nothing much to shout about. Besides, after all, it is Hell. Everything is dark and quiet, including the audience. Only an occasional muffled cough breaks it and a firefly flicker as here and there people bow forward to consult their programs. Ushers lean against the gilt pilasters with their white-gloved hands crossed in front of them. It's the old Met, of course—the great golden curtain, the Diamond Horseshoe with its plush-covered rails. Miriam and I were sent to hear *Hansel and Gretel* there once as children. I remember she wore a velvet dress and a velvet band to hold back her long hair.

As the light grows brighter, the tempo of the humming quickens somewhat, and it becomes possible to identify certain people. Adam is there and the patriarchs Abraham, Isaac, and Jacob with silver beards. There are prophets too, Isaiah and Micah. Habakkuk also is there, whoever Habakkuk was. There is no mistaking King David with a crown on his head and golden hair that curls down to his shoulders. The humming opens out into words, and "The people that walked in darkness have seen a great light," the chorus of shades sings softly, "and now hath it come and shone upon us that sit in death."

We sit there in the dark, my twin sister and I, and I wonder if at twelve or thirteen or whatever we were then, death was already in her like an ovary only waiting for God knows what or who to come fertilize it. Like the witch in the gingerbread house. *Ciao, Antonio.*

Simeon is there, the old Jew who was on hand when Joseph in knickerbockers and Mary in something filmy brought their child to present him at the Temple. John the Baptist is there, looking a little like Basil Rathbone. He seems uncomfortable and out of place in his leopard skin. Simeon and John come downstage and sing about how they both knew Jesus back when, and how much they are looking forward to seeing him again now that he has finally made it.

Adam is dressed in flesh-colored tights like an acrobat.

99

He seems too old for the part. His neck is stringy, and his legs have no calves. There is something soft and a little peculiar in his manner as he comes and stands so close to the footlights that his make-up shows. One expects a voice on the order of Richard Dyer Bennett's, but he turns out to be a baritone. In his aria he tells a story within a story within a story. And again within a story if you consider it as all part of my account of what happened that evening at the Salamander Motel in Armadillo.

Adam starts out very soft and *andante*, all head tones with his teeth showing, and you can see the conductor with his puckered lips and cautionary left palm trying to quiet down the strings. "*Mio figlio*," Adam begins, sustaining the phrase in a rather lovely, vibrant way but with something in his powdered face and the way he holds his hands that suggests it is really not a son he is talking about. There is some restive stirring among the patriarchs. Abraham is scowling down at his feet, and Isaac is twisting and untwisting a strand of his beard. Son or whatever, the name is Seth, and Adam tells about an errand he sent him on to the Archangel Michael at the gates of Paradise. "Entreat Michael to give thee of the oil of the tree of mercy that thou mayest anoint thy father Adam for the pain of his body," he sings, and you can see them there, Adam and Seth, on the beach together at Fire Island.

Spreadeagled in the full sun, Seth is moist and brown as a young pearl diver in his tight black trunks, but even under the striped umbrella Adam has started to peel. He reaches out and gives Seth's foot a little shove with his. "Now you just go *on* up there and get me some Coppertone," he says. *Mio figlio . . . Mio figlio . . .*

At first the Archangel is not encouraging. Five thousand and five hundred years must be accomplished before Adam can have oil from the tree of mercy for the pain of his body, but then, he tells Seth to go back and say, ah then . . . Adam sings it with his eyes half closed at the memory of how Seth brought back the message from the gates of Paradise: "Then the Son of God shall come down even unto Hell and will bring our father Adam into Paradise unto the tree of mercy." Not even the patriarchs remain entirely unmoved, and when Adam finishes and stands there with one knee slightly bent and his chin on his shoulder like a Picasso clown, the whole chorus of the dead rises and, joined now by the full orchestra, sings out fortissimo in praise and rejoicing.

During the intermission Miriam has to go to the bathroom, not because she has to *do* anything, she says, but because in theaters, restaurants, gas stations, even department stores and churches, she always goes to the bathroom just to have a look around. I remain in my plush seat, putting my overcoat and hat in my lap and drawing up my knees to let people squeeze out past me into the aisle. I wish that I hadn't been made to wear the hat. It is a gray fedora from John Ryan's, and because I haven't begun to get my growth yet, I am afraid it makes me look like a dwarf. The house lights have already started to dim by the time Miriam gets back. It is the fanciest Ladies' Room she has ever seen, with a dressing room full of tables and mirrors and a round, tufted sofa in the middle just like a whorehouse. Her breath smells of peppermint as she whispers this in my ear, and she has brought a Mound's back with her, half of which she gives to me. Even at the time, it occurs to me to wonder how she knows about whorehouses and the kind of sofas they have in them.

Hell is not only a place in Latin A, it is also a person. Hell and Satan are alone on the stage when the curtain goes up. Satan is dressed traditionally, like Mephistopheles in *Faust*—scarlet doublet and tights and a hat that comes down in a widow's peak in front and has several long feathers sweeping back. Hell cuts a very different figure. Short and on the flabby side, he is dressed in black leotards that are perhaps supposed to suggest a medieval torture chamber and is naked from the waist up. He is smudged here and there with soot and has those rolls of fat above the hips that Miriam calls love handles. He has a skin-tight helmet of black cloth which comes down low on his forehead and has loops cut out for his ears. His face has a worried, sweaty look which reminds me of the late Lou Costello. He and Satan converse in recitative with a single piano providing punctuation marks and stage directions in between.

Satan makes his point with his arms crossed at his chest and his feet planted wide apart. Jesus is on his way to Hell—there is no doubt about that—but they will make mincemeat of him once he gets there. But how can they be sure of that, Hell asks. That is easy, Satan says. He is afraid of death. Didn't he sweat blood in the garden and ask that the cup be taken from him? Besides, Satan says, he was able to tempt him just like other men. But he resisted, says Hell. Luck, says Satan. Three or four sharp, crisp chords on the piano, and then the entire string section introduces Hell's bass aria, "Remember Lazarus."

It is short, only twenty measures or so, and Hell sings

it with his hands clasped over his sooty navel. It is more plaintive than anything else, like a man not given to making scenes but forced at least to register protest. There was a man named Lazarus who died and was buried and Hell swallowed him down into his entrails as from the beginning he had swallowed down everybody. Then his belly pained him and he knew that all was not well, whereupon with not even the by-your-leave of a prayer but with just a word or two, somebody from the land of the living snatched Lazarus up out of Hell's entrails, and "he flew away from me not like to a dead man but to an eagle, so instantly did the earth cast him out." Hell draws his aria to a close by saying that he has every reason to believe that the one who did the snatching is the same one who is on his way down to make trouble now. In which case, who is going to make mincemeat of whom? Satan recoils with his caped arm crooked out in front of his widow's peak, and from offstage can be heard the chorus of the dead singing. "Remove, O princes, your gates, and be ye lift up, ye everlasting doors."

The longest scene follows then, and in many ways it is the least interesting. Everybody has to have his say as they stand around waiting. David the King and Isaiah the prophet come in and make the point that since they both predicted his triumph untold generations before, he is certain to be entirely triumphant here as everywhere else. Various saints echo these sentiments. Then King David and Hell have a rather florid duet where David echoes the earlier words of the chorus—"Be ye lift up, ye doors of Hell, that the King of Glory shall come in"—and Hell asks, by no means rhetorically but with the closest he can come to a sneer on his hopelessly sincere and anxious face, "Who is this King of Glory?"

The duet ends with Hell repeating his taunting question three times and David replying to each, "The Lord strong and mighty, the Lord mighty in Battle, he is the King of Glory."

It is at this point that the lights, which have been growing steadily brighter, reach an almost blinding intensity, and at the last of David's three *glory*'s, amid a blast of trumpets, horns, tympany, Jesus enters from the wings, and even Montague Rhodes James, you feel, must have had to sit on his hands to keep from putting in a footnote to the effect that at this moment all Hell breaks loose.

The Jesus I see looks less like the picture above Bebb's altar table than like Don Giovanni, the great lover himself. I see him all in white, but instead of that homespun garment with the *bateau* neckline, he is magnificently dressed in the height of eighteenth-century fashion with a cloak that flares out at his heels as he strides in and a plume in his hat and silver buckles on his shoes. He wears a grandee's little earring in one ear and carries a rapier in his hand. "Who art thou that didst lie dead in the sepulcher? Who art thou that settest free the prisoners? Who art thou that sheddest thy divine light upon them that were blinded by darkness?" Hell and Satan and the whole chorus of demons cry it out, and Jesus' response is a model of directness. He simply takes his rapier and runs Satan through the shoulder with it, not to kill him but to render him helpless. Then he signals to Hell, who comes up from behind and pinions Satan's arms to his sides as Satan's head drops to his chest in defeat.

Hell then sings his final aria, which goes on rather too long and during which everybody on stage including

Jesus freezes in place as though it is somehow the least they can do for Hell because he is so much shorter and stouter than Satan and looks so much less able to cope that you wonder if he will be able to pull things off after all. Satan should never have hanged the King of Glory on the cruel tree in the first place, Hell says, and now he will have the rest of eternity to learn what torments he must suffer in place of Adam and his children. Hell, Satan and the whole hellish multitude then depart.

Here, for the first time, Jesus speaks. He sweeps off his plumed hat, stretches both arms out as far as they will go to either side so that his white doublet glitters between the outspread wings of his white cloak, smiles a smile that would put Errol Flynn and Douglas Fairbanks, Jr., both to shame, not to mention Cesare Siepi, and says, "Come unto me, all ye my saints which bear mine image and likeness!"

Adam comes first. He walks perhaps a little too straight, a little too steady-hipped, but when he reaches the hand that Jesus is holding out to him, he falls to his knees at Jesus' feet with tears that are at least real enough to start some mascara running down one cheek and says, "O Lord, my God, I cried unto thee, and thou hast healed me, thou hast brought my soul out of Hell." Then David and Isaiah follow and behind them Abraham, Isaac and Jacob and all the patriarchs and prophets and saints until finally Jesus is completely hidden in their midst. "Sing unto the Lord a new song," David cries out, "for he hath done marvelous things." And the entire company replies with "Amen! Alleluia!" as the curtain comes down.

That is the end of it, really. There is a short last scene

or epilogue at the gates of Paradise not unlike the one in *Don Giovanni*, where Donna Anna, Donna Elvira and Don Ottavio come rushing in after the Don has descended into the flames and smoke. But, as in the case of the one in *Don Giovanni*, it is rather heavily moralistic and doesn't add much. So I skimmed it at the time there in Armadillo and do no more than mention it in passing here.

I preferred to go to sleep with the echo of David's last cry and that final rousing chorus still ringing in my ears, so, first depositing my quarter, I turned off the light and gave my sore muscles and frayed traveler's nerves over to the vibrating solicitude of the Magic Fingers.

CHAPTER SEVEN

I WAS AWAKENED the next morning by Bebb himself. He
didn't shake me or say anything, but even asleep I must
have sensed a presence, and when I opened my eyes,
there he was standing at the foot of my bed. He said,
"Antonio, you'll have to excuse me for busting in on you
like this, but it's after eleven. I was afraid you might be
dead."

It took me a moment or two to put it all together. I
had the sense of having slept too hard and deep for
dreams, and for a few seconds it was such a shock to see
the world again that it was as if I had been dead indeed.
The sunlight was flooding in between the slats of the

Venetian blinds, covering everything including Bebb with horizontal golden stripes. And there was Bebb himself, my victim, my San Graal, the Dr. Livingston to my Mr. Stanley, and the strangest thing about finding him there at the foot of my bed, of all places, was that it really wasn't so strange—as if I had been expecting him almost, or as if he had been waking me that way every morning for years. He looked slightly larger than I remembered him, both taller and stouter, or squarer anyway with his short neck and heavy shoulders and that rather massive bald head that reminded me a little of Daddy Warbucks. He was dressed much as I had seen him in New York in a nondescript dark suit with his four-pointed handkerchief and monogrammed B showing, but here in Armadillo it seemed to hang easier on him and looked less like a uniform he wasn't used to wearing.

"I took you up on your invitation," I said and realized that I didn't know what to call him. I thought of him as just Bebb, but that was pretty clearly out, and if Mr. Bebb seemed a little too much at this point, Leo seemed a little too little even though he did call me Antonio. So I called him nothing.

He said, "I had a feeling you would," and extended his right hand, which I had to crawl out of the covers to shake. Because of my disturbingly realistic dream on the train, I had rinsed out my pajamas in the shower the night before and gone to bed without them, so that when I look back on our second historic meeting as it took place in Armadillo, what I see is Bebb, the International President, standing there in his sober Mother Church suit and myself half crouching on the bed as naked as the day my poor mother bore me. We are reaching out over the covers toward each other, and our two hands are just touching. It is a picture which belongs in the Sistine Chapel.

Bebb said, "I had a feeling you might come, and I'm pleased as punch you did. I've got a lot to show you, Antonio, and I've got a lot to tell you about, so you just throw on your clothes and we'll grab you some coffee and be on our way."

My clothes were all of them right there in the bedroom, but finding myself reluctant to get dressed with those Open Sesame magician's eyes upon me, I muttered some vague explanation and carried them into the bathroom. I left the door ajar, and the mirror on the inside of the door allowed me to see Bebb without being seen myself. He sat down on the foot of my bed and talked to me while I got dressed.

"Antonio," he said, "I think that maybe the Kingdom has come at last. It is possible that Gabriel is finally getting ready to blow his horn. I've been to Texas. I just got back from Houston a couple of hours ago while you were fast asleep here in the Salamander Motel, and, Antonio, let me tell you Texas is not only a big state but Texas has got some big men in it. Ever heard of Herman Redpath? Red as in red and path as in path. Redpath. He says it's an Indian name, and he's got lots of Indian blood in him. You can see it right off. You could put his face on the head of a nickel and nobody'd hardly know the difference. Herman Redpath is a big man from a big state. And you talk about your Christians, why, he's—" I had forgotten about his habit of interrupting himself as he did here, looking out pop-eyed and intent into the empty room as if I'd been sitting right there on the bed beside him. "Antonio, that Herman Redpath is what I call a *Christian*. The Lord doesn't make them much like that any more. Why, all that man thinks about is giving. I doubt he even gets out of bed in the morning without he gives somebody something first just to get warmed up. I don't see how he's got anything left to call his own, except the more he gives away, the more he gets. That Herman Redpath," Bebb said, holding up one finger, and that eye, that marvelous, lazy eye, flickering shut for a moment and then opening again, "he is the givingest Christian it has ever been my privilege to meet. He is a blessing, that man. He is a light unto the gentiles."

"You've ordained him, have you?" I asked. I was standing in front of the shaving mirror, wondering whether Bebb would expect me to put on a tie or not. It was Florida and it was summer, but he was wearing a tie himself, and I had no idea what paces he might be planning to put me through. I had just about decided not to wear one anyway when I heard Bebb say, "Don't you go getting all dolled up now, Antonio, this isn't New York City. Just any old thing that's comfortable," and for a moment I thought he must have been able to see me in the door mirror standing there with the tie in my hand, but the angle of the door was all wrong. He couldn't possibly have seen me. "This Mr. Redpath," I said. "You've ordained him, you say?"

Bebb said, "That's what I'm getting at, Antonio. That is exactly the point. That is what I've just been to Texas about, and let me tell you all these airplane fares are setting the Mother Church back plenty. Herman Redpath has heard the call—just like you heard it yourself, just like thousands of others have heard it. But there's

110

one big difference. I say unto you—Matthew nineteen—
it is easier for a camel to go through the eye of a needle,
Antonio, than for a rich man to enter the Kingdom of
God. But for Herman Redpath it is as easy as taking
candy from a baby. It's like he's a thread was made on
purpose for that needle. It's what I've been down there
in Texas talking to him about. You should see this place
he's got. You could put Holy Love in one of his swimming pools and still have plenty of room left over for a
boat race. Just the room where he keeps his hi-fi and his
victrola records makes Holy Love look like a gym
locker."

I had finished dressing by this time and stepped out
of the bathroom in khaki slacks and a navy-blue polo
shirt Ellie gave me once with an alligator on the pocket.
It made me look like a Latin lover, she said. I had my
camera slung over one shoulder—it had occurred to me
that there ought to be some pictures to go with my
article, and if I got anybody else to take them, Bebb
was bound to get suspicious—and I had also put on the
dark glasses I had bought in Armadillo the day before,
so I looked like something right off the tourist special.
I wondered if even at that moment Persephone was
making her way down the Pullman corridors in her bathing suit, passing out reservation checks for lunch. I
wondered what she had done with my oranges.

There was no restaurant in the Salamander, but Bebb
took me across the street to a big gas station that had
food in slot machines, and I drank a quick cup of coffee
and ate an egg-salad sandwich which was so cold inside
that the first bite made my teeth ache. Then he said we
would stop by first at the Manse. He insisted we take

his car, and I found to my surprise that, like mine, it was a convertible. I had expected something more in keeping with the tight black raincoat and Tyrolean hat. It was a large convertible with fins, a plastic Jesus on the dashboard, and the initials L.B. on the door—was the L for Lucille or for Leo, I wondered. Bebb had the top down. As we drove to the Manse, Bebb continued to tell me about Herman Redpath.

Bebb said, "Herman Redpath is not ordained—he's not ordained *yet*. That's what I flew down to plan with him about. It was a planning trip, you see, so it's perfectly legal to write it off on the Mother Church. You'll never get into trouble that way. He wants to be ordained bad, Antonio. Why? It is not given to us to know why. Thy ways are not my ways, saith the Lord. And when you get right down to it, why does anybody want to be ordained? Why did you want to be ordained yourself, Antonio? Have you ever asked yourself that?" This was while we were at the gas station, and he caught me with my mouth full of egg salad, so that all I could do was nod yes, I had asked myself that question. For a moment I thought his lazy eye was going to perform again, but to my relief it did not.

Bebb said, "Herman Redpath has got everything a man could want, but he wants this too—*more*," he said, raising his finger. "He wants this more than anything else he's got. Think what that means. A man with his wealth—he drives a car makes this one look sick—and his influence . . . Antonio, I'm telling you this makes everything I've ever done before look like small potatoes. Meaning no slur on yourself," he added, "or any of the other Christians I've been privileged to draw into the

Gospel Ministry. In the eyes of the Lord we're all pretty small potatoes, Herman Redpath included. But speaking not in the language of Zion, Antonio, this is no jackrabbit. This is no red squirrel or gopher. This is a bull moose. This is a twelve-point buck, Antonio."

When we reached the Manse he pulled up at the curb just about where I had the evening before, but he held me there a few moments longer. With some difficulty because of the way the wheel was digging into his stomach, he turned in his seat to face me and placed one hand on my shoulder. He said, "Manna, Antonio. Riches. The green stuff," and he held his other hand in the air between us and rubbed his fingers together in the ancient gesture of avarice. "What is a man profited if he shall gain the whole world and lose his soul? And consider the lilies of the field, Antonio. Consider just that chickweed over by the sandbox. Even Herman Redpath in all his glory was not arrayed like one of these. Nobody knows that better than me. Horse shit." I was startled at first, but realized then that for Bebb the term was purely descriptive, like "bitch" for a dog breeder. "In itself, money's horse shit. But in terms of what it—put it to *work*, Antonio, and the sky's the limit. All a man's wildest dreams . . ." He took the handkerchief from his breast pocket and, without unfolding it, wiped the top of his head. Before he replaced it, I could see that on the inside, where it didn't show, it was grimy from what I presumed were many similar wipings. "What I mean is put it to work for *Christ*, Antonio," and this time there could be no doubt about it. The eye drowsed off and then came slowly awake again as if with a life or a death all its own.

Bebb gave three honks on his horn. My glance followed his toward the Manse, curious to see who would come out. Over at the gym set, one swing was stirring slightly in the breeze, and I wondered if it could have been for his baby that Bebb had originally bought it. If so, I gathered from what Lucille had said that the baby probably never got big enough to use it, and I thought of something I had bought to give Miriam the next month for Christmas—a long pair of wooden tongs with magnets on the tips for picking things up when you dropped them. She was always letting things fall off her hospital bed like cigarettes or Kleenex or the paper, and she said the nurses chilled her bedpan if she rang for them too often. Like the swing, it was possible that years might go by, I thought, and those tongs would still be sitting in the closet or wherever I'd put them, ungiven. I could always paint them with Rustoleum black, I supposed, and use them that way.

When no one answered his horn, Bebb blew it again —not just three snappy honks this time but six or seven long blasts without rhythm or pacing, like what you hear up around 125th Street on a crowded summer afternoon. In a moment or two the screen door opened and Brownie stepped out on the porch. He was wearing the same shorts and shirt he had had on the day before, but I was glad to see that as yet there were no stains at the armpits. Lucille probably didn't start sending for Tropicanas until later in the day. Even with my dark glasses on, he seemed to recognize me and gave a restrained little wave. I had not had time to wave back when Bebb cupped one hand to his mouth and yelled at him.

"Not you, deadbeat," he said. "The girl. Go tell that

girl to get her tail down here in five seconds or we'll leave without her."

It's surprising what subtleties you can inject even into a shout. I could tell perfectly well that when Bebb called Brownie deadbeat, he meant it, but when he said five seconds he meant thirty minutes or an hour or whatever it took. He might keep on honking the horn, but he'd wait. He could only mean Sharon, I decided. It was conceivable that he might speak of Lucille as a girl, but his referring to her tail was inconceivable. Brownie turned and went into the house again, and Bebb switched on the radio.

It would have seemed to me a reasonable time for him to explain where he was planning to take me and what he had in mind to show me once we got there. He might have dropped some hint about why Sharon, if it was indeed Sharon he meant, was going with us— whether she was to be just supercargo or part of the act. From his first appearance at the foot of my bed that morning, I had been waiting for him to open discussions about what had presumably brought me all the way down from New York in the first place, which was the matter of his proposal that I start an affiliate Gospel Faith in the metropolitan area for our mutual gain. This would have been a plausible time for him to open that up, and if he didn't, I was prepared to open it up myself, partly for the sake of making my disguise all the more secure but partly also because in the most idiotic way I found myself offended that he considered me so much less interesting a subject than Herman Redpath. But for the moment Bebb did not seem interested in further discussions of any kind. After the blast at

115

Brownie, his mouth had snapped tight shut on its hinges, and one after the other he was punching the automatic selector buttons of the radio with his finger. He was through with words for a while. He wanted music.

The music he found I can still hear in my mind's ear, and if when I think of Armadillo what I see is that useless stretch of sidewalk petering out in the scrub, what I hear when I remember Armadillo is the song that Bebb and I listened to as we sat in his open car in the sun waiting for the girl, whoever she might turn out to be, to get her tail down there. It was played on a honky-tonk piano, and you got the impression of a good deal of activity going on in the background, like glasses clinking and the hiss of draft beer being drawn and the sound of the saloonkeeper sliding the free-lunch platter down the mahogany bar to an old customer at the far end. It was the Yukon, it was *My Little Chickadee*, it was a Victorian whorehouse in Natchez, Mississippi, and if you'd listened hard, you could probably have heard the customers shifting around on one of those round, tufted sofas like the one Miriam had seen in the Ladies' Room at the Met the day we were sent to hear *Hansel and Gretel*. It was a bouncy little boilermaker of a tune, and just about the time I was getting to where I could have whistled it, somebody started singing the words. A man started singing them, a kind of shiftless, raspy bass, and I could see him in my mind as clearly as if he had been standing there on the lawn in front of the Manse. He was a big Victorian stud with a deep Southern twang and a handlebar mustache and a flashy stickpin made of paste and egg stains on his fancy vest. In between sing-

116

ing, he kept calling out in a loud, pleading voice, about as subtle in its suggestiveness as a rhinestone G-string, "Come on, Honey, you *know* what I like!" and you could all but smell his hairy, beery smile as he said it with the gaps between his teeth. I was unable to get many of the words at the time, and though I had occasion to hear it more than once afterwards, I have never been sure of all of them, but the chorus begins,

> *Chantilly lace*
> *And a pretty face*

and then there's something about

> *And a wiggle in her walk*
> *And a giggle in her talk*

and then maybe a few more "Come *on*, Honey"s and

> *Makes you feel all loose*
> *Like a long-necked goose.*

You could just see that big sweet-talking traveling man with his flat feet and his goose-greased lovelock and that twitching little butt in Chantilly lace he was salivating over. And then just as I was hoping I could get more of the words the next time round, I felt a touch on my shoulder and heard a girl's voice say quite close to my ear, "Big Bopper."

"Me?" I said.

"The man who's singing the song," she said.

"What's the name of the song?" I asked. "It's great."

"*Chantilly Lace*," she said, "but don't let it throw you. Bebb said, "Move it over, Antonio. There's room for us all up front. This is my daughter Sharon. The Reverend Antonio Parr from New York City."

If Bebb had chanced on some other tune when he was punching those radio buttons, would it have made a difference? If he had happened to hit on *Laura*, say, or *My Alice Blue Gown*, so that it was to those more subdued strains that I first came face to face with Sharon, would it have started our relationship out on such a different footing that everything from there on would have proceeded differently? I know only that from the very start my view of her, and perhaps in some way her view of me, was colored by that foolish novelty song played on the tinny piano as she squeezed into the front seat beside Bebb and me. She was wearing a pair of white sailor pants that she must have used a shoehorn to get into and a loose-fitting shirt the color of raspberry ice which hung outside. She wore rope sandals on her bare feet and carried a straw hat with a big, floppy brim. I haven't the faintest idea what Chantilly lace looks like, but as far as I'm concerned, that's what Sharon had on that first day I met her.

Chantilly lace and a pretty face. The face of Sharon Bebb. How do you describe a face like that, or any face, for that matter? In fact, the better you know it, the harder it is to describe. I have discovered that if I shut my eyes and try to see in my mind the faces of people I know, it is quite easy to summon up the fair-weather friends and casual acquaintances, the students I've taught, the vet who took care of Tom, but when it comes to somebody like Miriam whom I've known all my life, the best I can usually manage is a photograph of the face. I can't see it moving and changing the way faces do.

And so it is with Sharon.

In her case the photograph I see is one I must have taken later on that same day with my spy camera. She is sitting on a railing somewhere in the slightly round-shouldered way taller girls tend to. Her long hair looks as if it could stand a good brushing, and it has divided above one ear so that you can just see the earlobe through it. She is gazing down at something in a rather moody way—that straight nose, that almost somber tilt to the corners of her mouth, that curve of chin and throat arching down into the unbuttoned collar of her raspberry-ice shirt. I suppose that maybe, like mine, it is essentially an Italian face—a little sullen, a little self-indulgent, a little untrustworthy. A Florentine page boy caught peering through the keyhole at his mistress' bath. Some daughter of the lesser Medici given to lurking around the Colosseum by moonlight. Maybe there was something Italian too about the surprise of the face, which was the smile, that smile which is the only part of her face that I can sometimes make happen in my mind when I think of her. It was a surprise just because I would not have expected anything so unguarded and unabashed from that moody, downward glance. Whatever the secret of Sharon's face was, when she smiled the secret was out. Those wet white teeth. Those startling, minstrel-show eyes. There wasn't a wiggle in her walk exactly, but when she moved along in her lazy, loose-limbed way with that floppy hat in her hand and those white sailor pants, you knew there was a lot more going on than just somebody traveling from one place to another.

I shoved over into the middle of the seat as Bebb had

told me to, and with Bebb on one side of me and Sharon on the other and that plastic Jesus on the dashboard getting in the way of my view, we set off for I had no idea where.

It was Sharon who got this information out of him almost immediately. She said, "Hey, Bip, where are you taking us to anyway?" and Bebb said, "I'm taking you to the lions. Your old Bip's all wound up from his trip, and Antonio here is one of those city boys are tied up in knots most of the time anyway, so we're just going to find us some sunshine here in the Sunshine State and unwind. The lions are the unwindingest place I know."

It was the most expansive I had ever seen him, and I assumed it was Sharon's presence that had brought the change about. The raincoat tightness, the air he had even when glorifying Herman Redpath of keeping some vital part of himself buttoned up, the watchfulness that made that one drowsy eye such an anomaly in his face— all of this seemed to disappear as he drove along at seventy or seventy-five miles an hour back up some of the same pot-holed roads I had taken down from West Palm the day before. He kept the radio going and loosened his tie, and with his mouth snapped tight not so much now to keep something possibly incriminating from escaping, I thought, as to keep something particularly flavorsome from getting lost, he seemed for the time being quite oblivious to both Sharon and me. I tried at several points to make some kind of conversation with Sharon myself, but what with the roaring of the wind in our ears and the fact that we were squeezed in so tight that to turn toward each other to make ourselves heard was almost to touch noses, I finally gave up, so that the only communication between us was the soft collision of our flesh which Bebb in a sense forced upon us by taking up with his sizable bulk a good deal more than his third of the seat. It was only when we got out on the parkway and Bebb turned the radio off when the news came on that talk was possible again.

"Tell me about those lions," I said. "I never thought they were something Christians went out of their way to throw themselves to," but before Bebb had a chance to answer this rather pallid witticism, Sharon turned and said, "First tell me about that rich little Indian jerk. Luce says you've asked him home."

As she turned to speak, some of her hair blew into my face. It was the first time this had ever happened to me, and I remember it still. Such as it was, I had had my own hair blow into my face before, but never anybody else's. Unlike Ellie's hair, which smelled of shampoo, Sharon's smelled somehow of sleep is all I can say, smelled faintly musty and sweet anyhow, and before I had a chance to brush it away or whatever I would have done—a strand of it, I think, had even gotten into my mouth—Sharon reached up and did it herself. She did it by drawing her hand down from the top of her head to her cheek so that the hair came away by itself, and then she held it there close to her throat so it wouldn't blow again and looked past me at Bebb. This is another picture I can sometimes get of her in place of the one where she is sitting on the railing looking down.

Bebb said, "Herman Redpath is coming to Armadillo,

yes. Your mother was right. He's flying up from Texas in his private plane sometime—he'll be phoning to let me know just when—and I am going to ordain him to the Gospel Ministry personally right there in the church. It will be a great day for Holy Love. It will be a great day for all of us, Sharon, and don't you go around referring to him as a little Indian jerk."

Sharon said, "I referred to him as a *rich* little Indian jerk."

"I wish you'd take her in hand for me, Antonio," Bebb said.

Sharon looked at me and gave a little shrug.

"Sharper than a serpent's tooth," I said.

"Talk about your teeth," Bebb said. "How'd you like to try a set of those on for size? Puts even Brownie's to shame."

He was pointing toward a billboard that we were approaching. It showed the head of a lion with his mouth open in a great MGM roar and his upper fangs hanging down like stalactites.

Sharon said, "The last time we were here, one of them took a leak on the car. It was the high point of the day."

Bebb said, "Antonio, I wish you'd get to work on her language for me. It's the first thing needs to be cleaned up. But you know," he said, "the girl's right. It was the high point of the day, at least it was for me. Think of it, Antonio. There's no bars in this place. None of your little zoo cages with the poor jungle creatures wasting their lives away pacing back and forth, back and forth, on that cement floor until their claws are all wore off nearly—people throwing them peanuts and making crazy faces and poking at them with balloon sticks.

They're free as the breeze in this place, Antonio. Go anywhere. Do anything. If they get a notion they want to take a leak on somebody's car, they just go straight ahead and take it."

"You're going to have me in tears in a minute," I said. "I have a cat I live with in New York, and when I knew I was coming down here, I took him to the vet's to board. I hate to think of the size cage they've got him in right this minute. Probably even worse than a roomette."

Bebb said, "Well, but a cat's a cat. A cage gives a cat time for reflection. Keep a cat fed, and he'll make out just about anyplace. But a lion," he said, turning off at the next exit with so little reduction in speed that we were all tossed even more tightly against each other. "A lion feels a cage just like a man would—more," he said, reaching up to adjust the rear-view mirror as though he thought someone might be following us, "a lion feels it more than your average man would because he's king of the jungle. Five years, ten years, fifteen years. Think of it, Antonio. A king in a cage all that time, just wearing his claws off."

Now that we'd slowed down to park, Sharon had taken a comb out of the glove compartment and with her head tilted away from me was trying to pull it through a snarl at the ends of her sleep-smelling hair. She said, "What do you call your pussy?"

"I call him Tom," I said.

"Oh, it's a him," she said. "Hey, you've got a way with words. You ought to be a writer."

Bebb said, "I apologize, Antonio. Maybe you can knock some manners into her."

This time I was the one who shrugged. I could think

of nothing to say except something fatuous about ministers' daughters. There was something in Sharon's presence that made me feel fatuous in general—fatuous, phony, and very Madison Avenue.

Because Bebb's was a convertible, he had to exchange it for another car. He left his in the parking lot and rented another from a man in a concrete pillbox who explained the rules. You kept your windows closed tight and your doors locked. Under no circumstances did you get out of your car after you passed through the gates. If you needed help, you just stayed where you were and honked your horn until a hunter came—hunters were easy to spot because their cars were painted with black and white zebra stripes. Bebb had Sharon and me sit in the back seat because he said you could see more there, and he did the driving again although I had offered to.

Lion Country. I have never seen Africa, but the flat, mangy, zoo-colored acres we were driving toward with a palm tree sticking up here and there or a clump of brush by a water hole looked about as much like it, I thought, as anything I'd ever run across. At a gate in what must have been a twenty-foot-high fence of heavy wire mesh, a man with a rifle checked our ticket and let us through, and then in another few yards we had to go through a second fence just like it. Although, as the man in the pillbox had told us, the area extended over several square miles, we were, in effect, in the lions' cage, and I said as much to Sharon, who was gazing out of her window rather drowsily, I thought, with her chin in her hand.

"Don't panic," she said. "This kind of a hot day, they're probably all at the movies."

For a while I decided she must be right. Bebb was

cruising about ten miles an hour along the narrow, twisty road, apparently too intent on his own unwinding to pay any attention to his passengers in back, and there wasn't much to see except for an occasional snow-white cattle egret and in one scummy pond what I thought might be the snout of an alligator. There was another car parked around on the far side of the pond, but I couldn't see that they had anything more to look at than we did. A hawk or buzzard of some kind was spiraling slowly way up in the faded sky, and I was going to try out some quip about vultures on Sharon but thought better of it. She had leaned her forehead against the window, and I could see a triangle of cheek and one eyelid where the sun touched them reflected in the glass. I wondered if she could be asleep.

And then we began to see lions. Rather like Brownie calling me dear, it happened so gradually that it took a while before I realized it. There was a female lying in the rose-colored dust not more than a few feet back from the road. She was yellower than I remembered lions being except for her underbelly, which looked feathery and white, and she was licking her paw with her head tipped way over to the side and the paw more or less straight up, the way I have seen children trying to lick the drips off an ice-cream cone without dumping it. She gave no sign of noticing us as we drove past. I had seen Tom do his paw that same way, and the lion didn't seem much more than a somewhat larger version. A bit farther along we came across two males. One of them was rubbing his shoulder back and forth against a dead tree. He had a pained expression on his face as though he regretted either the necessity of scratching or its failure to help what was really itching him. The other was standing utterly still with his hind legs stretched back the way they make dogs stand at shows, and his tail, which had a slight S-shaped kink in it, bent almost straight up in the air.

Sharon leaned forward and touched Bebb's fat neck with one finger. She said, "Hey, Bip, eyes right," and it was only then that I saw the lion was pissing. Bebb didn't say anything, but glanced over where he had been told and smiled, I assumed—from behind I could see one cheek expand and the tip of his nose move. Without turning, he reached over his shoulder to touch the hand Sharon had touched him with, but by then she had withdrawn it and was using it to support her chin again.

At first it was like a zoo. We were here and the lions were there, and if you'd seen one lion, I thought, you'd seen them all, and the lions looked as though they had exactly the same feeling about people. But little by little this changed, although I couldn't say why. Little by little it began to get to me that they were lions and that they were here and that we were here too, Bebb and Sharon and I, not there but here with the scraggly palms and the water holes. It got to the point where lions' faces didn't even look like just lions' faces any more but like this lion's face and that lion's face. There was one lounging by a rock who looked a lot the way I imagined Herman Redpath did—all nose and mane and a rather undershot jaw. Another, if there is such a thing as a witty lion, looked witty to me—he was lying on his back with his belly in the sun, and as Bebb drove us by, he seemed to cover his eyes with his paws as though in some kind of arch reference to his comprehensively ex-

126

posed parts. When we rounded the next bend, we came upon a large pond where there must have been at least twenty lions all more or less together—a whole pride, I imagined, although I had no idea how big a regulation pride is supposed to be. Some were strolling near the water, others were squatting on their haunches in the dust. I saw no evidence of cubs anywhere and wondered if even such humane captivity as this inhibited their breeding. There were several padding toward us down the middle of the road, and Bebb pulled the car over to the ditch and stopped.

He said, "If you want to get some photos with that camera of yours, Antonio, here's your chance." Even as he spoke, one of the males who had been walking down the road reached the car and came abreast of Sharon on her side. Through the window you could just see his eyes and mane and the hairy tip of his tail. I took the camera off my shoulder and got a shot of him, aiming a little to the side in order to get a bit of Sharon's profile in too, I hoped—the nose and chin anyway and a little of the hair.

Bebb said, "You won't take any prizes that way, Antonio. The light's no good in the car. Go on outside where the sunshine is. Those lions are so used to people they won't hardly notice you. I've done it myself lots of times."

I thought at first that he was joking, but it became obvious right away that he wasn't. He turned around in his seat, laying his arm out along the back, and explained how if I took a picture from a shadowy car of a lion in the bright sun, it was bound to come out wrong. The difference in light would ruin it. I could leave the door open if I wanted to so I could get back in in a hurry if the occasion arose. And I could keep the car between the lions and me. There was no need to worry about the hunters. People did it all the time, Bebb said, and he knew quite a few of the hunters anyway. Then his mouth swung tight shut, and he lowered his chin to the back of his hand and waited for me to pull something out of my hat. The thought suddenly occurred to me that maybe this was some kind of initiation or ritual test. I remembered reading somewhere that before you got to be a full Druid, you had to lie naked in a frozen stream for a night or two. Would I or wouldn't I? Was I or wasn't I? Perhaps this was what Bebb was waiting to find out, I thought.

And Sharon was waiting. All I could see of her out of the corner of my eye was those white pants and a tan arm, but I felt her eyes upon me. If my Druidship was at stake, I felt sure, so was my manhood.

I said, "Look now, I'm sorry. I don't want to lose any more points than I have to, and I've got my pride just like everybody else. But I'm a city boy and an ex-schoolteacher. I do laps around the reservoir, and I don't smoke cigarettes. I watch my calories. So all in all I'm in pretty good shape for somebody my age. But I don't feel like tangling with a lion even if you leave the door open, and I'll bet I can buy better pictures back there at the gate than I'd get with my arm clawed off anyway."

Almost before I had finished speaking, Bebb had his hand out toward me. He said, "Antonio, I don't want you to think for one second I'm putting you on the spot or want to embarrass you in any way. Some folks are allergic to things other folks don't even notice. Me, I'm scared to death of heights. I'd rather have a tooth drawn than go up in an airplane. But wild animals I've never minded any more than bugs. You let me have that camera now, and I'll get you a picture that's a picture," and before I knew it, he was out of the car with my camera in his hand.

He didn't leave the door open, and he didn't make any effort to keep the car between him and the lions, and he couldn't have anyway because there were lions all around him, none so close that he couldn't have made a run for it if he'd had to, I suppose, but a lot closer than I'd ever seen a man and a lion before without so much as a ditch between them.

He stood there in his dark suit with the Florida sun glancing off his bald head and my own spy camera pressed up against his eye, and no more than a car's length away those lions padded around in the dust with their great, soft feet and tawny velvet flanks and wild, Old Testament manes. Androcles in the Colosseum? Jerome in the desert? Happy Hooligan meets Simba? All I know is that no picture he took was a match for the picture he made as I crouched forward there with my elbow on the front seat touching Sharon's elbow and watched him through the windshield of the rented car.

With an almost mystical smile, I thought, as though answering voices he hadn't heard distinctly, the most majestic of the male lions sauntered over to one of the females and mounted her. There didn't seem to be any passion about it as far as I could tell, but on the other hand it didn't seem perfunctory either—rather like two old friends seeking refreshment in each other's company toward the middle of a hot afternoon. Bebb swung my camera around and, as nearly as I could tell, got his shot in before they uncoupled.

"That Bip," Sharon said. "You've got to hand it to him." It was the first indication I'd had that, despite my failing the lion test myself, I still belonged to the human race in her eyes.

Another confirmation of this, I thought, came later. Once our safari was over and we were back out on the safe side of the two wire-mesh fences again, we had a late lunch at a combination hot-dog and souvenir stand near the entrance. There were a couple of round tables with umbrellas, and we sat down at one of them with our paper plates and bottles of soda pop. Neither Bebb nor Sharon had so far expressed any particular interest in knowing more about who I was or what I did with my life when I wasn't down in Florida going to zoos, but I had the impulse to tell them a little about myself anyway. There under false pretenses as I was, I wanted, at least within limits, to have some of the truth of me known. So with Bebb not really paying much attention as far as I could see and Sharon looking at me with a slightly puzzled frown—she seemed less puzzled at what I was saying, I thought, than at the fact I bothered to say anything at all—I told them about having taught English at a coed boarding school for a while and about the things I made with scrap iron. I even found myself telling them about Ellie. I don't know why I felt like telling them about Ellie. In part it may have been a kind of substitute for telling them about Miriam because I didn't feel like thinking about Miriam just then. But in any case I mentioned our orphan-asylum plans vaguely and how she worked at the U.N., and even as I was speaking I thought to myself how incongruous just the sound of her name seemed here among the three of us under our umbrella.

I tried to imagine Ellie and Lucille meeting, or Ellie and Brownie—it would be like the encounter of matter and anti-matter, I decided, one simply canceling the other quite out of existence—and I wondered what Ellie would have thought of Lion Country. I could imagine her little murmurs of wonder and surprise and how she would have pretended not to notice when the lion with the kink in his tail took a leak. And then I thought of the picture Bebb had snapped with my camera of the lions coupling, and how, if it turned out, I might bring it up to Manhattan House when I got back and Ellie could build a whole evening around it, maybe invite in some of her U.N. friends. I had paused to take a bite of hamburger, and at this thought I choked on it, and that was when I received what I took to be confirmation that, despite my failure at the lion test, Sharon accepted me as a member of the human race anyway. I choked on my hamburger, and the result was that a half-chewed crumb of it went shooting out of my mouth and hit Sharon somewhere in the neighborhood of the eye.

It is a nearly universal experience, I think, that when anything like that happens between people—you touch somebody's foot by accident under the table, say, or open the door when they're sitting on the can—the result is instantaneous apology on one side and embarrassment and confusion on the other. I apologized, all right, but Sharon—how can I say it? She didn't make much of it, didn't laugh or exclaim or anything like that, but the puzzled frown was shattered by that always surprising smile of hers—the smile of a gondolier who knows he has overcharged you and knows that you know—and what I understood her to be saying as she wiped at her cheek with the back of her hand was that something half-chewed had flown out of my mouth and hit her in the eye, and all in all, like Bebb's lions taking their pleasure by the water hole, it wasn't a bad idea for a hot afternoon with nothing much else to do. It livened things up a little. That crumb, you might say, was the first real bond between us.

Two more things. At the souvenir stand she bought Bebb an absurd hat. It was a black beanie with *Lion Country* written across the front in yellow, and at each side, so they stuck out over your ears when you wore it, a little propeller. She made the poor man wear it on the trip back to Armadillo, and of course the rush of air as we sped along the parkway made the propellers spin crazily. As I looked at him there with his fat, pale face zipped up against the wind and the glare, and the propellers sticking out of his head, I couldn't help remembering Lucille's words to me at the Manse the evening before. "Sometimes I believe Bebb is from outer space himself," she said, and for a moment I took the idea almost seriously.

When we got back to Armadillo toward the end of the afternoon, Bebb drove straight to the Manse instead of dropping me off first at the Salamander Motel. He opened his door and got out, at the same time indicating that Sharon and I were to stay in. Bebb said, "I'm expecting the call from Herman Redpath about now, so I want to get right on in to be there when it comes. Sharon, be a good girl and take Antonio back to the

motel. Antonio, you and I've still got a lot of business
to do, but I expect I'll be tied up with Texas most of this
evening, and yours and mine isn't anything won't keep
till tomorrow anyway. There's plenty to see in Armadillo.
Get Sharon to show you the sights. I'll tell you what."
He remembered here that he was still wearing the beanie
and took it off. He then reached into his trouser pocket
and drew out a little snap purse such as women use for
change in their pocketbooks. There was a small roll of
bills in it, one of which he peeled off and handed to me
before I had time to protest.

He said, "Antonio, how about you keeping Sharon
out for supper for me? I'll get a whole lot more done
with her out of the house. No, no." He pushed my hand
away as I reached out to return the bill. "We've got a
special entertainment account down at Holy Love. I
write it right off, and it's a hundred percent legal. Now,
you two young people have some fun together and get
something to eat when you're hungry, and that'll be just
fine."

It was the first time I'd seen Sharon show anything
like embarrassment, and for the first time too it made
me stop to wonder how old she was. Not more than
nineteen or twenty, I decided, twenty-one at the outside.
She said, "My God, Bip, you're one for the books all
right. What can the man say?"

I said, "Yes, Bip, and what can the child say either?"
and that was the second thing. It was the first time I'd
called him anything, and I called him Bip. I have never
particularly liked to hear adults calling each other by the
names that children call them. I have known grey-haired
men who called their blue-haired mothers-in-law things

133

like Nana and Googoo because those were the grand-
mother names their children used. And now I heard myself doing the same thing because Sharon had done it
and the name seemed to fit him somehow. Bip. Some
combination of Bebb and something else, I supposed,
or just a childhood corruption of Pop. The Grimm's
law of the nursery. In any case, I said, "Bip, for you we
are prepared to say anything or do anything. If it's O.K.
with you," I added to Sharon.

"If it's O.K. with you," she said, "then I guess it's
O.K. with me."

Chantilly lace, I thought. That slightly corrupt gondolier's smile.

CHAPTER EIGHT

I HADN'T REALIZED how hot it was till we got back to the Salamander Motel. I wanted to pick up my own car, and if I was to take Sharon out to supper later on, I thought I'd better change my shirt, so that's where we headed for first. There was no breeze, and there was no shade, just the little bits of eave projecting over the two rows of rooms which stuck out not unlike Bebb's propellers from each side of the small white stucco office. The immediate problem was what to do with Sharon while I changed my shirt. It didn't seem humane to ask her to wait for me in the hot sun or in the office, which as far as I could remember had nothing much in it but a desk and cigarette machine, and it didn't seem decorous to invite her into my room. Sharon, as it turned out, solved the problem herself. She said, "I feel like I've got lion all over me. Would you feel compromised if I came in and washed up?"

No one had touched the room since I left, and it was a mess. The bed lay unmade with the top sheet pulled down to the foot and half coming off onto the floor where I'd crawled out to shake hands with Bebb. Despite my effort to hide it behind the curtain, the Dewar's bottle was clearly in sight on the windowsill. The pajamas I'd rinsed out the night before in the shower were over the back of the one comfortable chair where I'd put them when they were dry. The only compensation was that no one had turned the fan off, and that, together with the fact that the Venetian blinds had also been drawn all day, made it somewhat cooler than it was outside.

"It feels like a movie theater in here," Sharon said, "or a cave." Her white sailor pants and her raspberry-ice shirt looked brighter in the artificial dusk of the Venetian blinds than they had in the sun, like flowers on a rainy day. I apologized for the mess and offered her the bathroom if she wanted to wash the lion off right away, but she seemed in no hurry about that and sat down in the chair with my pajamas on the back in such a settled sort of way that I found myself more or less obliged as the host to sit down myself on about the only place that was left, which was the foot of the unmade bed.

If my purpose in Armadillo was to find out as much as I could about Bebb, it occurred to me, this was about as rich an opportunity as I'd yet had—a daughter who would probably know most of the story from the inside and yet an adopted daughter who mightn't have the same hesitation about telling it. I felt no special remorse at the thought of pumping her because at this point the idea of getting back to New York and writing my article seemed so remote that I thought of myself as wanting to hear the story mainly just for the story's sake, particularly the story of Sharon herself. She sat there looking a little like a child called into the principal's office for copying somebody's homework—that grave, illegal face, yet with the perpetual possibility, I knew, of her secret-spilling smile—and yet I felt oddly that she was the one who was the principal.

"I feel all loose," I said, "like a long-necked goose."

"Like the Big Bopper," she said.

Come on, honey, you know what I want is what I might have said then, but I didn't. What I wanted, I might have said—and she almost looked as if she knew that I did—were the facts, the facts maybe most of all at that point about her, but the facts about Lucille too and Brownie and Herman Redpath and especially, of course, about Bebb. Not so much so that I could skin him alive just then, but so I could understand something about what went on inside that tight skin of his, that plump, pale sausage of a man with his rebellious eye and his heroism among lions. Rather have a tooth pulled, he had said, than go up in an airplane, and I thought of his flight to New York, to Texas, to God only knew what other places Holy Love took him to, and I wondered if he sat there every time with his coat buttoned tight as his safety belt and his mouth snapped shut to keep the terrible fear from showing. How much of a crook was he, and just how full was the accreditation of Gospel Faith? What was the truth about what had happened at Miami, and how had the trial come out? How about the five lost years when Brownie kept the files? And what about Lucille and the Trop-icanas and the dead baby and the silvers and golds from outer space? *Come on, honey, you know what I want,* I thought—knew more about what I wanted maybe than I knew myself, because in an odd way I think I had already sensed the answers to many of those ques-tions and thus must have wanted something else beyond them, which possibly she knew. What I said was, "Tell me about yourself," and I leaned back on my elbow in the twisted sheets and tried to look both casual and interested, whereas the truth of it, needless to say, was that I was not at all casual and a great deal more than interested.

It is the perfect sentence to stop conversations with, of course. I have been asked the same thing myself— Tell me about yourself—and my instinct has always been to flick my lower lip with my thumb, blub blub blub.

Sharon looked blank enough for a while. She had turned around in her chair and swung her sailor legs over the arm so she sat there sideways gazing out toward one of the drawn blinds with her hair dividing over her ear again. "I am adopted," she said after a while. "Bip adopted me when I was two, and I don't know a thing about my real parents, and if anybody else does, they've never told me. I don't know when my real birthday is, but we always celebrate it on Luce's because I was Bip's birthday present to her."

"They had their own baby once," I said. "I saw it in a photograph."

Sharon said, "It died." She looked back from the window to me at this and drew her hand down flat over her hair the way she had in the car when it blew into my face. "It was some kind of freak accident, and they don't either of them talk about it. Killed Luce, I guess."

"The Tropicanas?" I said.

Unexpectedly, she laughed. "That fruitcake Brownie," she said. "He told Luce she shouldn't offer you a Tropicana, being Holy Love and everything, and Luce told him you were from New York and go shove it. You should have seen your face the first time you tasted it wasn't just orange juice."

"You mean you saw my face?" I said.

"I was in the hall," she said, "and half the time Brownie didn't shut the door after him."

I said, "Spies get shot."

"We're all spying on each other," Sharon said. "Bip spies on the lions. And you spy on Bip. I can see you watching him just like the rest of them."

"Who are the rest of them?" I asked.

"All the Holy Lovers," she said. "The ones like you who come around, anyway. They're all trying to see if they can figure out how he does it."

"Learn his tricks," I said.

"You might say. Whatever you call it what he does."

"He loves you, doesn't he, Bip?" I said. "Just the way he says your name."

"He says it's a dime-store name. Luce gave it to me. He wanted something else," she said. "You know something about Bip? If you want to know about him, I'm the wrong one to ask. I don't know him all that better than you do, when it comes right down to it."

"Brownie said he went away for five years," I said. "By the way, Brownie shut that door on the bats last night. He pulled it till it clicked."

"You know what that Brownie drinks?" she said. "He won't touch Tropicanas or anything else hard, but he drinks after-shave. I caught him doing it once. I guess he figures if people smell it on his breath, they won't think it's his breath."

"Maybe it's what gives him such a sweet smile," I said. I didn't mean to be unkind about Brownie. When he waved to me after Bebb called him a deadbeat, it seemed to me that among other things there was some sweetness in it. "You come down pretty hard on Brownie," I said. "All of you."

Sharon said, "He's so soft. Maybe he needs something hard."

"Brownie said the five years Bip was away he was doing the Lord's work," I said.

Sharon said, "He was in jail."

It was like reaching out in the dark for your watch or a glass of water and finding that instead of having to grope all over the place for it, you've put your hand on it first thing. I had expected to have to knock over a lot of things in my clumsiness before coming on anything like this, and now that I'd come on it so easily, I was almost sorry. It was nothing I hadn't known, or all but known, right from the start, after all, and now that Sharon had confirmed it, I wanted to move away from it. Somebody else could supply the details if I needed any; in fact, there was no real reason I couldn't supply them for myself. I needed no one to help me imagine Bebb pacing back and forth in his cell wearing his claws off, I thought, or the way he had looked there in my room that very morning with the stripes of light from the blinds cutting across him. "That's tough," I said. "I'm sorry."

Sharon said, "A lot of people have it in for Bip. They got some kids to frame him, and the judge was in on it too, so they gave him five years. There wasn't a thing Bip could do about it."

"It must have been tough on you and Lucille too," I said.

Sharon yawned and stretched her arms up in the air till there was a bare strip between her white pants and her shirt like a dancer. One of her sandals fell off. "I hate to admit it," she said, "but Brownie looked after us pretty well. And there were always some Herman what's-his-names around too, only maybe not quite so loaded. Bip's got enemies, but he's got friends too." She reached down for the sandal. "Hey, is your name really Antonio?" she said.

I explained about my father's World War I romance and my Italian mother. I told her that, except for Bebb, most people called me Tono. Miriam said it made me sound less like an organ-grinder.

Sharon said, "Antonio, would you be shocked if I asked you something?"

If I was a spy, I thought? If I was still a virgin at thirty-four? Was I really in love with my twin sister? Did I believe in God? Did I masturbate? "I don't know," I said. "Maybe I would be."

She said, "I'll tell you how it is. The plumbing at home is about a hundred years old. They hadn't even invented showers back then, so all we have is bathtubs that sit way up high on claws. And they're so short you have to sit straight up in them with your knees pushed under your chin. What I'd like to know is would you be shocked if I asked could I wash the lion off here in your shower bath?" She sat there with the sandal in her hand and the one bare foot up on the arm of the chair. "I haven't gotten to have one since the last time Bip took me with him to Atlanta."

Looking back on it, I suspect we both knew what hung on my answer—not that I could have really answered anything other than of course the shower was all hers if she wanted it, but on how I answered it anyway, the look on my face, the way the air felt between our faces. She waited there in that one comfortable chair with her ear showing through where the hair divided over it and her cheek resting against the back where my pajamas were, and I waited. I was still sitting on the foot of the unmade bed, leaning sideways on one elbow. I glanced downward to rest from her eyes for a moment and noticed the little alligator on the pocket of the shirt Ellie had given me. Ellie. I could offer to get out of the room till she was through, I thought. I could do a couple of laps around the motel while I was waiting. I could find another room somewhere and take an ice-cold shower. In my mind, at least, I could light a candle to good Saint Anthony and ask that all not be lost forever, for me or for Sharon either. I crossed one leg over the other and, looking back up at her again with the steadiest glance I could manage, I said in a cool, Madison Avenue voice, "Help yourself. I think there's a clean towel in there, and I haven't touched the washcloth." Who ever heard of taking a shower with a washcloth? But I was grateful for whatever words came to my mind. It made no difference what they meant.

I remember the sound of the water splashing. Hot water splashing makes a different sound from cold water splashing—a finer-grained sound—and I could tell it was hot water she was using. I didn't try to picture anything, tried not to, in fact. I lay back on the crumpled sheets with my feet still on the floor, and with the toe of one and the heel of the other I worked off first one loafer and then the other. I looked up at the ceiling and thought of a line from *Madeline* that Miriam and I had liked as children about how on the ceiling of the hospital there was a crack "that had a habit / Of sometimes looking like a rabbit." There was no crack on this ceiling, just a light fixture which looked something like a pinwheel.

I suppose if I tried I could remember everything, the whole sequence of what followed from the time of Sharon's question and my answer up to the time we finally left that room a good while later. How one thing led to another, as the saying goes. Bebb's ad, Tom's eye, the dream on the train, "The Book of the Cock," the lion trying to get rid of its itch against the dead tree, and now me on my unmade bed with the Dewar's on the windowsill and the sound of the water splashing and all that came after. There can be no doubt about it. One thing does lead to another very much as the Hindu monkey swings from branch to branch and sometimes,

143

I am tempted to think, without much more in the way
of rhyme or reason.

I remember how after a while she was standing there
by the bed with the towel wrapped around her like a
sarong and holding her damp hair in a pile on top of
her head and asking me if I knew where something was,
though I haven't the faintest idea what it was she was
asking for and hadn't the faintest idea then. I remember
her face was wet still, and there were drops of water
caught in her eyelashes. And I remember how far away
and almost detached I felt as I reached up with one
hand and touched the place just below her shoulder
where she had the towel tucked in on itself and how at
my touch the towel didn't fall straight to the floor as
you might suppose but sideways instead and quite
slowly, catching for a moment on the way down.

If I forget thee, let my right hand forget her cunning.
If I do not remember thee, let my tongue cleave to the
roof of my mouth. And yet "O my America! My new-
found land . . . my Myne of precious stones, My
Emperie." It is Donne's words in the end that serve me
best. You do not describe such a moment. You lift it
up in both your hands as high as you can lift, and
there should be silver bells tinkling in the background
and boys in scarlet with their palms together and their
eyes lowered and their fingertips pressed to their lips.
Sharon—that dime-store name—frowned, did she? or
smiled her young thief's smile as she raised one hand to
her shoulder where my hand had touched, and stepped
free from the towel at her feet.

If I tried, I suppose I could remember how it all
went, one thing leading to another thing, and when it

comes my time to die and my whole life passes before me as they say a life does, I will see it all again and remember how it was with us there and what we did and what we said, which was not much, and how all the time the electric fan was going and if we had stopped to notice, we would have seen whatever there is to see of a sunset when the Venetian blinds are down. But "O my America! My new-found land," Donne wrote to his mistress on going to bed, that strange man, part priest and part satyr, who all his life was half in love with death. "License my roving hands and let them go / Before, behind, between, above, below," and then "How blest am I in this discovering thee! To enter in these bonds is to be free. Full nakedness! All joyes are due to thee." Anything I might add to that would have to be on the order of footnotes.

But as Montague Rhodes James would be almost certain to agree, a few footnotes are probably in order. The time finally came when I decided to take a shower myself, which I did, a rather brief one that was neither hot nor cold but pounded down hard on my neck and chest like needles, and when I came back into the bedroom again, dripping water all over the rug, I caught sight of myself in the dresser mirror and paused for a moment, God knows why, to get a better look. I was still soaking wet mostly, and my hair was in my eyes, and there were beads of perspiration on my upper lip and running down my sideburns. In the words of the Big Bopper, I looked all loose like a long-necked goose, and there was that about me which looked so particularly loose, looked such a limp and wretched souvenir of the thing it had been when we started, that with something like real indignation in my voice I said to Sharon, "Just see me. *See* what you've gone and done," and Sharon answered with something I can't remember except that it made me remind her that Bebb had said the first thing I was to clean up was her language, and Sharon said, "You better make that the second thing."

And I remember how later my strength returned and kept on returning so many more times than I would have thought possible that I told Sharon about the Hindu holy men who sometimes lavish all the vast accumulations of their abstinence on a single night that may last for centuries, and she seemed quite interested. I remember also how at some point I asked her if this was her first time. It was nearly dark by then except for a pearly greyness at the windows and the bluish-white sheen, almost like moonlight, of the sheets. She was lying on her side with her hands tucked under her cheek, palm to palm, like pictures of children asleep, and she said it wasn't her first time and it wasn't her last time either, and I wondered whether she meant that it wasn't her last time with me or just wasn't her last time. I wondered what difference it would make to me to know and what difference if any it made to her.

There in the Salamander Motel we went to bed together, Sharon and I, and I thought to myself that in the highly unlikely event that I was ever to tell Ellie about it, or even if I was to tell Miriam, that was the way I would probably put it—that we went to bed together. I would reduce it finally to that. It seemed such an impoverished expression, but then as we lay there side by side in the semi-dark, I decided that maybe it was not as impoverished as all that and there might be more to

146

it than first met the eye. Maybe from the very beginning what I had desired above all things was quite literally just to go to bed with her as we were in bed together there in that warm Florida night. For the second time that day, I had some of her hair in my face, but I let it stay there now, not smelling so much of sleep any more as of the shower. For quite a while we hardly said anything, and when we touched each other, it was as much like friends almost as like lovers. We'd gone to bed together, my new-found land and I, and maybe that was what had been at the heart of my desire all along.

Then after a while we talked, or at least Sharon did. She'd told me three lies, she said, and since I'd been decent enough to let her wash the lion off in my shower bath, she thought maybe she ought to come clean about them. The first lie was about Brownie. She had never really caught him drinking after-shave, she said. She believed that he drank it and Luce believed it too, but neither of them had any real proof. Maybe the only reason he smelled of it so was that he dowsed himself with it. The second lie was about Bip, and since I could not see her face very well—it was too close to see and there wasn't much light—I was not quite sure in what spirit she told about it. She was talking quite softly, half into the pillow, and there was an oddly deadpan quality to her voice. I could imagine her either smiling or frowning.

About Bebb's being in jail, she said, she wasn't really sure that he had been framed. Some said he was, and some said he wasn't. There were witnesses who claimed that they had seen the thing happen, and without any attempt to minimize it, Sharon told me exactly what they had said they saw. It was of course possible that they were lying because there was no question there were people out to get Bip for one reason or another. Bip himself had pleaded not guilty at the trial, but she had no idea what he had said in private because she had never heard him talk about it in private or anywhere else for that matter. Lucille talked about it sometimes when Bip wasn't around, but it was usually after a good many Tropicanas and you couldn't be sure what Lucille thought about it. The last time, Sharon remembered, Lucille said that people from outer space were queer as Hell. But you couldn't be sure what Lucille meant by queer.

The last lie was about Bip's baby, she said, but it involved Lucille and Bip too. She put both her hands flat on my chest as she started to tell about it and pushed herself a little bit away from me. Her hands felt cool against my sweatiness, and I reached for them in the dark and put one of them back on my chest and the other on my whiskers. It was true that the baby had died, she said, but it was not a freak accident as she had told me. Lucille had killed it, she said. A lot of people thought, as of course I had myself, that it was the baby's death that had led Lucille to Tropicanas, but actually it was the other way around. Bebb was away somewhere at the time, and Lucille was drowning her sorrows all by herself one evening when the baby, who was colicky and had given them lots of trouble from the start, started screaming its head off. Lucille went into the large, old-fashioned bathroom where they kept the crib and gave it a beating with a toilet brush. When Bebb got back the next morning, he found the baby dead and Lucille very nearly dead herself. She had tried to cut her wrists with a razor blade but had made such a bad job of it that they were able to save her. The coroner was a friend of Bip's, and between them they were able to fix it up somehow to look like an accident, but a lot of people had their suspicions, and it was not long afterwards that Bip moved to Armadillo. They had been living in Tennessee when the thing happened. In those days Bip had been a Bible salesman.

Bip himself, Sharon said, had told her this story. It was on her sixteenth birthday, thus also Lucille's birthday, and Bip had planned to take them both up to West Palm for a lobster dinner and the movies. But Lucille hadn't felt well, so Sharon and Bip had gone alone. After the lobster dinner, there turned out to be no movie they wanted to see, so they went to some professional *jai alai* matches instead. Bebb drank two bottles of beer, which was unusual for him, and it was on the drive home in the dark that he told her. She wasn't to think too hard of Lucille, he said. She hadn't been in her right mind when she did it. She had loved the baby more than her life, as proved by her attempt at suicide afterwards. He was telling Sharon, he said, because she had a right to know and because he needed to tell someone, but she was never to let Lucille know she knew.

When he finished, Sharon said, she told him she could not understand how in spite of all this he had ever been able to forgive her. And at this, Sharon said, Bebb had pulled the car off the road and stopped and then opened the door enough so that the light inside went on. He had looked at himself in the rear-view mirror and then turned to Sharon as if wanting to make sure that she could see his face as he spoke. "How do I know that I have ever forgiven her?" he said. And then, after a while, "How do I know that I have ever forgiven myself?"

It was not until almost eleven that Sharon and I left the Salamander Motel. There was no place left open for supper in Armadillo, and we decided we weren't hungry anyway, even though our only lunch had been the hot dogs at Lion Country. So I drove her home in Bebb's car in case he needed it the next morning, and I planned to get back to the motel on foot. It wasn't that far. There were no lights showing in the front of the Manse, and we kissed quite chastely in the shadows of the porch. Sharon had left her hat in my room, she said, and would I bring it around if I came the next morning. Would she be there if I did, I asked her, and as I waited for her to answer, I realized that in some way I had placed my life in her hands with the question. It was a feeling in the pit of the stomach like suddenly being afraid that you're lost as a child.

"This wasn't the first time," Sharon said, "and it wasn't the last time either," and then "Good night, Big Bopper," she said and had started for the door when I remembered the money Bebb had taken out of his snap purse and given to me for our supper when we left. I took it out of my pocket and handed it to her. Sharon tilted it into the moonlight to see what it was. "Five bucks," she said. "I guess he didn't expect us to eat much."

CHAPTER NINE

AS IT TURNED OUT, I didn't see Sharon the next day, not because she wasn't there when I arrived but because I never arrived. There was no phone in my room, but I had noticed a booth in front of the motel office and stopped there on my way to have a slot-machine breakfast at the gas station across the street. It was the second day since I'd last seen Miriam, and the way things were, I thought I'd better check in with her. She had her own phone, and it wasn't a bad time to call her because she would have already had her breakfast by then and the doctors didn't make their rounds until later.

Vast as the distance seemed in every way between the

Salamander Motel booth and that hospital room of hers with the storm-tinted window, I got through to her with no trouble at all, paying for three minutes with a whole fistful of change that I had picked up at the office. It rang out like the Bells of Saint Mary's as I deposited it coin by coin, and at the last peal of the last bell I could hear Miriam's voice at the other end. She made no introductory remarks, asked me nothing about how the trip was going or where I was calling from, but started right in with what was most on her mind.

She said, "Oh Tono, thank God it's you. Listen. Charlie phoned me yesterday. He's bringing Chris and Tony into the city today. They've got dentist appointments this afternoon and he's taking them to Radio City Music Hall afterwards, and in between times, around four or five, he asked if I'd like him to bring them up here to see me. I'm sure he had to take about six phenobarbitals to steel himself for the call, and it was sweet of him to do it, but I told him no. At least I told him I didn't want *him* to come. I think I could take it all right, but I know he couldn't. So what I suggested, Tono, was if I could get hold of you, maybe you could meet them somewhere and bring the boys up yourself, and he said if this was the way I wanted it, it was O.K. by him. Frankly, I think it was a huge load off his chest not to have to come himself. So, Tono, will you get hold of him this morning please—before they leave? That head doctor, the Groucho Marx one, says I seem to be holding my own, and I'd like to see the kids again while that lasts, before the fireworks start anyway. So I'm counting on you, Tono. Call Charlie and fix a place where he can hand the kids over to you."

While she was talking, I had been watching a Negro woman carrying a vacuum cleaner down the row of rooms where mine was, and I wondered if she would get to mine this time and if there would be anything there to tell her about Sharon and me and what she would think about it if she thought about it at all. The whole time Miriam was talking, I had been waiting for pause enough to tell her that what she was asking was totally impossible. Here I was fifteen hundred miles away or whatever it was on a summer's day with a floppy straw hat in my hand that belonged to a girl I had gone to bed with the night before and a queer floppy feeling in the pit of my stomach at the thought that when I got to the Manse maybe she would not be there or maybe she would. What Miriam was asking was a complete impossibility, as she herself would surely realize if I just reminded her of the geography of the thing, and as soon as she stopped talking I would remind her. Then it occurred to me that of course Miriam had no idea I was in Florida at all.

Her only world was the world of that hospital room, and if she had even been listening the day I told her I was planning to take the train down, she must have put it out of her mind long since or assumed vaguely that I must be back. In any case, I was not in Florida because basically, for her, there was no such place as Florida. I was only twenty or thirty blocks away at my apartment with Tom, and thus when she said she was counting on me, she was really counting on me, and what she was asking me was not an impossibility that I could make her understand in a minute but an urgency that I could not refuse. What she was asking me was to make it possible for her to see her two sons once more while she still had eyes to see them with, and when you came right down to it, there was no reason I couldn't do it. Though I was no more of a flier than Bebb, there were planes, after all. I could be at the airport in West Palm in an hour, three or four more to Kennedy, say another hour into the city. It was only about eight thirty now. The Negro woman had just set her vacuum cleaner down two doors from mine and was fumbling with a ring of keys when Miriam stopped and I heard myself saying, "I'll get Charlie on the phone as soon as we hang up, and I'll bring Chris and Tony up around four."

Miriam said, "Thank God it was you, Tono. I don't know what I'd have done. Don't you forget, now," and I told her I wouldn't forget.

I had to go back to the office for some more change and then called Charlie. He sounded sleepy and confused but finally understood what I was getting at and confirmed all that Miriam had told me. The dentist's office was across Forty-second Street from Grand Central, so why didn't I plan to look for him and the boys under the clock at the Biltmore a little before four. The dentist was just for prophylaxis this time, so they should be no later than that. The boys and I should be able to have a good hour with Miriam afterwards because the Rockettes didn't go on until seven and that would still leave him and the boys plenty of time for supper. The dentist, the last meeting with their mother, supper, the Rockettes—we plotted the boys' day out, Charlie and I, and I could see him sitting there in his pajamas on the edge of the bed, his face still blurred with sleep. I was going to tell him where I was so in case I didn't make it on time he would understand and wait, but then I thought better of it. If Miriam didn't know, I didn't want Charlie to know either.

My third and last call was to Bebb to tell him that I wouldn't be able to keep our appointment that morning. Brownie answered. Bebb hadn't come down yet, he said. He had been on the phone most of the evening and hadn't gotten to bed until late. I asked for Sharon, and Brownie said, "Dear, you don't see Sharon up and around much before ten unless it's for something special," and I wondered whether, if I had come over as I'd said, the sound of my voice in the hall would have counted as special enough. I thought of her asleep with her two hands tucked under her cheek. I asked Brownie to tell Bebb that I had been called back to New York unexpectedly but hoped to return to Armadillo the next day and would call when I did. I thought of adding something about Miriam and why I was going, thought for a moment even of asking if Bebb would hold up my name in prayer for the plane trip, and Miriam's name too, but Brownie said, "I'll have to go now, dear. The bacon's burning," and hung up.

I left all my luggage at the Salamander, thinking to be back so soon, and took only my overcoat for when we got to New York and it would be November again. The weather at the airport was perfect, warm and bright and without a cloud in the sky, and I felt eccentric and valetudinarian with the coat over my arm and wondered if that explained Bebb's inadequate black raincoat the day I had met him in the city—not that he didn't have something heavier but simply hadn't felt like getting on the plane with it. I thought also of how Bebb said he

155

was scared to death of planes and wondered if he really was or had just said it to make me feel better about not wanting to get out of the car in Lion Country. As for me, I wasn't so much scared of planes as I was irritated by them. Life was full of risks that it was neither possible nor wise to avoid, but flying was not one of them. As long as there were means of surface transportation, flying was one of life's avoidable risks, and I found that anything that tried, however tacitly, to persuade me otherwise irritated me. Planes themselves irritated me, for instance, with all their misleading look of sleek invulnerability, and the hostess who came down the aisle as we were about to take off from West Palm taking drink orders irritated me too. What a far cry from my Persephone of the trip down, I thought. She looked like the president of the student council at a Baptist college, and for all her professional solicitude to the contrary, I had the feeling that anybody who ordered a drink at ten thirty in the morning would find a rather unpleasant quotation beneath his photograph in the yearbook. I ordered a double martini, therefore, following it shortly with a second, and slept most of the way to New York.

"With the first dream that comes with the first sleep," Alice Meynell wrote in a sonnet which my former students always rather liked despite its Victorianisms, "I run, I run, I am gathered to thy heart," and as soon as I closed my eyes there some thousands of feet above the earth, I found myself starting to think about Sharon. I thought of the way she had looked as she stood there holding her wet hair in a pile on top of her head and how she had said she didn't know when her real birthday was. I thought of how Bebb had made her look at him when he answered her question about how he had ever been able to forgive Lucille for the baby. But I did not want to think about Sharon until I found a time and place for thinking about her properly, and made myself look elsewhere for something to fall asleep on.

I decided to think about my article on Bebb. How would I begin it, I wondered, and what would my approach be? In one sense I didn't know enough yet for a real exposé, and in another sense I knew too much. It was one thing to expose the fat stranger who had put sugar in his chocolate milk and talked about making checks out to cash to keep the Internal Revenue Service out of your hair, but Bebb in knickerbockers with the faceless baby in his lap, Bebb standing unarmed among the lions, even Bebb doing whatever he had done and for whatever reasons in front of those children in Miami. . . . Not that the second Bebb was any less of a crook than the first, maybe much more of a one, but how did you expose such a person, and in the long run what would you actually be exposing? And was it possible for me any longer to expose Bebb without at the same time exposing myself, I who had drunk Tropicanas with his wife, who had let him risk his life to get a photograph for me of lions copulating, who had accepted money from him to take his only child out for supper and had then taken her back to my unmade bed at the Salamander Motel instead? And photographs—how could I get a photograph of Bebb's eye lazing shut, what kind of Cartier-Bresson or Karsh would I have to be in order to capture the expression I had seen in his face when he was looking at Sharon as she put the beanie with the

157

propeller on it upon his bald head? Despite all my efforts, Sharon kept drifting back into my mind, and, groggily poised as I was on the very sill of sleep, the thought of her and the thought of Bebb became all confused with one another, even their faces, and I could not think clearly which of the two of them my article was to expose or whether it was they who were exposing me or I who was exposing myself and whether it was a good thing or a bad thing. I remembered how I had stood there in front of the dresser mirror shouting to Sharon, "See me. See what you've done," and then gradually the two double martinis and the hum of the engines pushed me over the sill, and I slept until we reached New York.

It was typical somehow of Charlie Blaine to pick under the clock at the Biltmore for the place where he and the boys were to meet me. Juniors up from Princeton and sophomores down from Smith, young ensigns on leave from the Pacific and girls who wept at *Mrs. Miniver* and did their turn at the USO, attractive young people all the way back from himself and Miriam, I suppose, to Zelda and Scott—this was undoubtedly the way Charlie thought of the Biltmore, and of course he was dead wrong on two counts. Number one, if it was still the kind of place he remembered its having been, it was the wrong place to meet the brother of your ex-wife when she was dying of myeloma. Number two, it was no longer the kind of place he remembered and hadn't been for years. When I got there the only people sitting on the curved banquette under the clock

158

were an elevator man picking his nose and a fat woman with an orchid corsage pinned to her coat who was reading the *Daily News*. In a moment, around the corner from the newstand where they must have seen me walk in came Charlie with my two nephews.

Tony, the ten-year-old, was dark and had something of Miriam around his eyes and nose. He was a lot fatter than I had remembered him and looked sleepy. Chris, who was twelve, was a shadow of the shadow who was his father—his face and hair were both about the same color, which was dimly blond. I could see right away that Chris had been weeping, and since he had always been the closer of the two to Miriam I was not surprised. His eyes were pink, and there was a damp smear on his cheek. The boys were both wearing grey flannel suits with long pants, and Chris had on a hooded jacket that was approximately the same color as his hair and face. Charlie stepped forward to greet me with a warmth that made me remember Miriam's speaking of his love-making as importunate but strangely passionless. He was glad to see me, I think, not because of who I was but because of what I was about to relieve him of. Tony and Chris both shook hands and called me Uncle Tono.

I said, "Hey, Chris, I can't take you up to see your mother looking like that. We've all got to put on a good show for her this afternoon."

Charlie said, "That's all right. It's not about Miriam. The nurse found a bad cavity, and the dentist decided he'd better fix it then and there. Chris says it still hurts from the drilling."

"The Novocain's all worn off," Chris said, "and it feels like he must have left something in there under the filling by mistake. I think we better go back and have him look at it." Even as he spoke, I could see the tears well up in his eyes again.

Charlie said, "It's just the reaction to the drill. It will go away. Besides, you've got to go up to see your mother with Uncle Tono. You know how sick she is, and she's been expecting you all day."

Tony yawned. "Maybe if he could suck on a piece of ice, that would help," he said, and I said that sounded like a good idea to me and gave them a dollar to go downstairs to the grill and get something in paper cups with ice in it and then Chris could suck it. I did this partly because it seemed to me it might help and partly, I think, because, although we were all there well ahead of time, Charlie was obviously eager to get rid of us and I saw no reason why he should be let off as easily as all that. If Miriam was right that he couldn't take going up to the hospital, he could at least take this. As soon as Tony and Chris had gone, I said, "Charlie, have you told them how sick she is? Do they have any idea they may be seeing her for the last time?"

"I don't know why you say that," Charlie said. There was a faint smile on his face, but I thought I could see that he was irritated. "I understand the doctors say she may go on a lot longer, which means this probably won't be the last time at all."

I said, "Even if she does go on a lot longer, this may be the last time she'll be able to see them in any sense that means much. So I think she's going to make it her business to have it be the last time."

Charlie said, "Well, I don't think the boys have any idea of that. At least, I'm sure Tony doesn't. He was up so late watching TV last night, he's half asleep anyway. Chris maybe. He's the sensitive one, and I think his tooth really hurts him. Do you suppose I ought to take him back to the dentist?"

I said, "That's up to you, Charlie. You know him better than I do."

Charlie seemed to give the matter serious thought. "No," he said at last. "On second thought, I think definitely not. If this really turns out to be the last time, it would hurt him more later to know he didn't go than his tooth hurts him now."

"How about you, Charlie?" I said. What I think I meant was how about him in a general sort of way—how was he getting on, how did it feel to be losing a wife he had already lost—but he took me to mean how did he himself feel about not going up there to see Miriam this afternoon now that he had firmly committed his sons to it.

He said, "I'll tell you how it is with me, Tono," and his rather faded blue eyes took on a faraway look as though he was remembering some old script he had worked on for educational TV but was mistaking it for something out of Kahlil Gibran or the Psalms. "I'd like to go up there with you in many ways, but in another way I'd rather not. You see, I prefer to remember her the way she was."

I said, "That's great for you, Charlie. You'll be able to keep your happy memories intact that way. But suppose everybody decided the same thing? Then everybody would stay away so they could remember her the way she was, and she would die all alone there the way she is."

Charlie said, "You're her brother, Tono. You belong there with her, no question about it. And Chris and

Tony too. They're her flesh and blood. But, to tell you the truth, I don't think Miriam wants to see me. She told me she didn't think she could take it if I came."

I said, "What she told me was she thought she could take it all right, but she didn't think you could." As soon as I said it, I regretted it. I regretted it because Miriam wouldn't have wanted me to say it and because I could see that it had left its mark on Charlie. It was the first time since we had started talking that he looked fully awake.

"Oh God," he said. "Did she say that?" I nodded, and he sat down there under the famous clock not far from the fat woman with the corsage, the skirts of his overcoat touching the carpet and his fedora on his knee. "The truth of it is she's right, Tono. I'd be scared to death to go."

I felt suddenly so sorry for him that I reached out and put my hand on his shoulder. I said, "Well, Charlie, don't take it too hard. I didn't mean to put you on the spot. Everybody's scared to death of something, and you just happen to be scared to death of death. For me it's life."

"Thanks," he said, although I was not sure what he was thanking me for, and then the boys came back up the stairs, and Tony said, "The man told us there hadn't been a grill down there for years. It's a florist shop."

"We'll get Chris some ice at the hospital, then," I said, and then added to Charlie, "You and I, Charlie. We belong to another age."

When we got to Miriam's room, we found her sitting up straighter than I had seen her for some time. They had cranked the bed up higher and put an extra pillow behind her, and there was something about the way she was propped there with her shoulders slightly hunched and one hand lying palm up at her side that made me think of a large doll. Her other arm was in a plaster cast from the wrist to above the elbow, and this was the first thing the boys asked her about once they had kissed her and taken off their coats and sat down side by side on the broad windowsill where she directed them.

Miriam said, "Isn't that the last straw? I tripped and fell on my way to the john the other day and broke the damned thing," and then she started right in asking them about themselves, how the dentist had been and how school was and if they had been taking their vitamins as though lining up in advance enough questions to keep them going the whole hour. It was at this point that I gestured to her that I would leave the three of them alone together for a while and had just started for the door when she interrupted herself in the middle of a sentence and said, "For Christ's sake, don't leave me, Tono," which was the only time that afternoon that I saw anything like terror in her eyes. Chris had started telling her about his tooth, and she was asking him about it, and then she stopped so utterly dead in her tracks at the sight of me heading for the door that it was apparent even to Chris, I think, that the words we were all using seemed to count for a good deal less than words usually did, or at least to count for something quite different. It took a moment or two to get conversation started again, and this was the only difficult part of the whole time, those few moments when we sat there with nothing but silence to hide our nakedness behind. It was Chris who saved the day by asking if he could get some ice for his tooth. There turned out to be some in the water pitcher, and in trying to crack it on the radiator he smattered some on the floor, so that Miriam had to tell him to get a Kleenex to wipe it up, and suddenly we found that we all had words to wear again and familiar parts to play in their familiar garb.

Tony got started on the movie he had sat up so late the night before watching on television, and before he was through he gave a fairly complete outline of it. It was an old Abbott and Costello film called *Abbott and Costello Meet Frankenstein and the Wolf Man*, he thought, or something like that, and as I sat listening to him tell it—he was perched there on the windowsill in his long grey pants with the fly half unzipped because of his paunch and waving his hands around and rolling his dark eyes—I thought to myself that the operatic Italian strain from my mother had survived another generation. There was one part of the story that had particularly appealed to him, and his account of it went into particular detail and became at times particularly operatic.

By a series of blunders, Abbott and Costello had found themselves on an island somewhere which was inhabited by what seemed to be the whole infernal pantheon of Hollywood monsters. Frankenstein was there and the Wolf Man and Count Dracula and others whose names Tony couldn't remember but whose appearance and personality he managed to convey by a number of heavenward glances and small, rapid intakes of breath as he described them. They were all out to get Abbott and Costello for one reason or another, and Count Dracula with his special proclivities was peculiarly attracted by Costello because he looked so fat and juicy. The Count spent a good deal of time trying to catch Costello in dark places where he could sink his fangs into his neck and drink his fill without interruption, and things were looking pretty bad there for a while until by some fluke Costello managed to give them all the slip.

Tony was especially good at conveying the suspense of it—fat little Costello running down to the shore where a motorboat was moored and hopping into it and fiddling with the controls until suddenly the motor gave signs of starting and you felt that maybe he was going to be safe after all. Only just at that point, back among the rocks at the mouth of a black cave, Dracula appeared. He had on his opera cape with his arm crooked out in front of his face so that just his tortured, piercing eyes showed above it, and with his other arm he started making hypnotic gestures at Costello's back as he was about to make his getaway. Tony imitated the hypnotic gestures, and then he said, "All they show you is Costello's face, see? The whole screen. He's standing there just about to make a break for it and this Dracula's up there in the cave zapping him from behind, and you can tell on Costello's face how it's working. He starts to sweat and go duh-duh-duh and everything, and you can tell he can't resist because Dracula's too powerful for him, and so finally he turns around and gets out of the boat and starts walking back up the beach toward where Dracula's waiting in the cave. He starts walking back real slow and sad because he doesn't want to do it at all and is just going because Dracula's zapping him and he can't help himself, and then the best part is when little by little he gets going faster and faster back up the beach till finally he picks up his shirttails like a girl and gives this dopy smile and starts *skipping* back there to old Dracula. You should have seen it, Mum." It was Tony's one aria that afternoon and he got through it well and only when it was over, as though the strain of it together with his late hours the night before were too much for him, lapsed back almost immediately into drowsiness.

Miriam also seemed drowsy for a moment, I thought. She had been listening to Tony more attentively than I felt she'd listened to anybody else up to then, and when he finished, she kept on looking at him as though he were still talking. Then both her eyes did a very Bebbsian thing—they fluttered lazily shut for a moment and then came open again. Her hair was pinned back behind her ears with too many bobby pins, and I wanted to take the bobby pins out and let the hair fall down over her shoulders the way I was used to seeing it. I wanted to open the louvers on either side of the picture window and let some fresh air in and the smell of the hospital out. I wanted to tell her about Sharon and about the lions screwing and the fat lady with the orchid corsage. And that broken arm—the only good thing about it was that she said she'd fallen on her way to the john and I hadn't thought she could even get to the john any more.

A little incoherently because of the ice in his mouth, Chris was telling her about school—how he hated science and math and loved English, and I saw a whole life flowing out from there. That great watershed of the young: do you like science and math, or do you like English and possibly history? If it's the first, then your life goes one way, and if it's the second, then your life goes the other, and the whole thing's usually settled before you even get to high school. Chris had a poem in the magazine, he told his mother, and he hoped to get a part in the play, and maybe he would end up in educational TV like his father, I thought, or writing novels up to page thirty-four like his uncle, or even explaining how they used to heap coals of fire on people's heads like Brownie—who could say? But at least in a general and rather depressing way, I felt sure, you could say plenty, and I wondered what Miriam was thinking as she lay there watching him too and possibly even listening—his face and hair that were nearly the same color or absence of color, his wiry hair itself that curled flat to the scalp, the faded eyes of his father. I remembered Miriam's saying she was afraid Charlie and his housekeeper might turn her sons into fairies if they weren't careful, and in Chris's case I could picture it easily enough. Not that there was anything particularly feminine in his manner any more than there was anything particularly masculine in it—at twelve he stood just on the fringes of that great, sweaty free-for-all and hadn't chosen his side yet —but I could imagine its happening the way his mother feared. Chris in his forties teaching English at Choate, say, or Hotchkiss, taking his pets out to dinner in town, telling risqué stories in class, keeping photographs of former students tucked into his dresser mirror and inscribed to him by his first name.

Miriam said, "There's a color TV down at the end of the corridor in the sun room. Why don't you kids run take a look while I talk to Tono about a couple of things? We'll call you back," and when they had gone, she let her head sink into the pillows in a way that made me realize for the first time that she had been working at holding it up. "Jesus Christ, Tono," she said, and when I came over and offered her a cigarette from the pack on her bedside table, she waved them away with her good hand. "I've given them up for keeps," she said. "They're bad for my health."

She lay there looking off toward the window. It was getting quite dark outside, and I thought I saw signs of a little snow flurry in the air. Her good arm was still lying at her side much as it had been when we first came in, and I had the impulse, which I resisted, to reach down and touch the upturned palm.

"I lied to the kids," she said, and remembering Sharon's three lies, I wondered what there was about me that made people keep confessing their sins. "I didn't have any fall going to the bathroom. I've been using that damned bedpan for weeks. You'll never believe it, Tono, but you want to know how I broke my arm?"

I nodded, I guess, standing there at the side of her bed looking down at the pack of cigarettes she'd given up.

"Night before last I woke up and reached out to get a glass of water from the table, and it just broke. I could hear it, Tono. It sounded like when you step on a stick in the woods."

I have never been a cigarette smoker, but I took one out of the pack, and with the matches that had been tucked in under the cellophane, I lit it. It tasted rather like dust.

"Do you think anything happens?" Miriam said. "After you're dead, I mean. I'm not being morbid, I'm just damned curious."

Three or four times in my life it has been given to me, as Brownie might have put it, to say the right thing, and this was one of them. I take no credit for it anyway. The Hindu monkey just happened to reach out for the right branch at the right time, that's all, and was lucky enough to catch hold of it. I remembered Montague Rhodes James and Latin text A and the part where Christ enters at the end in a blaze of light as Don Giovanni, and I started to tell Miriam about it. I described his glittering white cloak and doublet and the silver buckles on his shoes, and I pictured his smile to her, the flashing white teeth and pointed beard like Errol Flynn or a young Ronald Colman. I told her about the little earring in one ear and how he drove his rapier through Satan's shoulder and signaled to Hell to pin his arms to his sides. I told her how he stretched his arms out wide and said, "Come unto me, all ye my playfellows who bear my image and likeness." I had a feeling I was confusing it somewhat with what he'd said to the children he'd changed back from goats again, but it seemed to fit, so I said it anyway. And I told her how Adam had come up, and then King David and all the patriarchs and prophets.

She really listened to the whole thing, I could tell, and when I finished, she reached out for my cigarette, which I gave to her. She took a puff on it and said, "*Bene, bene, Antonio,*" then after another puff handed it back to me, and I stubbed it out in the ashtray for her. "Go tell the kids to come back in," she said, "and then you better get them back to old Charlie."

There was a button hanging by a thread on Chris's hooded jacket, and she told him to get somebody to sew it on for him before he lost it. She asked him how his tooth was, and he said it was some better. Tony, she said, shouldn't watch television so much. It ruined the eyes. He was to tell Charlie that for her. Charlie was going to take them to see the Rockettes, they told her, and she said she'd never been crazy about the Rockettes herself but everybody ought to see them at least once.

After she had kissed them goodbye and we were about to leave, Tony gave an enormous yawn, stretching one fat arm up into the air and knuckling his eyes with the other, and it seemed to rub her the wrong way because she sounded quite angry when she spoke to him and in some ways more like herself than I'd heard her for a long time. "Now you stay awake, Tony," she said. "You just keep your eyes open and stay *awake*."

There was a lot of life in her voice, a lot of Wop, and I can hear her saying it still. *Stay awake*, she told him as we left, and part of what she had in the back of her mind, I suppose, was poor Charlie with his naps and his kapok pillows sleeping his life away. *Stay awake* were the last words she spoke to my younger nephew and namesake, and looking back on it, not just the words but the fire inside them, what I think she meant was stay alive. "You just stay alive" was what she told that fat little boy with his zipper half unzipped, or there would be Hell to pay. And then we were gone.

After I delivered the boys back to Charlie at Reuben's on Fifty-eighth Street, I thought of spending the night in New York. As much as I'd had a plan, that had been it. I could ring up Ellie, I'd thought. I might even drop in at the vet's the next morning and see how Tom was getting along. But at the last minute I decided against it. Instead, I caught a night flight out of Kennedy and was back in West Palm by about midnight, where I picked up my cream-colored convertible. I had not realized when I left how homesick I would be for Armadillo.

CHAPTER TEN

I DREAMT that night about Sharon. We were walking
through the grass somewhere, and the wind was in her
hair, blowing it against my face again, and when I
reached up to brush it aside, she wouldn't let me. "Don't
touch me," I thought she said, and it made me feel sick
and lost until I realized that she had her hands on my
cheeks and was gently nodding my head from side to
side. "Rise and Shine, Big Bopper," she was saying,
"rise and shine," and her hands felt cool on my face, and
I felt that something was rising somewhere and for all I
knew shining too, and when I opened my eyes, I found

171

that Sharon herself, no dream of Sharon, was there beside me. "You're the one," she said. She was holding my face in her hands as though it was something that interested her.

You can never step into the same river twice, as whichever Greek said who said also that the only permanent thing about life is change. It was different with Sharon and me that morning from what it had been two evenings before, in no sense less than it had been then and in some ways possibly even more, but different anyway. She was not my new-found land now but a land that I had touched on before and where I had left a flag against my returning, a land that as soon as I touched it again I knew I had never stopped being homesick for and that I returned to now like a king returning from exile who stoops to kiss the earth beneath his feet. It was not Venetian-blind dusk in the room as it had been the first time but Venetian-blind morning with the sun streaking in through the slats and fanning out across the wall above our heads; and from what must have been the room next door to mine, to ours, we could hear the sound of a vacuum cleaner as the Negro woman whom I had observed from the telephone booth the day before drew every day closer like Fate itself.

Sharon's dress was a circle of green and yellow on the rug where she must have stepped out of it while I was still asleep, and one of her sandals was poking out from underneath. I drew her eyelids sideways with my thumbs, and she became the shimmering young ranee or fragrant-limbed houri and I the fallen holy man with his hair every whichway, bleary-eyed, unshaven, and unwashed. We were not together for anything like as long as the first time, but we were together long enough to be quiet and still for a little while too, and then Sharon said, "I came to pick up my hat. Bip saw your car outside and told me to come get you. When you've had breakfast, he wants to see you down at the church."

I said, "It was nice of you to come, and I hope you'll feel free to come again any time you take a notion to. I've been keeping your hat in the closet for you."

"It's nice to come together this way," she said, and then, "Come," again, standing there by the side of the bed now and reaching out to take my hand. "You better get up and get dressed now. Bip needs you. He's in a real sweat, you should see him."

And he was, figuratively and otherwise. I dropped Sharon off at the Manse after a slot-machine breakfast which I ate with her floppy straw hat on my head where she had put it—it made me look like a half-breed, she said—and then I drove on to Holy Love. I stopped in for a moment at the souvenir stand first and bought a shrunken head for Tony, a wickerwork monkey for Chris, and a small rug with a Red Indian on it for Ellie. I considered one with a sunset on it for a while, but then decided that the Red Indian might do more to liven things up at Manhattan House. I wanted to get something for Miriam too, but I couldn't find anything that I thought she'd like. Maybe on the way home on the train I could get her a bag of oranges, I thought, but then I realized I wasn't even sure they'd let her eat oranges. When I entered the church, I found both Bebb and Brownie there.

Brownie was up on a chair washing the glass-brick windows. He had shorts on again and sneakers with bobby socks, and he smiled as he greeted me, his glasses fogged up and the stains under his arms bigger and darker than I had seen them before. Bebb was dressed in what I began to think must be either his only suit or one of a perfectly matched collection, but this time he had laid the jacket over the top of the lectern and was standing there with his shirtsleeves rolled up and his face damp and shiny. He was vacuuming the carpet, and the folding chairs were all folded up and stacked against the walls. He switched off the vacuum as soon as he saw me come in, and "Herman Redpath," he said, wiping his handkerchief over the top of his head. "Herman Redpath is flying up in his private plane first thing tomorrow morning, and I am going to ordain him personally right here at Holy Love. Thank the Lord you've come, Antonio. I need somebody to talk to. Brownie, you pismire, watch what you're doing. You're dribbling dirty water all over the floor."

I would never have thought Bebb capable of looking so overwrought. Whatever might be stirring down underneath somewhere, I had always thought of him as keeping it pretty well tucked in with only that occasionally giveway eye to hint at its hidden presence. A parlor magician keeps himself buttoned up pretty close against the possibility of exposing his trick, and just the look of Bebb suggested as much—the skin stretched tight almost to splitting over the plump flesh, the nutcracker mouth snapped shut, that skimpy black raincoat I had first seen him in which bound him under the arms and across the rump. But on this occasion his jacket was off, his shirt was undone at the collar, his tie pulled loose, and he seemed prepared to express himself without con-

174

straint. He unfolded two of the chairs and set them up for us in front of the altar table and proceeded to range over a number of different topics, all the while playing with the vacuum-cleaner hose, which he would double up in his fist or snake along his knee or shake back and forth like a rattle, while off to one side Brownie got on with his glass-brick windows.

On Herman Redpath: "Antonio," Bebb said, "twenty-four hours from now I will be—twenty-*three* hours from this moment almost to the dot—I will be laying my hands on the head of Herman Redpath. The wealth of that man is beyond the dreams of avarice, and he made every nickel of it himself. He is a fine Indian Christian and one of nature's gentlemen, and he will be flying here to Armadillo with a whole planeload of close friends and kinfolk to be present at the ceremony tomorrow. Brownie, unless you put some elbow grease into it, you're wasting your time. You're so flabby and hopeless, it looks like you're up there wiping an old lady's tail, and that is about what you're good for anyway. Brownie and me, we've got to lick this place into shape so when Herman Redpath and his party get here I won't have anything I've got to be ashamed of. Herman Redpath will stand just about where you're sitting now, and I will stand up there behind the altar table. Then at the proper moment Herman Redpath will kneel down, and I will move down to in front of the table and lay my two hands, like this, on top of his head—if there's any other clergy present, it's etiquette to invite them to step up and lay their hands on his head too—and then I will call upon the Almighty to send down upon him the gift of charity—charity is the most important gift of them all, Antonio—and the gift of faith, and the gift of the word of wisdom. Those three are absolute musts. Without them you're licked before you start. And for Herman Redpath I may also request the special gift of healing because as a direct descendant of the American Indians he probably has a potential for healing already. Herbs, Antonio. Herbs and roots and an understanding of many growing things that the white man knows not of."

On his dreams: "Scripture tells us how the devil took Jesus up unto an exceeding high mountain and showed him all the kingdoms of the world and the glory of them, and then the devil saith unto him, 'All these things will I give thee if thou wilt fall down and worship me.' The kingdoms of the world, Antonio, and the glory of them. Who hasn't seen these things, if only in his dreams? Show me the man who says he hasn't been tempted to bow down and worship Mammon for these things, and I will show you a liar. I have dreamed, Antonio, and God knows I am not beyond temptation. I am chief among sinners. And the wealth of Herman Redpath . . . the cash-on-hand, the blue-chip securities, the oil leases, the cattle lands . . . He has put nothing down on the dotted line yet, but hints have been dropped, promises have been made. Herman Redpath has extended to me the right hand of fellowship, Antonio, and I would not be human if I had not given some thought to what that— to what it all *might* mean. The things of this world and the glory thereof. A fine new car with air-conditioning for this infernal heat. A bungalow along the coast some-place where Sharon could go for a week-end with her young friends, where I could send Lucille for July and August when she gets her rash. A new color TV—the

176

one we've got gives us nothing but trouble. Cameras, clothes, transistor radios, money in the bank, not to mention power and influence and a voice that when you say something, people are going to listen to you the way they listen to Herman Redpath. I believe I would be able to resist these things, Antonio, although in my dreaming I have not always chosen to resist them. I believe that when Herman Redpath and I have joined forces, together we will take the great riches that he has earned by the sweat of his brow and put them to work for Jesus, Antonio. I see Holy Love swelling like a mighty stream. I see Gospel Faith expanding its activities. I see more and better ads, Antonio, and more personalized attention to each one of them, more follow-up. And at the end of it all, I see an old man named Bebb living out his declining years in peace. There have been deep hurts and bitter memories for me, Antonio. There have been fierce battles where blood has been shed. But I dream of a time when the lion shall lie down with the lamb right here in Armadillo, Antonio, and in my heart. And no longer shall they hurt or destroy in all my holy mountain, saith the Lord."

On Sharon: "When King David was an old man, Antonio, they brought him a maiden named Abishag to warm his heart and give him strength again. I am no King David, and I am not what you would call exactly an old man either, but from the moment she first entered our house at the age of two years—a poor, wizened little thing didn't anybody want, with no daddy to give her his name and a mother totally without means—from that moment I began to see what the love of God was all about. The love of God is a wizened little thing doesn't anybody want, Antonio, but once you receive it into your heart, it gives you your strength again. We had a little bit of a baby of our own once that didn't live, Lucille and me, and Sharon brought us healing and forgiveness for our grief. And trouble, Antonio. I won't let on for one moment she didn't bring us plenty of trouble too. A child that's not your own flesh and blood, you try to make up to it for what you aren't. You lay your heart open before it. You expose your tenderest part to it to love or to hurt or to run away scared from, however it happens to feel. When you love a child, you put yourself at that child's mercy, Antonio, and there has never been a child, but one, was always merciful. Sharon more than most maybe. We have been fortunate. You have seen her for yourself now, Antonio, 'Who is she that looketh forth as the morning, fair as the moon, clear as the sun, and terrible as an army with banners?' She is the warmth of my heart and my strength, Antonio, and I want her to be happy more than I want anything else. I want her to settle down with a good man—not one of your world-beaters or a millionaire or a Rudolph Valentino—but a man with a patient heart who will see to the good in her even when she is sometimes crazy and spiteful and who will treat her with courtesy and use her kindly. I would fly from here to Timbuktu to find such a man for her, Antonio, and I've told you I would rather have a tooth drawn than go up in a plane."

On Antonio Parr: "You and me, Antonio, we have business together. The first time I set eyes on you in that greasy spoon in New York City, I said there's a man I respect. He is a smart man who doesn't hardly ever say more than he means and who may sometimes say less than he means but probably only if he thinks it's easier on you that way. I won't say I trusted you right off, Antonio. That would be an exaggeration. On account of my ads and Gospel Faith and all of it, I have had my run-ins with the authorities. The IRS goes without saying and I have already mentioned it to you, but the Better Business Bureau, the U.S. Post Office, the Federal Trade Commission, and the U.S. Department of Education—at one time or another they have all been on my tail, trying to prove what I do is illegal. Everything I do is legal, Antonio. I have seen to that. I am vigilant because I have to be vigilant, and when a young fellow writes a letter like you did and expresses an interest in talking with me, I am suspicious. It would not be the only time that even high-up officials have stooped to that kind of stunt with me. When I first saw you, Antonio, I wasn't sure what you were up to, but whatever you were up to, I could tell you had a kind heart and wouldn't ever do anything on purpose to hurt a person. So I trusted you up to that point, and I would trust you farther than that point now. You told me once your mother was Italian, and you have some of the Old World in you. You have an old look in your eyes even though you are young, and if I believed in reincarnation, I would say you have lived more lives than just one on this earth or on some other earth like it. If you are really interested in starting a branch of Gospel Faith up North, you just stay around a few days more and we'll talk about it. I want you to do this very much, Antonio. Don't go away until after the ordination anyway, because if I am talking inches now, after Herman Redpath joins us I will be talking miles. I like you, Antonio. Lucille likes you. She says you have

fine manners and are a gentleman. And Sharon likes
you too. To be frank with you, she has never said she
does, but she doesn't have to. If she said she liked you,
chances are it would be one of her jokes. So you hang
around a couple of days longer, Antonio, and we'll have
a chance to do some business together."

On Brownie: (Bebb did not make this whole speech
at once. It came out at various points during our conversation as Brownie did various things to prompt it, like
dribbling the water or not rubbing hard enough and
sometimes things that I did not notice myself like just
the expresion on his face, I suppose, or the way the back
of his neck looked.) "Brownie, you wash those windows
like you teach Scripture. You just skim the surface. You
just smear around a little soft soap and water, and it may
look good while it's still wet, but when it dries, any fool
can see what a mess you've made. You've got to get in
there and sweat and rub till your arms ache so the light
can come through. Same way with Scripture. Sweat and
grunt and maybe the light that comes through blinds you
almost, but at least it's the light. It's the light that
shineth in darkness even if the darkness comprehendeth
it not. There's a sermon in that, Antonio. Brownie, the
way you pour on that after-shave, you've got this church
smelling like a whorehouse. Now, you take a man like
Brownie, Antonio, and you ask yourself where the Almighty went wrong. Well, I tell you it's not the Almighty went wrong, it's Brownie went wrong. The
Almighty gave Brownie life, and Brownie never lived it.
He just shoved it up his ass. But it's not too late for him,
Antonio. Even for Brownie there's hope. There's got to
be. Because if there's no hope for just a single one of us,

then there's no hope for any of us. Brownie, he does most of the work on the courses. That's why he's Dean and why his signature's on the diplomas. The way it runs is you pick out of the catalogue which course you want to have and just send in a check or money order made out payable to Gospel Faith for the tuition fee. Then Brownie sends you back the required reading. Good paperback books, Antonio, none of your cheap stuff. You write out full outlines of all those books and mail them off on eight-by-eleven paper to show you've done the work. If they meet our standards, Brownie mails back your diploma. Services rendered for cash received. Is there anybody would like to explain to me what's illegal about that? I don't hold a man's past against him any more than Jesus did. Remember the good thief, Antonio. Remember the woman taken in adultery. But there's people like Brownie that hold their own past against them till it gets where they can't break loose out of it any more. Brownie did a little time here something like twenty-five or thirty years back. Cashing bad checks. You ever noticed his smile, Antonio? That's a smile you turn on the warden or the judge. It's a smile to use on cops. It's a smile says *Who, me?* It's a smile says *Kick my ass, and I'll still kiss yours.* What have you got against getting married, Brownie? The trouble with you is the only sex you get is in the bathtub. I don't mean to take off on you like this all the time. It's just something about the way you are and the way I am. I'm sorry. Forgive me, Brownie."

There was more which I do not remember, and although I listened to it carefully, all the time Bebb was talking I kept thinking in the back of my head that not an hour earlier I had been in bed with his daughter, and not for the first time and probably not for the last time either. Bebb sat there in his folding chair, tipping back in it sometimes and playing with the vacuum-cleaner hose and mopping the top of his head as the morning wore on. I didn't do much talking myself, and Bebb obviously didn't expect me to. It was his time to let things out, and I had a feeling there might be still more to come when he looked at his watch and rose quickly. He said, "Herman Redpath. He's supposed to be calling me at noon to confirm plans. If you would stay here and help Brownie get things set for tomorrow, I would be much obliged, Antonio."

As soon as he had gone, I said to Brownie, "Brownie, how can you just sit there and take it from him like that?"

Brownie had moved his chair over to the next window and was standing on it with a wet rag in his hand and several dry ones hanging out of the rear pocket of his shorts. He turned as I spoke and, removing his glasses, wiped each eye with the back of his wrist. He did not put his glasses back on right away, and looking at him without them, I felt the way I remember feeling as a child when I went to my science teacher's house for an assignment once and found him in his pajamas. I had caught him off-duty and out of uniform, and our usual relationship seemed so totally altered thereby that I could no longer be sure who either of us was. Seeing Brownie without his glasses was like seeing Mary Baker Eddy on the can, and I was prepared for anything.

Brownie said, "I've taken a lot from him, it's true. But I have been given a lot by him too, dear."

I said, "What have you been given, if you don't mind my asking?" Tropicanas to serve, I thought, and suppers to make, and windows to wash. Eight-by-eleven outlines to read and diplomas to sign. For the first time in a long while I found myself wanting to skin Bebb alive again, and although I thought then that it was for Brownie's sake, I have thought since that it was probably because of Sharon. I had made clandestine and illicit love to the warmth of Bebb's heart, and it made me hate him. "What has Bebb ever given you that entitles him to treat you like shit?" I asked Brownie. Saying *shit* in Bebb's church, I suspect, was another way of getting back at him.

Brownie said, "He has given me my life, dear. Leo Bebb raised me from the dead."

"I'm not sure I follow you," I said.

Brownie smiled at me, and without his horn-rimmed eyebrows it was much vaguer and more random. He said, "I mean like Lazarus. Dear, I was laid out dead in Knoxville, Tennessee, and Leo Bebb came in and raised me up."

Brownie told me the story standing in the chair with his glasses dangling from his hand. I had crouched down to change the head around on the vacuum cleaner and remained there—Bebb had been using the brushy side on the rug rather than the plain one, I discovered. As Brownie talked, I was looking up at him from below and Jesus was looking as usual toward the hot-air register. Behind Brownie I could see the glass brick drying in cloudy streaks just as Bebb had predicted it would.

It was back in the days when Bebb had been a Bible salesman, Brownie said, and just after Lucille's baby was born. Brownie himself was a salesman working on commission in a used-car lot and came to know Bebb through doing business with him. Bebb had a large territory to cover with his Bibles, and over the course of a few years he bought and traded in several times. They were not close friends, Brownie said, but they were more than just acquaintances because he remembered that when the baby was born, Bebb came by the car lot on purpose to hand him a cigar and tell him it was a boy and they had named him Herman, which, as soon as Brownie said it, made me wonder if this might be part of the reason Bebb had such a warm spot in his heart for Herman Redpath. Within a day or so after this, Brownie said, he, Brownie, died.

It was a freak accident. There had been a heavy rainstorm with high winds the night before, and a power line had blown down along the street that Brownie walked every morning to work. Brownie noticed that it was down, but didn't realize the danger, and about a block away from the car lot he stepped into a puddle where the line had broken in two and received such a jolt of electricity that it stopped his heart and killed him. There was no doubt about its killing him, he said. His boss from the car lot saw it happen and got help, dragging Brownie out of the puddle by a rope he'd managed somehow to loop around Brownie's foot without getting electrocuted himself. They tried to administer artificial respiration, at the same time sending for a doctor, but their efforts were unsuccessful, and when the doctor finally arrived, he pronounced Brownie dead.

Brownie said, "At that time I was sharing a couple of rooms with a friend of mine who was a barber, and since

I had no wife or family—I've never been married, dear
—they got hold of my friend first thing, and he came
right down in his white tunic, leaving a customer in the
chair, they say, with only half his face shaved. All of them
except Billy—that was the barber—were in favor of
taking me straight to the undertaker, but Billy was a devoted friend and he wanted me brought back home
first. I was quite a mess to look at, as you can imagine,
and he felt it wasn't right to let a stranger handle me, at
least not until he cleaned me up and got a chance to say
goodbye first. It was a touching gesture and also a very
fortunate one, as it turned out, because if they had taken
me straight to the undertaker, the chances are he would
have slit me up under the arms the way they do and
started draining me right away, and in that case it is
doubtful if I would be here telling you the tale now.

"Well, news travels fast in a town the size Knoxville
was then, especially bad news, and it wasn't more than
an hour or two before Mr. Bebb heard it, and as soon as
he heard it, he came right down to where Billy and I
lived to see was there anything he could do. Being
friends, I had also made him a very good price on a
Chevy wagon he was considering at the time, and I believe he wanted to find out if I had left anything in
writing on it, knowing I was in the habit of setting such
things down in a notebook I carried around in my
pocket. When he came into our room, there was nobody
there except just Billy and I, and Billy is the one who
gave me a full description later on of what happened.
But there is no need to go into the details. We've got our
work to get on with."

"Please," I said. "Go into the details." I was as curious

to hear them as Brownie was plainly eager to tell them. You could see that he'd told the story before—the form of it was not quite fixed yet, but I felt sure, for instance, that this was the point where he always paused about not going into details—and yet I don't believe that he'd told it often before. The words of it were perhaps no longer new to him, but I had the sense that to some degree he was still able to re-live it as he talked. He hadn't told it too often for that.

"Billy had me lying on the bed in my underclothes," Brownie said. "He had scrubbed me up and trimmed my hair around the ears and combed it. He had laid out a clean shirt and tie and the suit I wore to church Sundays, and he was just fixing to get me dressed when all of a sudden Mr. Bebb came in. He didn't even knock, Billy said—just walked right in and stood there at the foot of the bed and looked down at me lying there dead. 'Billy,' he said, 'tell me exactly what happened,' and Billy told him.

"When Billy was done, Mr. Bebb looked at me awhile longer and then finally he said, 'Billy, do you believe in the Holy Ghost, the lord and giver of life?' Poor Billy, he was not what you would call a religious man. He was of French Canadian extraction and had been raised a Roman Catholic, but he ran away from home when he was only thirteen and hadn't been to church since. So when Mr. Bebb asked him the question point blank like that, Billy told me he didn't know what to say. But we had been devoted friends and roommates for several years by then—I was thirty-three at the time and he was still in his twenties—and the sight of me laid out there cold and still on the bed that way made him feel like he had to believe in something, he said, so he told Mr. Bebb yes, he believed in the lord and giver of life, and Mr. Bebb said, 'Well, Billy, that makes two of us, not counting Brownie. And counting Brownie makes three because Brownie was a believer too.'

"Being in the business of selling Bibles, Mr. Bebb knew his Scripture even back then, and going by what Billy told me later, I think he must have had John eleven in the back of his mind the whole time. He said, 'Billy, our friend Brownie sleepeth, but I go that I may awake him out of sleep.' Then he walked up to the head of the bed and laid both his hands down on top of me where Billy had my hair all fixed up and combed. He raised his eyes and seemed to be praying, Billy said—I am the resurrection and the life; he that believeth in me, though he were dead, yet shall he live—and then, after a few moments of silence when Billy said his face got as red as though he was holding his breath, Mr. Bebb called out in a loud voice almost as if he was mad, *'Brownie, you stand up!'*

"Billy said at first he didn't think anything was going to happen. I just kept on lying there with my face about the same color as the pillow, but then Billy thought he saw something move. Now, because I am not telling this in mixed company, dear, but just to another member of the male sex, I do not mind telling you that what Billy said he first thought he saw move was one of my private parts—just a very faint movement down there the way it can happen sometimes to anybody for no reason and you don't even notice it, but I was wearing only my underdrawers at the time and so Billy noticed. Then he thought he saw some color returning to my face, and Mr. Bebb held his arm out, crooked at the elbow, and after a while I reached out and grabbed hold of it and pulled myself up to a sitting position. Billy said he did not know if what he saw running down off Mr. Bebb's face was tears or sweat.

"From then on I can tell the story myself, and there is very little left of it to tell. The first thing I remember was, it was as if I was lying at the bottom of a deep pit and way up at the top I could see this arm, and I knew if I could only manage to reach it, I would be all right. I did not know or care whose arm it was. I just knew I had to reach it or perish, and fortunately I reached it. When I opened my eyes, it wasn't Mr. Bebb I saw first, it was Billy. The light seemed so bright it made my eyes ache, and for a moment I thought he was on fire."

Brownie had been standing on the chair all this time, and when he finished his story and kept on standing there without his glasses and so plainly carried away by his memories, I was afraid he might have a bad fall and got up to my feet in case it proved necessary to catch him. But then he hooked his glasses back over his ears again, and his whole face seemed to come back into focus —the smile I had grown accustomed to, the heavy, plastic eyebrows. I said, "Brownie, are you sure you were really dead?"

He said, "Dear, I would not tell such a story if I was not sure."

"Do you remember what it was like to be dead?" I said.

He said, "There is nothing to remember about that because there was nothing there, and there was nothing left of me to do the remembering with even if there had been something there. Death is zero, dear. It is zero minus."

188

I said, "Well, it was a miracle then. It was one of the miracles of the age, and I don't see why it didn't put Knoxville, Tennessee, on the map. There should be a shrine there with little girls in white dresses marching around with candles and piles of crutches stacked up. Bebb should be riding around in a white Cadillac with virgins to scatter rose petals before him wherever he goes."

Brownie said, "Yes. Only that wasn't the way Mr. Bebb wanted it. First thing he said when he had me sitting up again was for me and Billy not to go around shooting our mouths off because there would be an awful fuss if we did, and it would probably lose him his job with the Bible company because they were very conservative and wouldn't want the publicity. He said that losing his job would probably kill Lucille, who had just had the baby and was feeling blue anyway and wasn't getting much sleep nights. But of course it was bound to get out, whether we shot our mouths off or not, because there were plenty who had heard about the accident, and then the next thing they knew, there I was back at work again as good as new."

"Exactly," I said. "So how come there's no shrine and piles of crutches? How come Bebb's still driving a Dodge with fifty thousand miles on it that doesn't even have air-conditioning?"

Brownie said, "There is a very simple explanation for that, and with your interest in religion, I am surprised you have not thought of it for yourself. When you come right down to it, dear, you see, people don't want miracles."

"But that's just what they do want," I said. "Get the

189

rumor started that a statue of the Virgin's nose has started to run, and within twenty-four hours people will be lined up six deep."

Brownie said, "Little miracles, yes. People will flock to anything that seems to mean there is still some magic left in the world, some little leftover piece of holiness. But a real miracle—something that makes everything you ever thought you knew about the world look kind of sick and that doesn't leave you much choice except to believe in something—nobody wants one of those kind, dear."

"Speak for yourself," I said. "That's just the kind I do want, the only kind." I suppose I was thinking about Miriam at the time, but also about Charlie Blaine sleeping his life away, and even that fat woman with the corsage sitting all by herself under the clock at the Biltmore.

Brownie said, "Well, maybe. For you. But in the case of most people, a real miracle upsets too many apple-carts and leaves too little room to turn around in. So they explain it away. Take the miracle of life, for instance. People say it's all just acids."

"I'd be interested to hear how they explained it away about Bebb's raising you from the dead," I said, "if that's really what he did." It wasn't Brownie I wanted to skin alive, it was Bebb, but I kept being afraid that my knife would slip and cut the wrong man, so I tried to control myself although to my surprise I could feel my hands trembling.

Brownie said, "Oh, that wasn't very hard, dear. They made out that the power in that broken line had been turned off way before I stepped my foot into the puddle and I just blacked out for some reason. I took a little something every now and then back in those days, and people said I was probably under the influence that morning. It is true that the night before happened to be Billy's birthday."

"But how about the doctor?" I said. "The one they sent for who pronounced you dead."

"Clyde Binney," Brownie said. "A clean, nice-spoken young fellow who got to be a friend of Billy's later on. It's strange how our lives cross and crisscross each other, almost like there was a kind of pattern to it. Clyde wasn't exactly a doctor, dear, although he'd spent a couple of years in medical school before circumstances forced him to leave. He was more what you would call a chiropractor. He said he could have been mistaken when they asked him about it later. It might have been just a very weak pulse rate and in all the confusion and everything . . . he could have jumped to conclusions."

"But what about Bebb's part in it?" I said. "What did people say about that?"

Brownie said, "A lot of them made a joke out of it. They said Bebb just wanted to make sure he got that Chevy wagon at the price I'd made him. It was a very generous price because he had given me a lot of business in the past."

"But what does Bebb think about it himself?" I said. "Does he really believe himself he raised you from the dead?"

Brownie had started to work on the window again, rubbing hard at the cloudy streaks with one of his dry rags, but he turned here and looked at me over his shoulder. He said, "We almost never discuss it any more—this happened twenty years ago, dear—but I hardly see how he could believe anything else. Billy said that when he touched my body, it was cold as ice and had already started to go stiff. There was no color in my face. I do not think there is a single doubt in Leo Bebb's mind but that he raised me from the dead in Knoxville, Tennessee. And I think it is also a clue to why he sometimes treats me the way he does."

"You mean like what he said?" I asked. "The Almighty gave you life, and you've never lived it?"

"Just shoved it up my ass," Brownie said in a rather slow, dim way as though he was translating from some original tongue. "Yes, that," he said, "but more than that. Sometimes I think Leo Bebb thinks he didn't quite get the job done that first time. I think that sometimes with his cruelest words he's just trying to bring me back from the dead again, only this time all the way back."

I started the vacuum cleaner. I did not mean to start it, but I was standing there with one foot on its torpedo-like back, and by accident my foot slipped and turned on the switch. That droning, whining roar, that sudden flooding back of reality. I think Brownie was grateful for the interruption because he immediately went back to the glass brick with fresh vigor, and I was grateful for it myself. I had nothing more to say to Brownie just then and nothing more to ask him. He had taken me with his story down a queer and twisted street that branched off finally in two opposite directions. One of them was my need to believe in miracles, and the other was my need not to believe in Bebb, whose hide I was after both as a corrupter of innocence and as the father of Sharon, whose already frayed innocence I was myself in the process of further corrupting. I could not move in one direction without doing serious mischief to the part of me that needed to move in the other, and thus I chose not to move in either but picked up the vacuum gratefully and started cleaning hell out of Holy Love. I wondered if the Negro lady at the Salamander had hit my room yet.

Bebb returned after a while, carrying several long florist boxes full of green tissue paper and cut flowers and bringing Lucille with him to arrange them. Lucille had her black glasses on again with her eyebrows arched above them, and she moved around through that sunlit church in a rather abandoned way at first, I thought, like a groundhog on Groundhog Day hoping to see his shadow so he can return to his dark burrow for six more weeks of winter. But she settled down to the flowers eventually, and while Bebb and Brownie started to set the folding chairs back up in their neat rows again, I tried to help her with them.

I remembered the photograph I had seen on the wall of Bebb's office and tried to read back from what I could see of her face now to the face of the young woman in the filmy dress and shingled hair gazing down at the baby in her husband's lap. After a while I thought I could almost do it—something about the angle of her cheek as she laid the flowers down on the altar table, something about the way her hair was combed out from the temples. It is easier, of course, to read back to a face that used to be than to try to read ahead to a face that will be someday, as, sitting in Miriam's hospital room, I had looked at my nephew Chris and tried to read ahead

to his face at forty. And I thought of the curious pre-
science of the photographer who had caught Lucille's
baby in a way that showed no face at all.

Lucille did not talk to me much, and at first I did not
think she knew who I was or could see me clearly enough
through those black glasses to be sure, but at one point
she dropped her lower jaw in what I felt certain was a
smile and said she heard Bebb had already taken me to
see the lions. "That Bebb," she said, "he's just like a
kid. He's never learned to keep his shirt on. He gets so
excited he wants to show everybody everything the first
day and have them be crazy about it like he is, be crazy
about him."

"These people from outer space," I said, "they're
different from the rest of us."

Lucille said, "You're telling me?" standing there
cradling a skinny armful of gladiolas, but what I had
wanted to do was say to her Is he or isn't he? did he or
didn't he? could he or couldn't he? and looking into her
black glasses, I wondered how much she knew and how
much she would tell, or even how much she had told me
already. Had she had to bite her tongue not to say that
Bebb had never learned to keep his pants on, not his
shirt? But then Bebb himself interrupted us.

He took me by the elbow and led me to where he had
the entrance door propped open to let the dust out and
the fresh air in. We stood there under the frosted-glass
cross, and he looked me straight in the eye and said,
"Antonio, she'd spit right in my eye if she knew I was
saying this and don't you ever let on I put you up to it,
but I happen to know Sharon is itching to go to the
beach this afternoon. She's laying around the back yard

194

in her bathing suit right now with the sprinkler on, and I just know if you dropped the word, she'd jump at it. I'd take her myself or send Brownie, but we've got our hands full right here."

Whereby he added another question to my already impossible list. I could no longer escape the suspicion that from the beginning he had gone out of his way to bring us together, Sharon and me. But at this point it occurred to me to wonder for the first time if, even back there on Lexington Avenue in the rain, that was what had led him to suggest in his offhand way that I come down to Armadillo and see the whole operation through from A to Z. And if that could possibly have been the case, what had been his motive? Was it simply to catch for Sharon a man about the right age for her who evidently didn't have to work for a living and seemed to have his heart in the right place? Or could it conceivably have been somehow for my sake as well as hers? "I am here to save your soul, Antonio Parr," he had said. Did he know as he stood there under the cross, mopping the sweat off his head, that we had made holy love together, the warmth of his heart and I?

CHAPTER ELEVEN

MY TRIP TO the beach with Sharon turned out to be less than a success. I found her behind the Manse stretched out in the sun in her bathing suit with the sprinkler adjusted so that it kept up a steady patter on her bare feet, and, as Bebb had predicted, she seemed glad enough to go once I suggested it. She was ready to leave in minutes, just slipping on what I believe is called a muu-muu over her bathing suit and tying a yellow scarf under her chin to keep her hair from blowing, but almost as soon as we were on our way she began to seem moody and withdrawn. It must have taken the better part of an hour to reach the stretch of public beach she knew about at

Hobe Sound, and I don't suppose we talked more than three or four times the whole way.

We stopped along the road somewhere for ice-cream cones, and the one bright spot of the trip that I can remember happened in that connection. I was eating my cone as I drove, a double-dip chocolate one, and at some point a bit of the overhang dropped off and fell half into and half on top of the open neck of the navy-blue polo shirt that Ellie had given me. We had some paper napkins, and with one of them Sharon got what she could off my shirt for me. She then reached down inside the neck and wiped off my bare chest, and I remember still the curious thud of something like panic that I felt in my stomach at the touch of her hand there as we drove along with the sun bright in our faces and the warm air roaring in our ears. But this didn't last long, and the rest of the drive was, at best, uneventful.

When we finally got there, the beach was dotted with Portuguese men-of-war, those creatures from outer space with their transparent bladders of turquoise shading up into purple and those long, wispy stingers that I am told burn like red-hot steel if you touch them. They looked quite beautiful floating here and there in the water, especially when a wave picked one up so that you could see it tipped for a moment against the glassy blue-green wall, but they pretty well eliminated the possibility of swimming, and we were reduced to splashing around in a few shallow, tepid pools left in the sand by the ebbing tide. The men-of-war that had washed up on the beach were so dried out by the sun that the bladders were stretched drum-head tight, and we amused ourselves by popping them with bits of shell and stones as we walked up the beach. We kept on walking until we left the public part behind and started passing the houses of the rich people, houses so rich and elegant that they didn't have to look it but sat back almost inconspicuously there among the palms and sea grape, each with its own little flight of steps leading up from the sand to the green lawn, each with its low cement groin projecting out into the sea to keep the beach from washing away.

Ellie, I knew, had visited here several times, and she had described to me with a curious mixture of disapproval and fascination the extraordinary lavishness of the place that seemed all the more lavish for being so pastel and hushed, like the sound of whitewall tires on an oyster-shell drive. She described the rich people themselves, her parents' generation for the most part but dressed in the cockatoo colors of childhood, the starched nannies wheeling the great-grandchildren of Presidents down to the sandbox and swings near where the yachts were moored, the little fringed golf carts and the masseuse arriving at the door with her collapsible table. I remembered particularly her telling me how when she asked some retired tycoon in canary slacks and an avocado blazer how he liked retirement, he replied that all in all he liked it well enough except that he missed the vacations.

I was haunted by my memory of all this as I walked along the beach with Sharon Bebb of Armadillo. I thought of Ellie going out to dinner in one of these very houses perhaps and conscientiously trying to talk civil rights to the Goldwater Republicans or, out of consideration for her hostess, tactfully trying not to. I

thought of the old Yales and Harvards with their prostates and hearing-aids padding over to the edge of the
heated pool for one quick dip before the pre-lunch
martinis. I thought of how I myself belonged neither to
their world nor to Ellie's nor to Sharon's either but how,
like my scrap-iron sculpture, I could be arranged in different ways to suit different worlds, and before long I
found that I was becoming as depressed and withdrawn
as Sharon seemed.

We got back to Armadillo toward sunset. We were
sticky from the salt water, with sand in our hair and
tar on our feet, and when I asked Sharon if she'd like to
come back to the Salamander with me for a shower, I
think she considered it for a minute. She had drawn her
hair into a long, loose braid and somehow looped the
yellow scarf in and out of it. Her eyes looked more green
than brown as she squinted into the sun at me, frowning,
and then finally shook her head, no. She said, "Bip put
you up to taking me, didn't he?"

"Is that what's been the trouble?" I said.

"Didn't he?" she said.

I nodded.

"Oh well," she said. "It was better than if Brownie
had taken me."

I thanked her.

"That's all right," she said. "The lions won't do it
every time you pull your camera out. There'll be other
times." It was the kindest thing that I think she'd said
to me up to that point, and after dropping her off back
at the Manse, I lay down on my bed at the Salamander,
slipped a quarter into the Magic Fingers, and fell asleep
on the memory of it. There would be other times, she

had said, and I found myself not only looking forward to those times whenever they should come and whatever they should bring but also enjoying this time to myself before they came. You don't lose the habits of a lifetime all in a minute, and for the space at least of that long nap—I woke up a few hours later just long enough to phone Bebb that I would be at the Manse first thing in the morning to help get things ready for the big show —I returned to my celibacy and my bachelor solitude with a zest no less keen for knowing that they would not last forever. Although I did not know it then, it was the last peaceful moment I was to have for some time to come.

When I arrived at the Manse the next morning, it looked like an Italian wedding. There must have been four or five limousines parked along the street with their uniformed drivers lounging around in various attitudes, one of them apparently asleep in the back seat with his visored cap pulled down over his eyes, another with his cap pushed back, idly buffing a piece of chrome with his handkerchief. There seemed to be children everywhere, dark-haired, dark-eyed children from kindergarten on up and all of them dressed as if for a wedding or a first communion in white dresses and uncomfortable, boxy-looking little white suits with their hair slicked back or frizzed up with white flowers in it and here and there a lopsided veil pinned on. Some of them were at the sand-box and swings, others climbing around the porch and in the palmettos, and as I got out of the car, a couple of them came tearing around from behind the house with what I recognized as the hose and sprinkler Sharon had been using to keep her feet cool the morning before. By the porch steps, filled with white glads, there were several tall baskets with high, arched handles such as are sent to funerals or *bon voyage* parties on ocean liners, and there was one elaborate arrangement of white carnations laid out on an easel-like frame in the shape of a cross. Sitting near the front door there was a bulky object about the size and shape of a garbage can which on closer inspection turned out to be a rolled-up length of red carpet. When I knocked at the door, it was Brownie who came.

It was the first time that I had seen him in anything but shorts, and the change it made in his whole appearance was quite startling. He had on a double-breasted powder-blue suit with a silvery clip-on bow tie and a sprig of lily of the valley pinned to his lapel. He could have been the owner of a successful haberdashery store or the president of Armadillo Fire Insurance, and the fragrance of his after-shave was even more powerful than usual. His forehead was wet with perspiration, and the smile he gave me seemed so much the product of his dentures alone that I felt Brownie himself could hardly be held responsible for its almost total failure. He said, "Herman Redpath and his party arrived earlier than expected, and the Bebbs are entertaining them till it's time to go to the church. I know they'll be glad to see you, dear. They were about to send me to the motel," and then he led me down the hall, past the bathroom under the stairs with the brown toilet seat, and all the way back to the sitting room where Lucille had received me that first night in Armadillo, which seemed to me already to have taken place as many months earlier as it had actually been days.

The room was crowded with people. Lucille in dark glasses was seated in her high-backed wicker armchair in a dress that might almost have been the filmy one from the photograph, and she was holding, clamped between her knees, a glass which I took from its color and height to be a Tropicana. On the arm of her chair sat Bebb speaking with great animation to someone, his mouth snapping rapidly open and shut on its hinges with his magician's eyes open-sesame wide and his bald head buffed to a high polish. He did not stop talking when I came in, but I could tell that he had seen me. At his elbow the color TV was on. A man with a green face and a reddish-purple aura around one ear and under his chin seemed, like Bebb, to be making a speech of some kind, but it was impossible to know what he was saying because the volume was turned off. All around the room, particularly on one sofa, there were Indians.

Perhaps if I had not already known from Bebb about Herman Redpath's ancestry, I would not have recognized them as Indians, but as it was, there could be no doubt of it. Their clothes, which, like the children's, were predominantly white, only served to emphasize the fact by making their skin look even swarthier than it was and their hair look even blacker. There must have been between fifteen and twenty of them all told, fat ones and thin ones, old ones and young ones, more women than men. There was a plump one who looked like Jack Oakie sitting on the floor with his arms around his knees and an old woman with a face like a relief map of the Rockies wearing a peekaboo blouse. Sharing an ottoman there were three young women with so nearly the same face—a flat, nostril-splayed face suitable for patching teepees with or trapping small game—that it would have taken their mother to tell them apart. And their mother, I felt sure, was also there. She was one of the ones on the sofa and as large a woman as I have seen before or since. She had to sit sideways to make room for all the others, with one mighty leg thrust out into the room and her daughters' features lost in her face like a button or two in a basket of laundry. The arrangement on the sofa in general reminded me of Sargent's portrait of all those sisters sitting on top of each other, or at least a somewhat more populous and overblown version of it. It was all white skirts and sleeves and corsages, all piled black hair and buffalo-counting eyes, and then somewhere in the center—like the sight of your own face in a group photograph which at first you don't notice and then can see nothing else but—there was Herman Redpath. He was made entirely of chocolate.

Herman Redpath was wearing a brown suit with a brown shirt and, in place of a tie, a medallion of horn with two strings hanging down. He had on a brown, broad-brimmed felt hat of a kind that I associate less with the Wild West than with Methodist circuit riders, and his brown face was the face of an ancient Pharaoh. It was a narrow, wedge-shaped face with a large, high-bridged nose and the skin pulled so tight that it seemed to keep his thin lips from quite closing over his teeth and his eyes from opening much wider than a horizon-scanning squint. I could not make out whom he was talking to, and everybody else seemed to be talking at the same time, but his voice was the one I heard through all the others and recognized immediately as his. What he was saying was, "I bet you can't guess what it cost me to fly all these sonsofbitches out here not even counting the limousines and the drivers at the airport cost me somewhere in the neighborhood of three four thousand dollars but I don't give a fart how much it cost because it's worth it to me and it's worth it to Leo hey Leo," he called out, pushing a white elbow aside in order to catch Bebb's eye, "bring that long glass of water over here and introduce us," and I realized that he was referring to me.

Herman Redpath took an immediate liking to me, and as soon as I saw him, I could have predicted that he would. All my life it has been that way. The boy with the worst breath in school, the aunt who has made ouija-board contact with Lillian Russell, the one alcoholic in the room or the only person who has recently had his gallstones removed and is carrying them around in an envelope—I have inevitably been the one that they felt especially drawn to. Ellie always said that it was my sympathetic El Greco eyes and Miriam that it was because they recognized me as a brother under the skin; and in some ways these both come down to the same thing which may be the truth of it. But whatever the explanation, it was not Bebb or Brownie, not Sharon or Lucille or anybody else in Armadillo that day whom Herman Redpath took a shine to. It was me.

He cleared several Indians off the sofa and made me sit down beside him and then talked to me for a long time without interruption, by which I mean not just that he did not pause long enough between sentences for me to interrupt with some comment of my own but that he did not pause long enough between sentences for me to know where one sentence ended and another began, so that listening to him was like trying to translate from an ancient scroll where all the words have been run together and the vowels left out. As nearly as I could tell, he was talking about God, although his approach was not theological and his images were drawn from un-expected places.

He said, "You take your Ezekiels and your Jeremiahs and your Saint Paul the Apostles and all your kiss-my-ass holy men and they were always seeing God somewhere God was always jumping out at them got up like a wheel with eyes in between the spokes or a plumb line or some damn thing like a blinding light when they were going someplace so as far as I can see they must have spent most of the time shitting in their pants I know I would just the sound of a rattler when I don't expect it knocks the shit right out of me I have never seen God any place or talked to him direct and I not only don't expect to see him hell I don't even want to see him I couldn't take that much God all at once and he couldn't probably take that much Redpath I've got Indian blood in me what do you think these freaks I've brought along with me are a bunch of Irishmen I never once come up on God with his pants down nor him me as far as I know I could tell you plenty other things I've come up on walk-ing around out there from the time I was a kid jacking off every chance I got sometimes twenty twenty-five times a day and still plenty seed left where the rest come from you don't have to believe it round about when the sun starts going down and there's everything looks like it's on fire and the wind blows till you think you'll freeze your balls off tumbleweed blowing and some old squaw

205

itching herself front of the fire the things I've seen the things I'm always ready to see you never know when so you got to be ready any minute I still am ready now I'm pushing seventy-five can't hardly keep it standing two minutes any more and all that comes out is a little piddle of dust I don't say I ever saw God direct but what I saw you got to be quick as hell to see because it happens quick right up from behind a rock or flapping out of a tree once a cactus opened up like a pair of hands you say something alive yes something alive by Jesus comes rushing out it's gone before you can say jack-rabbit what was it you tell me what was it it was not a snake or a rabbit or a bird or a coyote life life it's like life gets so hot sometimes it starts to boil a bubble comes up and breaks that's what I see maybe the life busts out sometimes can't nothing hold it in I've never seen so much as God's hindparts Leo here says it's God is the fire makes life boil I don't give a fart long as it boils maybe God is the name of it he says the holy spirit I like him he doesn't kiss my ass like most of them he's no holy man they say he's done time so what if he's done time he's got the life in him when he lays his hands on my head he says the Jesus life comes through the fingers it's not the Jesus I want it's the life I want those kids out there you think they're my grandchildren hell they're my children mostly some women in this room probably got my children inside them right now but I'm pushing seventy-five and the sap's drying up the sap's drying up to where soon it's going to be nothing except dust comes piddling out when I shoot let Leo Bebb see can he give me the life back give me the seed back and I'll build him all the churches he wants make this one look like shit you seen that daughter of his Jesus Christ if she was just to rub her tight little ass against me I'd get one on might last me ten minutes or more and what come out wouldn't be dust either not by a damn sight you look like you got Indian blood in you too I noticed it as soon as you poked your head in the door."

That Tutankhamen face, those delicate brown hands on the chocolate pants, that sofa full of squaws in white dresses with gardenias and lilies of the valley in their hair. I could see Bebb trying to signal me from the door, and as soon as Herman Redpath drew a brown silk handkerchief out of his breast pocket and pressed it against his mouth for a minute as if to spit something out, I made a break for it. Looking back over my shoulder, I saw that he was talking again to someone else or to no one else or to everyone, and I do not think he even noticed that I had gone. He had his hand on the huge white knee of the fat woman sitting sidesaddle next to him, and it lay there fragile and sere like a dead leaf.

Bebb drew me out into the hall. He said, "Antonio, the hour is at hand. I'm going to take Herman Redpath and his party down to the church. I want you to stay here so if anybody comes to the house you can direct them. Herman Redpath is an important man, and there may be reporters. Sharon's going to stay too case there's any ladies come who need the facilities. When the time comes, you bring her down to Holy Love with you."

Sharon and I stayed, but nobody came. We stood on the front porch watching the withdrawal of the Indians. The children were rounded up, some of their white clothes the worse for wear after their rout in the sandbox and among the palmettos. The tall baskets of flowers were somehow loaded into the limousines, and it was Brownie who staggered down the steps under the weight of the rolled-up red carpet. The fat mother of the three daughters got in beside one of the uniformed drivers by sitting down first and then having the Jack Oakie man pick up her legs and swing them in after her. The old lady in the peekaboo blouse ended up sitting on somebody's lap. I could see her through a window perched there like a medicine man's poppet.

The last ones to leave the house were Bebb and Lucille themselves with Herman Redpath following behind them. It was like the royal family coming out on the balcony at Buckingham Palace. They stood there at the top of the porch steps for a few moments while an Indian with a Graflex took pictures—Bebb on one side, plump and glittering, Lucille on the other with her lower jaw dropped and one skinny arm on the railing, and between them Herman Redpath, who stood little higher than a child. He had removed his hat, and his brown scalp was almost completely bare except for a few wisps of black hair, one of which the air stirred so that it stood up like a feather. When the photographer finished, Herman Redpath raised his arm and waved at the waiting limousines. There were several answering honks, arms reaching out of windows, handkerchiefs and flowers waving, and then the party descended the stairs, got into Bebb's car—Bebb and Lucille in the front seat, Herman Redpath by himself in the back—and drove off with the limousines following behind.

Sharon and I waited around on the porch for a few minutes, but when nobody seemed to be coming, we went back inside. We still had a quarter of an hour or so before the ceremony was to begin, and it was cooler out of the sun. We stood there in the hall in that trance-like way people have when there is nothing to do but wait, and all by ourselves in that old house as we were, and both dressed up for Herman Redpath's ordination, for a few moments it was as if we were strangers. For the first time Sharon's hair looked properly brushed to me, sleek with a glint to it and not divided above the ears, and she was wearing gold hoop earrings as big around as silver dollars. After our day on the beach, she was almost as brown as one of the fairer Indians, and stepping out of her sandals, she stood there barefoot. I could think of nothing either to say or to do, and neither apparently could she, so I stuck out my hand finally and said in my Madison Avenue voice, "I'm Antonio Parr. Wesleyan '55," and she said nothing at first, just stood there with her hand in mine, looking rather somber and illegal. Then she gave my hand a little jerk and said, "Come on up while I wash the Indian off."

I am no fool. Even at that instant I knew perfectly well what would happen if I followed her. She had already started up the stairs, but paused for a moment and half turned with one hand on the banister and the toes of one bare foot resting on the instep of the other. I knew that if I followed her up, there would be no one to direct the reporters if they came. I knew that any ladies who might appear would have to find their own way to the Victorian facility under the stairs. I knew, or thought I knew and perhaps actually did know, that Bebb had left me there believing that I would carry out my charge and then get both Sharon and myself to the church on time because in different ways he needed us

both there as much as he ever could be said to need
anybody. All this and more I knew, but I am no hero. I
followed her up two steps at a time once I got started,
and that is how it happened that we missed the ordination of Herman Redpath as I knew we would from the
moment my foot touched the first stair and as Sharon,
I suppose, must have known even sooner.

We missed the ordination of Herman Redpath, and
how, if at all, it would have proceeded differently had
we not missed it, and how a number of lives including
our own might have been changed either for better or
worse thereby, must remain forever among the other
what-ifs of history. We missed it, and we knew that we
were, and we didn't even stop to mark the moment's
passing if it could even be said to have passed, because
there are times beyond time or this side of time when
moments do not pass so much as they accumulate like
different colored filters on a camera lens, bringing the
clouds out and making the shadows look deep and rich.
The curtains moved, I remember, muslin curtains as
soft as cobweb from years of washing. They floated in
and out of the open window to the smell, I think, of
honeysuckle—or could it have been some lingering trace
of Brownie's after-shave?—and there was a soft rattle
way off in the distance of somebody's lawnmower.
George Hamilton and Ringo Starr were there on the
wall together with several nameless young men, one in
an airforce uniform who looked like an advertisement
for Bryl-Cream and another crouched on a beach with
his mouth open and holding what looked like either a
football helmet or a horseshoe crab between his thighs.
Bebb was there shaking the hand of somebody who

might have been Oral Roberts, and there was a Florida State pennant, a water-color sketch of a palm tree with a sailboat way off in the water behind it. We didn't have all the time in the world and we knew it, but we took our time anyway, and if a reporter had wandered in on us to ask the way to Holy Love or if Lucille had come back for her dark glasses or Brownie for his teeth, I suppose we would have noticed them, but I do not think it would have mattered much any more than the curtains mattered or the sound of the mower.

And then all hell broke loose. The door slammed shut downstairs so that you could feel the whole house vibrate from it, then the sound of Brownie's voice calling something I couldn't make out, footsteps hurrying noisily down the hall, another door closing or opening, and the sudden, hard splash of water in a sink. They were the unmistakable sounds of catastrophe, and we both knew it, and yet we stayed there for a moment or two longer as if we didn't know it, and I remember thinking for no reason of Robert Frost's "two roads diverged in a yellow wood" and deciding that Sharon was both the two roads diverging and the yellow wood too. And then, as soon as we could, we went down.

We found Brownie and Lucille in the kitchen, and I have wondered since why it is that at times of crisis it is so often the kitchen that people repair to as if there among the pots and pans the bitterest pill or craziest salad can be somehow swallowed down and cleared away like a meal. Lucille was sitting bolt upright at the kitchen table with one arm hanging straight at her side and the other stretched out on the table in front of her as though she was about to give blood. Brownie was standing bent over at the sink, where the water was running. He was holding a wet dishrag to his face, and his nose was bleeding. I do not know to this day what caused Brownie's nosebleed, but I assume that it was either just nerves or possibly something to do with the slamming of the door.

Under different circumstances they might well have asked us how we happened to be there then, I in my shirtsleeves and Sharon barefoot and without her gold hoop earrings. They might have asked us why it was that we hadn't shown up at the church an hour before as we had been told to, but there was obviously no place in their minds for such questions as those, and if there had been, I do not know how we would have answered. Their story, as it gradually emerged, came partly from Brownie and partly from Lucille, sometimes in sequence and sometimes simultaneously, but I can no longer disentangle the strands of one from those of the other, and where their two accounts differed, sometimes quite radically, I can no longer be sure on what grounds I made my choice between them. I have since listened carefully to one or two other people tell about what happened at Holy Love that day when Sharon and I were not there, and even certain photographs were at one point made available to me, but I am under no delusion that mine is the definitive account. It is just a version like everybody else's, and I suppose it is no less flavored than all the others by the cask that it was aged in.

At the beginning, apparently, everything went along much as might have been expected. Bebb noticed that Sharon and I had not yet arrived by the time things were supposed to start, so he tried to stall for a while, but then some of the younger children began to get restless and there seemed to be some danger that the old lady with the blouse might be overcome by the heat if she had to wait much longer, so finally Bebb had to set things in motion without us. He and Herman Redpath sat alone together in the front row and behind them Lucille and Brownie with the Indians, a reporter from Fort Lauderdale, some hard-shell Baptists who were there primarily for the music, and a handful of passers-by who had simply wandered in, attracted by the crowd.

The Baptists had lent their junior choir for the occasion, and the service began with a half-dozen hymns or so, including "Throw out the life-line" and "When the roll is called up yonder," after which most of the Baptist parents of the choristers pointedly withdrew. Then there were some free prayers offered by Brownie, after which Brownie gave a kind of charge to Herman Redpath, reminding him of his sacred obligation to propagate the Gospel faithfully and above all accurately, and taking for his text Matthew eighteen six, where Jesus gathers some children about him and warns the disciples that rather than cause one of those little ones to sin, "it were better for him that a millstone were hanged about his neck and that he were drowned in the depth of the sea."

In explicating the passage, Brownie drew attention, as might have been expected, to some facts about the ancient world that illuminated the meaning and prevented the possibility of certain obvious misunderstandings. In the time of Jesus, he pointed out, G. Zuss, the grain was of such poor quality and so easily pulverized that millstones were often made of a very light, porous stone resembling pumice. This stone was, indeed, so unusually aerated almost in the manner of styrofoam that, combined with the fact that the salt content of the Dead Sea was so notoriously high that even fat men could float in it like corks, a millstone around the neck might under certain circumstances serve the function of a life-preserver. And this was clearly what the passage intended, Brownie argued: it was better not to cause one of the little ones to sin—there could be no question about that—but if you slipped up, then out went the life-line with a millstone tied to the working end, and very few people ever drowned in the Dead Sea anyway. Then there were some more hymns, some more prayers, and finally Bebb rose for the ordination itself.

Bebb was dressed in his white robe, and what with the heat and the fatigue of the day, his face was apparently more drained of color than usual, so that when I try to picture him standing there behind the altar table, I see a palely shimmering Moby Dick or Taj Mahal of a man, and in front of him, with his back to the congregation and facing Bebb, that little chocolate-colored Choctaw, that Mohawk midget, who was Herman Redpath.

Bebb prayed some general prayers first. He prayed for rain to come so the citrus crop wouldn't be ruined, but not too much rain for the visitors from the North. He prayed for the sick and the dying and asked the Almighty to provide them with healing where he could and with courage and comfort where he could not. He prayed for the President and the Congress and for all judges everywhere that they might perform their duties faithfully but always remember that Jesus was a friend of sinners and temper justice with mercy. He prayed for all prisoners. He prayed for old people in nursing homes and for little children. He prayed for the Armed Forces and for all men who did battle everywhere, especially, he said, for those whose battle was a secret one that went on inside their skins. And then he stepped around in front of the table and placed his hands on Herman Redpath's nearly naked scalp.

Except for Brownie's address about the millstone, the prayer that Bebb delivered at this point was the only part of the service, as far as I know, that was written down, and I record it here as I have myself read it.

"O God mighty in battle and the sinners' friend, thou who hast counted up the very hairs on our heads and callest forth also the stars and the planets of outer space by name, send down the snow-white dove of thy holy spirit to roost upon thy servant Herman Redpath. He is here to feel thy life throbbing through his veins, so bestow life upon him. He is here that he may mount up in thy service like an eagle, so grant him the strength of a young man to mount with. Herman Redpath is here to receive from thy hands the holy power to love, so of thy love-power give him good measure, pressed down and shaken together and running over so that he may receive it into his lap and scatter it abroad like seed. Grant him the gift of charity so that he may be very charitable. Grant him the gift of faith so that he may always keep faith with us who are his faithful friends and with thee. Grant him the word of wisdom so that his word may be his bond and as sound as a dollar. And finally grant him the special gift of healing so that whomsoever he lays his hands upon in love may respond yea even beyond his fondest dreams. Amen."

At this point Bebb stepped back a few steps from

Herman Redpath and, raising first his face, pale and moist as cheese, he started slowly to raise his arms also until like great white wings they were stretched up on either side as far as they would go. Some say that he called out something unintelligible here—some final glossolalia or paean perhaps, like a Druid at the moment when the first ray of the midsummer sun shoots in across the great lintel stone—but some say that he made no sound at all and just stood there with his arms spread and his head thrown back. In any case, virtually everybody agrees that it was at this moment rather than earlier that it first became apparent that during all the time he had been raising his arms, his white robe had been coming farther and farther apart up the middle until here, as his arms reached their zenith, it could be clearly seen that the veil of the Temple had been rent asunder and the Holy of Holies exposed. It was here that the terrible mystery was made manifest, the rabbit pulled white and squirming out of the magician's darkness.

You see in this world mainly what you expect to see, and what you do not expect to see you are usually blind to, and this was apparently the case for a few moments there at Holy Love while the Indians and the Baptists and the passers-by and the reporter from Fort Lauderdale no less than Brownie and Lucille themselves sat there not simply not believing their eyes but not even believing that something had happened for their eyes to try not to believe. When finally they did see, I suspect they were all struck blind in some measure, or at least this is suggested by the fact that each of the various accounts I have heard has differed substantially from the others as to exactly what there was to see and in what state and with what apparent motive and to what supposed end. Of the six or seven flashbulb shots that the Fort Lauderdale reporter somehow mustered the presence of mind to take, all but one either failed to turn out or showed only a blaze of white robe, white face, white wall, with the shadowy figure of Herman Redpath standing in just the wrong place, or right place, depending on the side you took. A copy of the one picture that is said to have turned out reasonably clearly came into my possession much later on, but after giving the matter a great deal of thought, I decided finally to destroy it without looking at it. When it comes to the truth of the matter, the real truth, a camera is no more to be trusted than any of the rest of us.

So what exactly happened there no one will ever know, I suppose, but that something seismic happened there can be no doubt, because within a matter of minutes there was neither a Baptist nor an Indian nor a passer-by left in the place, and within minutes of that, Brownie was back at the Manse with his nose bleeding into the sink and Lucille was sitting there reaching out with an unsteady hand for the Tropicana that Sharon had made for her.

Once Brownie had gotten his nose under control and Sharon had taken Lucille upstairs to lie down, Sharon and I drove down to the church to see if we could locate Bebb. Neither of us, I think, expected to find him. Brownie said that he had seen two state troopers leading him out the back way through the fire-insurance office, and he feared the worst. It was Mr. Bebb's second time, he said—the only reference I ever heard him make to Bebb's five missing years except that time he spoke of it as having been spent on the Lord's work—and to make matters worse, Brownie added, there had been a number of children in the congregation. Lucille said that she had not noticed any troopers but had seen Bebb jump into his car and start south, which meant that he was heading for the Keys very likely and then on to Cuba. This well exemplifies the difficulty of putting together a story from such witnesses because both Brownie and Lucille seemed quite sure of their conflicting reports, and yet, as it turned out, neither report was true. When we got to the church, Bebb was sitting there on the stoop under the frosted-glass cross.

It was just a little past noon with the sun almost directly overhead and no shadows. The souvenir-stand people must have gone off to lunch leaving their shrunken heads behind them because there was a sign with a clock-face on it hanging from the knob of the screen door. There seemed to be nothing going on at the barber shop unless perhaps among the miniature turtles in the front window. It seemed a deeply yet precariously quiet moment like the lull between breakers at the seashore when one wave has just been sucked back hissing down the sand and the next one has not yet broken.

Bebb sat there in his shirtsleeves with the jacket to his suit folded neatly beside him so that the four-pointed handkerchief in his breast pocket faced up. He had his chin in his hands and seemed so lost in thought as he gazed down at his feet that at first I assumed he hadn't seen us. Then Sharon said, "Bip," and at the sound of his name, without looking up but as if he had been talking to us for some time and was simply resuming where he had left off a few moments before, he said, "Herman Redpath was all shook up, you could see that, but I don't doubt for a second that when he gets back to Texas he will feel like himself again. That man is generous to a fault, Antonio, and no power on earth is going to make him withdraw the right hand of fellowship or go back on his word. I could see it written on his face when he left as clear as day. That place is as full of flowers in there as a funeral parlor, glads lying around everywhere. Sharon, you see somebody gets them to the hospital or the old folks' home."

Sharon said, "How come you did it, Bip?"

He said nothing for a while. Sharon had dropped down to the stone step beside him, and he reached out and laid his hand on top of hers, carefully, as though to leave nothing of her hand showing. He said, "Sharon, it was an accident—it was," interrupting himself with one finger raised, "it was not an accident, you see, but— you might call it something more on the order of—" and as he kept breaking in on himself, I thought, it was as if he was taking her always down, down to some deeper sub-cellar still of what might be the truth of it or just another urine-smelling level of the IRT. "I have nothing to hide, Sharon. That is for sure, even if nothing else is. I have nothing I've got to be ashamed of. A man opens himself up sometimes. He lays himself on the line, and he says love me or leave me, but anyway look and see who I am. He says keep your eyes open for Jesus' sake, and pay attention. You say how come Bip did something.

Honey, some things you don't plan out ahead of time so you can say later on you did it for such-and-such a reason. There are things happen all by themselves, and they're the things you remember out of your life. There comes times when a man takes crazy chances. You shake them up good and roll them out, double or nothing, with your fingers crossed. Play it too safe and you end up something on the order of Brownie. I expect you left Brownie back home to look after your mother."

Sharon nodded. Beside her, Bebb looked bigger and whiter than ever, but with some of the bounce gone, like a New Year's Eve balloon the next morning.

I said, "Bip, what are you going to do next?"

He said, "Antonio, I'm not kidding myself. What I do next may be in my hands or then it may not be, and that's what I'm waiting here to find out. They're always locking people up for the wrong reasons—the right people maybe, but the wrong reasons and the wrong times. Think of it, Antonio—this thing I've been dreaming about come true at last. I threw out the life-line, and the one caught it was Herman Redpath in all his wealth and power. And now the lock-up. But my ways are not thy ways, saith the Lord. Antonio, you take a man's been in prison a couple years, and he's ready for Jesus like he's never been ready any place else. He's ready for anything has got some hope and life in it. Life, Antonio, is what a prisoner's ready for. Freedom. Lion Country. It's worth breaking the law just so you can get put in the lock-up, where the grapes are ripe for the harvest and the Lord needs all the hands he can get for the vineyard. You should hear the way they sing hymns behind bars, Antonio. Makes you go all over gooseflesh."

220

"Give us one, Bip," Sharon said. She drew her hand out from under his and let her head come down to rest on his shoulder.

The noon sun was almost blinding, but Bebb looked straight out ahead of him without so much as blinking and, with his mouth snapped shut even tighter than usual and his nostrils swelling, started to hum a few tentative, uncertain things that could have ended up being almost any hymn in the book. The one he finally settled on was "Rock of Ages," and although Sharon's head was on his shoulder as he sang it, he did not sing it to her or to me or to Jesus or anybody else as far as I could tell, but more to himself or possibly even to Herman Redpath up in the sky there somewhere on his way to Texas.

"Rock of ages, cleft for me," Bebb sang in a kind of 1930's radio voice. "Let me hide myself in thee. . . . Nothing in my hand I bring, Simply to thy cross I cling," and over his head, I noticed, almost too good to be true, some Indian I suppose had flicked on the light in the frosted-glass sign so that even in the daylight it shone out a little with HOLY LOVE written up and down it like the cross on a Bayer aspirin tablet.

CHAPTER TWELVE

DURING MY YEARS as an English teacher, students were always handing in stories that ended up with a sentence or two to the effect that the next morning they woke up and found out the whole thing had been just a dream. It is one of the easier ways, certainly, to bring a story to a close—it saves you from having to draw all the loose ends together, for one thing, and excuses you for any improbabilities you may have committed along the way, for another—and for reasons like that most of my colleagues regarded the practice with considerable disfavor and docked the grade accordingly. I, on the other hand, always tended to like such stories. In life as in fiction, it

222

seems to me, the richer and more memorable moments inevitably do take on a dreamlike quality once you emerge from them. The birthday party, the walk through the park in the snow, seeing the old man with the umbrella knocked down by the taxi—did they happen really, or did you just dream that they happened? It is De Quincey's essay on *Macbeth* all over again—the knocking on the gate, the drunken porter's bad jokes about liquor and sex, the *realia* of life, in other words, and by contrast the bloody end of the old king takes on the quality of nightmare.

In the case of this story about my days in Armadillo, on the other hand, just the reverse is the case. When I got back to New York and to the routine again of my life there, I had the feeling that it was they that were dreamlike and that it was in Armadillo that I had left reality behind. Just the difference of season was part of it, I suppose: the grey and ghost-like city winter with the lights going on early down the center of Park Avenue and the tops of the buildings lost in dusk, whereas in Armadillo the blaze of summer that was almost too bright to see by and either no shadows at all or shadows as clear-cut as life and death themselves. I moved a little like a dream or a ghost myself those first days especially of being home, and it was only when I thought back on how it had been for me in Florida that I could feel something like a real heart beating against my ribs.

I flew back to New York the same day as the climactic events surrounding the ordination of Herman Redpath, and the reason was Miriam. I called the hospital to check in with her, and they gave me a doctor who said they had been trying to locate me for over a day to say that she had taken a decided turn for the worse and I had better be prepared to stand by. No one had known where I was, of course. Miriam, who probably wouldn't have remembered anyway, was past remembering, I had never told Charlie Blaine, and no one thought about Ellie, who would have been able to put them on the right track. So, with Miriam so much on my mind that I had a hard time focusing on anything else, I left the Bebbs and Brownie in the hour of their need without any clear notion of what I was leaving and said goodbye to Sharon as though goodbye was only a poor translation of some word which in the original tongue meant something quite innocuous.

Miriam lived for several weeks after my return, and I saw her again a number of times, but although there may have been moments when she was trying to respond, I am not certain that she ever again really saw me. Other bones broke, broke like her arms for no cause other than that she moved them the wrong way or simply tried to shift her position in bed, and in the end there was apparently not a major bone in her body that remained intact. The last time I saw her, they had her in a giant cast that resembled the letter A with both her legs sheathed all the way down to her ankles in plaster and in between a crosspiece to keep them from moving. The nurses advised me to go home and get some sleep because she was under such heavy sedation that she couldn't possibly know or care whether anyone was there or not, but I stuck around on the off-chance that she might come to if only for a moment and I didn't want her to find herself alone in that room that for so many weeks had been her only world.

Part of the time her eyes were open—there was never anything broken-looking or sick about her eyes, which to the last seemed to have more anger in them than anything else—and during those times I talked to her, even though there was no indication that she could hear a word I was saying. In that sense it was a little like praying, and like it also because it was more for my own sake, I think, than for hers, just as I have always suspected prayer is more for man's sake than for God's—it is not God who needs to be praised but we who need to praise him, whether we believe in him or not. On the other hand, there was nothing especially prayerful in what I talked to her about. I talked to her a lot about how it had been when we were children, and I went on at some length about the radio programs we used to listen to—*Mr. Keen, Tracer of Lost Persons* and *Uncle Don, Easy Aces*, where we always got a kick out of Jane Ace's saying "You could have knocked me down with a fender," and one called *Omar the Mystic*, which nobody but me seems to remember, where at the end of each episode they used to tap out a secret message on bells which you could decode for yourself if you sent in a boxtop of something for one of their secret decoders. I reminded her of the time we were sent to the Met to hear *Hansel and Gretel* by Humperdinck—or was it *The Harrowing of Hell* by Montague Rhodes James?—and I talked about the smell of our apartment on winter evenings and the sounds of the horns heading home up Park Avenue.

At one point I even tried to give her a picture of some of the things that had happened while I was in Armadillo. I tried to describe Brownie and his smile, for instance, and Lion Country and the way Bip had looked driving home in his beanie with the propellers on it. What I wanted to describe most to her, of course, was Sharon—my sister might have liked Sharon, I suspect, in a way that I'm afraid she would never have liked poor Ellie—but partly because the nurse kept coming in and out, and partly because for reasons that I suppose Dr. Freud would have found interesting I never was much good at telling Miriam about the women in my life, I stayed away from Sharon and told a little about my meeting with the girl in the bathing suit instead.

When I finally left—whatever they try to say, even the bonds between twins can hold only so long, and I reached the point where I was literally unable to keep my eyes open any longer—I knew without any doubt for once that I was seeing her for the last time. There was something oddly anti-climactic about it. The real last times, I think—the last times I had really seen *her*— were when she had tossed that vague little wave to me as she was stubbing her cigarette out in the ashtray and when with such ferocity in her voice she told her younger son, Tony, to stay awake. My actual last sight of Miriam was last only in a chronological sense, because it seemed not so much Miriam I was seeing but rather the first letter of the alphabet. It was a giant A—so meaningless by itself, though so rich in combination—lying there, white on white, on that hospital bed. I made no attempt to say goodbye and neither shed any tears nor felt like shedding any but just left when the time came and closed the door behind me. If A stood for anything, I thought, it stood for *andiamo* or *avanti*, meaning *Let's get the Hell out of here.* I could imagine Miriam thinking that somewhere deep inside all her sedation and plaster, and I thought it also myself.

She was buried on Christmas Eve day in an enormous cemetery in Brooklyn because our father had had Brooklyn connections and both he and his Italian bride were buried there. No one came except Charlie with his two boys and me, and the service, such as it was, was conducted by a young Episcopal priest, an acquaintance of Charlie's, who looked about as pale and helpless to me as Charlie himself did. Because of the divorce, it was really up to me to make the arrangements, but Charlie seemed so eager to handle them himself—perhaps, I thought, to make it up to Miriam for not having gone to see her that day he took the boys to the Rockettes—that I let him do it. He decided against having any funeral, just the brief Episcopal business there by the graveside, and the reason he gave was that Miriam wouldn't have wanted any fuss, by which I understood him to mean that he himself didn't want any. Miriam, I suspect, might have enjoyed a real Wop affair with everybody sobbing noisily and a lot to drink afterwards, but Charlie Blaine didn't want to make any fuss about death any more than he wanted to make any fuss about life. His idea was to get through both as quietly and painlessly as possible, with plenty of long naps along the way.

Everything the priest read was familiar to me until he got to a passage which included the words "make me to hear joy and gladness that the bones which thou hast broken may rejoice." It is the Fifty-first Psalm, I discovered later, and maybe Episcopalians always use it, but if so, I had never happened to notice it before. The peculiar aptness of it struck me first as grisly and depressing and then almost immediately as just right. I didn't like the thought of God's being the one who had broken Miriam's bones, but, remembering Don Giovanni with his rapier in Dr. James's Hell, I decided that he had always been one to play rough, and if the last word was really going to be one of rejoicing, I could forgive him almost anything—like Adam when he finally got that oil from the tree of mercy for the pain of his body. Charlie stood there with a Vicks inhaler—his sinuses always kicked up in damp weather, he said—and the boys got through it all right. Chris got through it almost too well, I thought—maybe he was thinking about the poem he would write about it afterwards, or maybe his tooth was hurting him again—but Tony pleased me by looking as though at any moment he might burst into great, fat cadenzas of Italian grief. He didn't, I'm happy to say, but I think his mother would have been pleased to note that he almost did. It proved, among other things, that he had stayed awake.

The dreamlike quality of those first weeks after my return from Armadillo, or maybe just the dreamlike quality of myself, was increased by the unexpected behavior of both Ellie and Tom. Given the undemonstrativeness of cats generally, I didn't expect Tom to burst into the Halleluiah Chorus when I went down to get him at the vet's, but I expected more than I got. The vet opened the door of the cage where Tom was sitting on his haunches with his tail curled around in front of him in one of his Egyptian moods, and without so much as a sidelong glance at me, he went stalking straight across the linoleum to the radiator where he sat down and with determined upward sweeps of his tongue started cleaning one of his wrists. Perhaps he was just showing me how deeply offended he still was by my having abandoned him all that time to a prisoner's cell, but I remember wondering at the time if I had become so ghostlike and transparent that he simply hadn't noticed I was there.

Ellie's reaction struck me as essentially the same thing transcribed for piano and strings. We kissed when I met her out on the plaza in front of the U.N.—there were snowflakes in the air, with the flags of the nations hanging spent and limp from their staffs—and she asked me all the proper questions about Miriam and Florida and Tom, but I could see that her heart wasn't in it. I think she may even have forgotten why I went down in the first place. She made some vague reference to my writing, but I do not believe she could have told me, if I'd asked her, exactly what I had gone down there to write about. And I was in no hurry to put her to the test.

The only writing I ever actually did on the Bebb article was in the form of a few notes I jotted down on the back of a receipted Salamander Motel bill on my late flight back to West Palm the same day I'd flown up to take the boys to see Miriam—the management had said they'd hold the room till my return, but asked me to pay for the two nights I'd already spent there. All I'd written on the back of the bill were a few incomplete and in most cases inaccurate sentences. "Nobody calls him Leo," I wrote. Herman Redpath called him Leo, but I didn't learn this until later. "Tropicanas two orange to one gin." Though only a guess, I eventually discovered from Sharon that in this case I was one hundred percent accurate. I wrote, "Brownie must hate his guts—B. treats him like shit." Nothing could have been more inaccurate than the first part—if Bebb died first, Brownie would probably see to it that his guts were enshrined somewhere like the Buddha's tooth—and as for the second part, though forced to agree that Bebb treated him like shit, Brownie would probably say that Bebb did it the same way the Lord did when he picked up that handful of shit in Eden and formed it into the shape of a man, breathing into its nostrils the breath of life so that it might become a living soul. "Toilet brush," I wrote down, and "Framed or not framed?" and that was about the sum of it. I realized by now that I hadn't the faintest intention of writing any article and was grateful to Ellie for not bringing the matter up.

Like Tom, Ellie seemed to regard me as the Ghost of Christmas Past, and since, chronologically speaking, little more than a week or ten days had gone by since our Beef Stroganoff supper when Tom had so nearly succumbed to the vet's anesthesia, I can explain her attitude only on the grounds that, like me, she sensed that on the eve of my departure for Armadillo we had approached what might have been the point of no return in our relationship and then, unaccountably, returned. I remembered how we had sat there in Manhattan House over our scotch and sodas with the rain coming down outside and how I had thought that things might possibly take place between us then that had never taken place between us before. The time had been right, and we were both lonely, and her hair smelled sweetly of shampoo, and then Tom had gone eerily into his dance of life-in-death or death-in-life, and the golden rug became damply stained, and as quietly and inexorably as a man's last breath, the golden moment passed.

At some level of her cautious and sensitive being, Ellie too must have marked its passing, I think, because though only a week or ten days went by before we met again there in front of the U.N., it had been time enough for her to immerse herself even more passionately than before in a world where passion was not a private possibility but a public cause. I took her to supper at Giovanni's that evening, and her talk was all of Red China and low-income housing and the Job Corps, and although she pressed my hand and gave me her loveliest pre-Raphaelite smile as we kissed goodnight at her apartment door, I felt that it was a parting of phantoms. It was bad in its way but, like Miriam's death, not quite as bad as I might have thought. The one advantage I know to living in a dream is that in dreams you may never get more than a shadow of the things you really want, but you also never really get hurt either. You can fall out of a window or sleep with your sister or preside stark naked over the Security Council, but in the end you always walk away more or less intact on your shadowy feet.

I wouldn't want to live there, but dreams are not a bad place to visit, especially after an overdose of reality, and that is probably why I delayed as long as I did before trying to reestablish communication with Armadillo. Miriam was buried on the day of Christmas Eve, I spent a cheerless Christmas watching TV with Charlie and the boys in Westchester, and it was not until the day after Christmas, that low ebb of the year, when I was back in my apartment again with Tom, that I tried putting in a call to Bebb. I put it in person-to-person, although I do not know why since there was no one in that house I wouldn't have been glad to talk to, even Lucille. Maybe it was just that I wanted to talk to Bebb first so that there would be no suspicion, especially not in my own mind, that I was doing things behind his back. The article having long since been abandoned, my concern by that time was in no sense conspiratorial. Somewhere along the telephonic process my Northern operator in her impersonal efficiency exchanged words with a Southern operator whose voice sounded rich and slow with compassion, and the next thing I heard was Brownie fifteen hundred miles away explaining to one or the other of them that Mr. Bebb was no longer in Armadillo, he had left no number where he could be reached, and there was no telling when if ever he might come back. I told the operator that I would talk to Brownie instead. Even across all those miles then I could almost hear his smile as he recognized me by my voice, and by way of demonstrating the uncanny sharpness of human perceptions, especially when fresh from a long sleep, I even thought I could detect a whiff of after-shave.

Brownie said, "I can't talk over the phone, dear. They left just a day after you did, all three of them. I would have left too, but Mr. Bebb asked me to stay and straighten things up here. I've got all their belongings to pack and the house to close, and you wouldn't believe the heat we're having."

"Where did they go, Brownie?" I said. "Was there any trouble, or did everything just blow over?"

Brownie said, "Dear, you never know who's listening. I can tell you this, though. Before they left, they asked me to give you a message."

"Sharon did?" I said.

Brownie said, "No, it wasn't Sharon. It was Mr. Bebb. He said if you called, to tell you to remember how when Moses led his people out of bondage in Egypt, the Lord opened up a path for them right through the Red Sea."

"How could I forget?" I said.

Brownie said, "There are many treasures hidden in Scripture, dear, and many things written that he who runs may read."

"He who runs where?" I said.

Brownie said, "There's never any telling where a man may run to except that even if he takes the wings of the morning and flies to the outermost parts of the sea, he can never run away from the Lord."

"Not even in Texas, I suppose," I said.

Brownie said, "I certainly wouldn't think so, dear."

"Not even in Dallas," I said.

"Not in Dallas and not in Houston either," Brownie said.

I said, "Brownie, I miss you. I miss you all, and I even miss the Salamander Motel. By the way, by mistake I took *The Apocryphal New Testament* edited by M. R. James home with me in my suitcase. How can I get it back to you?"

Brownie said, "Don't you worry about that. Just keep it until we meet again someday, and that will be time enough."

I said, "I hope we do meet again someday, Brownie. All of us."

Brownie said, "If not in this world, dear, then in a

better world to come," and when he hung up, I could see him there with the smile already fading and the sweat stains dark on his shirt as he turned back to the debris of Gospel Faith—the half-filled suitcases, the bulging cartons, and, for all I knew, even the rugs rolled up in the downstairs hall and Lucille's color TV in a crate. Had Brownie, that disentangler of meaning and lover of clarity, resorted to the veiled language of espionage as an act of midsummer madness, I wondered, or did the walls really have ears listening for just the faintest echo of Bebb's footsteps so that the pursuit could begin? I did not know, but, deciding that even the most ingenious pursuer would be unlikely to overhear me at so great a distance, I got Herman Redpath's number in Houston from information and put in a second person-to-person call to Bebb. The phone was answered by what I took to be the voice of some Indian, and in minutes I found myself talking to Bebb himself.

He said, "Antonio, this is the day that the Lord hath made, let us rejoice and be glad in it," and I could tell right away that it was the old Bebb still. I could tell that nothing he had let loose or that had been let loose upon him had taken the bounce out of him permanently, and I suppose the fear that it might have been otherwise was part of the reason I had delayed so long in calling. Though obviously glad to hear from me at last, and eager, I thought, to tell me many things, Bebb was almost as guarded over the phone as Brownie had been, and I was able to get virtually nothing out of him about what had happened in Armadillo after my departure or what he was doing in Houston or what he was planning to go on to next. Even on the subject of Herman Red-

234

path he was unusually reticent except to say that although they were guests in his house and beneficiaries of his fathomless generosity, they had not seen a great deal of Herman Redpath himself because he was much occupied elsewhere. It was when I inquired for Sharon in as restrained and casual a manner as I could manage that Bebb came out with what must have been on his mind from the beginning. He said, "Antonio, maybe you better hop on a plane and see for yourself. In Herman Redpath's house there are many mansions, and there isn't anybody here wouldn't welcome the sight of you with open arms."

The apartment that Tom and I shared was on the third floor of a brownstone on upper Madison Avenue, and I remember that as Bebb made his suggestion, I was sitting in the front room with my feet up on the radiator. It was the room I used as a studio, and it was littered all over with cans of Rustoleum black and newspaper spread around to catch the drippings and a great many pieces of scrap iron both assembled and unassembled. I remember the greyness of the day and the look of the apartment building across the street with its narrow concrete balconies and its picture windows that pictured nothing but other people's windows on my side of the street. I remember the sound of a Madison Avenue bus starting up from the bus-stop at the corner —that pneumatic hiss followed by the world-weary groan of the gears. "Maybe you better hop on a plane and come see for yourself," Bebb had said, and in response to his words certainly, and to the sense of great promise that seemed somehow implicit in them, but in response also to the bus and the scrap iron and the grey New York day generally, I heard myself saying that it didn't sound like a bad idea at that, and if I could get things in order in time, I'd fly down the next day and call him from the airport.

On such slender threads hang the destinies of men and nations. For want of a nail the kingdom was lost, the old poem says, and I have thought since that if any one of a great number of factors had been missing at that particular moment on the day after Christmas—if it had been the day after the day after, say, or if the Madison Avenue bus hadn't chanced to start up just then with those ghostly sighs of weariness and despair as it shifted from low gear into high—there is no telling how differently I might have responded to Bebb's invitation or what kingdom, what mine of precious stones, might have been forever lost to me. But whether by chance or by providence, things happened precisely and encyclopedically as they did happen, and I told Bebb I would go, and I went. With a sense of guilt so acute that I could hardly bring myself to meet his eye on the taxi ride down, I left Tom once again at the vet's and arrived at Houston the next afternoon.

I will make no attempt to give a full account of all that happened there. It would take too long, for one thing, and it would be misleading, for another, because the Cecil B. DeMille quality of it, the cast of thousands, the pageantry, the drama, would tend to give it more significance than it really had. With time as with everything else, needless to say, it is not the quantity that counts, it is the quality, and under certain circumstances a sunset glimpsed through a Venetian blind or even not glimpsed can count for more than two weeks in Venice

236

with your eyes open the whole time. Let a single scene out of the whole Texas extravaganza, then, represent all the others.

Bebb himself met me at the airport and drove me out to the Red Path Ranch, and that same evening there was a big barbecue. Up to that point I had seen nobody, not even Sharon, who had been supposed to come with him to meet me, Bebb said, but had gone out on horseback earlier and hadn't returned in time. Bebb told me little I wanted to know—he seemed much more interested in pointing out to me the splendors of the ranch as we drove through—and almost as soon as we arrived at the building where I was to stay, he left me, saying that he was already late for an appointment with our host and would see me at the barbecue that evening. My building was a one-story stucco affair with a tiled roof and built around a quadrangle with a swimming pool at the center. I took a dip in the pool to wash the city off and then clocked about three miles on an exercycle which I found under the pillared roof of the walk that ran around the quadrangle on all four sides.

Lying there in the sun afterwards, I kept thinking that maybe Sharon would return from her ride and come looking for me, but she did not come, and after a while I fell asleep and had a dream. It was a very short dream, and it was about Miriam. I cannot remember how she looked or where we were, but I remember the sound of her voice and the sense of calm after storm, the sense of walking out into the fresh air again after a bad movie, as she said, "My God, it's good to get that cast off, Tono." That was all there was to it, but it was worth going to Texas to hear. When I woke up I couldn't stop thinking about that giant A—how they must have taken it off before they let the undertakers have her and how some remnant of it was still probably lying around somewhere at the bottom of an incinerator or in the city dump just as, for all I know, there are old books or old coins lying around that Shakespeare must have held in his hands once or at the bottom of the Jordan maybe a piece of rock Jesus threw out at some moment of frustration or somewhere else a boulder that he stepped behind to take a leak. The world must be full of such lost souvenirs, and I suppose no one has ever lived without leaving many of them behind. But of course what I was gladdest to take back with me out of that dream was the idea that wherever my sister was, if only in her Brooklyn grave, she at least didn't have that A to contend with any more. "That the bones which thou hast broken may rejoice," the pale priest read, and if I could not think of it yet as A for *alleluiah* or *amen*, I could at least hear it as a long-drawn *ah-h-h* of relief and astonishment as somebody's scissors, or possibly even rapier, cut the damned thing away.

And then, that night, the barbecue. It reminds me of a book Miriam and I had as children called *Great Characters out of Dickens*, I think, where many people from many of the different novels are brought together between the same covers—Mr. Micawber and Sarah Gamp, old Magwitch and Pickwick and Tom the copper's nark. Bebb was there, and Lucille, and Herman Redpath, and eventually Sharon, not to mention a number of Indians that I recognized from the ordination—Jack Oakie, for instance, and the old lady who some said was Herman Redpath's wife and others his sister and Sharon said both—and a number that I had never seen before. Just about everybody was there except for Brownie, who was still back at Armadillo packing things up. A whole steer was roasting on a huge spit, and there were accordions and a marimba band and Japanese lanterns. There was beer and champagne and even Tropicanas, for all I know, plus a portable outhouse with the Red Path brand painted on the door in case anybody needed that out there under the Texas stars. There was a pit full of red-hot coals, and it was there, squatting beside it, that I found Herman Redpath again. He was wearing the same brown suit, brown shirt, brown hat, and he reached out and grabbed me as I passed by.

He said, "That sonofabitch Bebb I don't give a fart what he is or what he did time for all I know is soon as we got back here that same day after he pulled Jesus knows what-all kind of a crazy trick damn if the thing didn't start working right off the life the Jesus life any name you want to call it why I'll kiss your ass if that same night we got back I didn't get one on stiff as a poker must have lasted better part of twenty minutes maybe more if I haven't planted me a pack of seed around here since then you can bet your balls it wasn't the want of seed or there was anything wrong on that end it was something wrong with the hole I planted it in I got the life in me again thanks to that bastard you seen the little brown tits on that daughter of his what I wouldn't give for a handful like that the life I got back I'm not tear-assing around spending it just any place I'm saving up and spending it where you bet your sweet ass it counts don't do much days any more stick pretty close to home I wouldn't be out here now spending the life in me on all these sonsofbitches weren't it for Leo asking me to he wanted something special for you your first night I took a shine to you myself soon as you poked your tail in the door looks to me like you got Indian blood in you it's nights not days I spend the life I got you take that Leo Bebb I don't give a fart what he done time for he give me back the life again every week he lays his hands on me another time I got me a six-shooter now like the old days I can keep it in firing position twenty twenty-five minutes maybe that's his daughter over there now take a look at the pretty little ass she's got on her," and with a wrench no less than the one John Glenn must have experienced when he blasted off from his thundering pad into the silences of outer space, and making an ascent no less great, I turned from the firelit face of that old sachem just in time to see Sharon coming through the place between the marimba band and the roasting steer in a dress the color of moonlight with a glint in her hair and her arm in a silk scarf tied into a sling.

"Terrible as an army with banners" were among the words Bebb had quoted from the Song of Solomon in an effort to describe her to me once, and for the first time I realized that what Solomon if not Bebb must have meant by such a curious image was that one way mortal man has always reacted to beauty like hers is with terror in his very bowels. I was scared stiff as I saw her picking her way toward me through all the Indians, and as nearly as I can tell, I was scared not so much because of the terrible power her beauty gave her over me as because of my own terrible inability to respond to it in anything remotely like the way the stars themselves cried out for me to. In face of such a sight and mystery as a girl can present when she walks toward you through the firelight in a moon-colored dress, it is possible for any one of us to be like whichever prophet it was who, when he beheld the Lord himself sitting high and lifted up among his angels, could only cry out, "Woe is me, for I am undone . . . I am a man of unclean lips. . . ." Nor, Brownie would be pleased to note, is that the only reference to Scripture that this moment of seeing Sharon again at the barbecue recalls, because Bebb had come up behind me by this time and said softly into my ear as she approached, "Behold, I saw the holy city, new Jerusalem, coming down out of heaven like a bride adorned for her husband," and the next moment she was there holding out her good hand toward me and saying, "Take it easy, Bopper. Herman's mare threw me, and it's taken till now to wash the horse shit off"—*horse shit* not as an obscenity but the way Bebb had used it once as a technical term for something that smells of grain and musk and sun and makes the vegetables grow.

It was later that same night that I asked her to marry me. It wasn't much, I realized even at the time, but it was the best I could find to do.

She said, "Bip put you up to it, didn't he?"

I said, "Bip certainly had his hand in things right from the beginning. There's no getting around that."

"Didn't he?" Sharon said.

"Not in so many words," I said.

Then she said, "Well, at least you're better than Brownie," and I interpreted that, correctly for once, to be an acceptance.

*　*　*

Ellie was wonderful all the way through. There was no need to be wonderful about letting me go because that had already happened—like people shaking hands through a car window, we had come apart finally not because either of us especially chose to but because life moves, that's all—but she was wonderful in her way about Sharon when I brought her back to New York as my bride. We were married in Texas early in the new year, not by Bebb as it turned out—there was some question as to whether Texas law would recognize his ordination—but by an Episcopal priest in a mission church packed full of Indians on the fringes of the Red Path Ranch. Bebb gave his adopted daughter away and pronounced the benediction afterwards, Lucille held the bride's bouquet while we exchanged our vows, and Brownie arrived from Armadillo in time to stand up in a cloud of after-shave as my best man. It seemed fitting that we should go back to the Salamander Motel for our honeymoon, but, fearing our presence in Armadillo might stir up trouble for Bebb, we flew to Nassau instead. It was when we returned from there that Ellie went out of her way to be nice to Sharon and showed her around the shops, talked to her about clothes, and took her on a tour of the U.N., where Sharon sat in the visitors' gallery in the General Assembly with a set of those instantaneous translation earphones on her head and looking, I'm sure, as much like something from outer space as Bebb ever had. Matter and anti-matter, they met without mutual annihilation, my young bride and my old comrade, and like one of those human-interest photographs at the back of *Life* that shows a cat and a mouse, say, sharing the same bowl of milk, I think

242

they even took a rather eccentric fancy to each other.

Not least among Ellie's kindnesses was that she took Tom off my hands. The first moment she saw him, Sharon took a dislike to that cat—among other things, he made her itch, she said—and Tom seemed approximately as enthusiastic about her as he had been about me when I went to get him out of his cage at the vet's. So he moved into Manhattan House, and I saw him there occasionally when Ellie asked us in for an evening with some of her U.N. friends. He made a place for himself on the golden rug under the piano and spent most of his time either there or in the corner where the hot air came through.

For the first three months we lived on in the Madison Avenue apartment, Sharon and I, but it was not a happy arrangement. The apartment seemed cramped and airless after the Manse in Armadillo, and as for the city in general, every time she came back from wandering around in it, she said that she had the feeling she'd been mixed up in a fight she'd somehow lost. So when spring came, we rented a house in Connecticut not far from the Sound, and in the fall I went back to teaching—four classes of English and coaching track at the local high school. It was not a bad place to live, and although the beach was a far cry from the one at Hobe Sound we drove to once, Sharon enjoyed it in the summers, and at least there were no Portuguese men-of-war.

Miriam's two boys came to live with us eventually. There was never any one decisive moment when the move was made, and I cannot say that I ever consciously reached the point even in my own mind when I decided that the time had come to grant the last request that my sister had charitably never quite brought herself to make of me. Charlie's house was only a few hours away, and gradually my nephews just took to spending more and more time with us—only week-ends and vacations at first, but eventually through his educational TV connections Charlie decided the school where I taught was better than theirs, so they ended up moving in with us on a more or less year-round basis. Charlie fretted about them and missed them and in many ways was a good father, but in the long run I think he was just as glad to be rid of them. Boys are a good deal of fuss when you come right down to it, and it was fuss that he spent a lot of his waking hours and all of his sleeping ones trying to avoid.

It was a good move for Charlie and by and large also a good move for Sharon and me, but whether it was a good move for Chris and Tony themselves, time alone will tell. During those early years of our marriage when we had no children of our own and lived in a town where neither of us had any roots or knew anybody very well, we needed people besides just each other to bounce our lives off of. In fact, we needed not just people in general but people more or less like the people we had had before, so that without realizing it we tended to assign those two boys roles they could hardly have been aware of but were always in some danger, I suppose, of taking up on their own. Chris in many ways became Tom for me—the silent awareness by the fire as I corrected themes in the evening, the all-knowing gaze that I would talk to myself to when nobody else was around, the dignified presence whose eccentricities I tended to publicize as a kind of joke on us both. And Tony, I think, filled part of the place in Sharon's life that Bebb had occupied. He was fat and she loved deviling him, and at one level of their being or another they were always catching each other by surprise—being or doing unexpected things to each other at unexpected times—and thus bringing out both the saddest and the gayest in each other. On the whole, however, I think Miriam would have been pleased. In addition to everything else, especially after Sharon took up the guitar and I put a ping-pong table in the cellar for the boys, we tended to get too little sleep in our house rather than too much. And with the aerial we had, we could get only two channels on the TV and those not very well.

Bebb stayed on at the ranch in Texas, Lucille and Brownie with him of course. Evidently no one ever pressed charges for whatever had gone on at Herman Redpath's ordination—perhaps because it was his own church where it happened and most of the Baptists had already left with their children—so conceivably he might have returned to Armadillo. But he never did. He continued to serve as Herman Redpath's beadsman or medicine man, and the weekly laying-on of hands apparently never entirely lost its magic, or, if it did, Herman Redpath kept Bebb on anyway as a souvenir of splendors past and in hope perhaps of others still to come, or maybe just as a charm against the evil eye. But Bebb's labors in the vineyard didn't end there. Good to his word, Herman Redpath built him another Holy Love much larger and finer to replace the one that he had to abandon in Armadillo. It was built on the ranch property to resemble the Alamo, and on Sundays he held services of some kind there which were attended faithfully by Herman Redpath and the Indians. The *Put Yourself on God's Payroll* ads continued to appear among the glow-in-the-dark Virgins and hemorrhoid cures, and the files of Gospel Faith kept on growing.

I pulled my own folder out once when Sharon and I were down there on a visit and nobody was around, and the code letter that Bebb had written on it long before in his own hand was, curiously enough, an A. Average? Appalling? Article-writer? Or possibly an eerie foreshadowing of Miriam's last days? I do not know. I never asked either Bebb or Brownie about it and never shall. Like most oracles, I suppose, it was destined to mean whatever I chose to make it mean, maybe that in the end I would become just Antonio again or in a way, you might say, Antonio for the first time, since for years almost everybody except Bebb had called me Tono. Sharon didn't like Tono—she said it came too close for comfort to her baby word for number two, which had been nono—so Antonio I became, except once in a while Bopper or Bop. Bip and Bop. I told her once that she should have us framed on either side of the mantle clock like Mike and Ike or the Gold Dust twins.

Down and then up again, south and then north again. If these events in my life had a pattern, it was something like that. If a shape, then a V, or even, by stretching it somewhat, an upside-down A, I suppose, with the little bar in between representing the bridge that always connects the present with both the past and the future. Because when I was on my way down in my roomette as Tono, I had in me already seeds of the Antonio I was to become; and when I finally went up again with Sharon as my bride, I carried as part of my baggage and will carry always the celibate dabbler in unwelded scrap iron that I had been on the way down. All of which goes to show, as if that were necessary, that you cannot escape the past or the future either, and at my best and bravest I do not even want to escape them. Miriam's death, the faceless baby, Lucille's Tropicanas and in a way also Brownie's smile and that slightly mad and rebellious eye of Bebb's—all the sad and hurtful things of the past I would prevent having happened if I could, but, failing that, I would not wish the hurt of them away even if that were possible.

When Miriam's bones were breaking, for instance, if I could have pushed a button that would have stopped not her pain but the pain of her pain in me, I would not have pushed the button because, to put it quite simply, my pain was because I loved her, and to have wished my pain away would have been somehow to wish my love away as well. And at my best and bravest I do not want to escape the future either, even though I know that it contains what will someday be my own great and final pain. Because a distaste for dying is twin to a taste for living, and again I don't think you can tamper with one without somehow doing mischief to the other. But this is at my best and bravest. The rest of the time I am a fool and a coward just like most of the other lost persons that in the end it will take no less than Mr. Keen himself to trace.

FREDERICK BUECHNER

Frederick Buechner was born in 1926 in New York City. He was educated at Lawrenceville School and Princeton University, where he graduated in 1948 after two years in the army. In 1950 he published his first novel, A Long Day's Dying. After teaching English at Lawrenceville, during which time he published his second novel, The Seasons' Difference (1952), he attended Union Theological Seminary. In 1958 he received his Bachelor of Divinity degree and was ordained a Presbyterian minister. In that same year his third novel, The Return of Ansel Gibbs, was published to wide acclaim. From 1958 to 1967 he served as School Minister and chairman of the religion department at Phillips Exeter Academy. During that period he wrote his fourth novel, The Final Beast, and two volumes of meditations, The Magnificent Defeat and The Hungering Dark. In 1970 his novel The Entrance to Porlock was published. He is presently writing in Vermont, where he lives with his wife and three children.